CW01573211

The Edge of the Cemetery

The Edge of the Cemetery

Ghost Killer Book 2

Margaret Millmore

Copyright (C) 2016 Margaret Millmore
Layout design and Copyright (C) 2016 Creativia
Cover art by http://www.thecovercollection.com/
Edited by: Maxine Bringenberg 2016
This book is a work of fiction. Names, characters, places, and incidents are the product of the author's imagination or are used fictitiously. Any resemblance to actual events, locales, or persons, living or dead, is purely coincidental.
All rights reserved. No part of this book may be reproduced or transmitted in any form or by any means, electronic or mechanical, including photocopying, recording, or by any information storage and retrieval system, without the author's permission.

Prologue

My name is George Sinclair, a once ordinary thirty-something guy, who, several months back, discovered he could see ghosts. But seeing ghosts was one thing; realizing they were plaguing people with illness and disease for the sole purpose of inflicting a life of pain, or in some cases, killing them, was another. And realizing that I could kill these demons and alleviate their victims' pain was another altogether. Suddenly I was a ghost killer, and my life as I knew it was over.

Ghosts aren't rare; in fact, they're everywhere. They linger in-between our world and whatever comes after death. Some get lost in transition and can't figure out how to keep going after they die…I call them "lost souls". They're usually harmless and uninterested in the living, but are attracted to yours truly. They seem to beg with their eyes, asking me to send them on, and with a gentle jab they swirl away into nothingness. However, there are those that won't move on; they know they can do more harm staying connected to this realm than moving on to the next. There's also the possibility that there really is a heaven and hell, and they know damn well they're headed south. So they stay and wreak havoc on those of us with a solid body. Those are the ones I kill…those nasty little bastards that just want to hurt people.

Ghosts and demons are different, yet the same. Let me explain. They all died at least twenty to thirty years ago (although the longer they are dead, the more powerful they become), they all wear the vintage clothing of the time of their deaths, and they all have round-rimmed glasses on. When they re-materialize as ghosts they immediately seek out a victim and plague them with a disease or deformity, haunting slowly, causing a life of pain and suffering. The most powerful ghosts—demons, as I prefer to call them—have been around for a very long time and have had multiple victims. They have the power to accelerate their victim's pain and illness, which in turn will expedite their death.

Perhaps this all seems rather unbelievable. I thought so too…in the beginning, that is. And if discovering ghosts and demons exist, *and* killing them (after all, how can you kill something that's already dead? Most of you can't, but I can!), isn't enough to make your head hurt, let me tell you about the longaevus…the word is Latin and means "long life". In our world the term is used to describe a type of person…usually they're good, but not always. They are the result of an accidental confluence of events; it involves a powerful demon, its victim, a powerful ghost killer, and perfect timing. If a ghost killer kills a demon at the same moment it is killing its victim, the victim doesn't die, causing a third reaction, thus the confluence. Instead, the victim sort of absorbs the power of the demon and a little of the ghost killer's power too, which in turn gives them a great deal of physical strength and allows them to live a long, long time with very little aging.

But wait, there's more (my apologies if I'm beginning to sound like a TV infomercial…); we should discuss the Watchers as well. They are a group of people, some ghost killers themselves, others just ordinary folks, that are aware of our unordinary situation. The Watchers have been around for centuries, and their primary purpose is to protect ghost killers from those that want to harness our power. They also guide us when we have no one else to show us the way. In addition, they know everything that goes on in the world of ghosts and demons, and if an infestation arises that can't be handled locally, they will send in reinforcements. Aris Galanos, a high-ranking official in the group, lives right here in the city, and although he calls San Francisco home, his reach and obligations extend to most of the country.

There are a couple more terms I'd like to familiarize you with before we go on. The first is the "convergence," an event that takes place when a demon merges with a human. It's quite similar to the confluence that creates a longaevus, but instead of the bespectacled vintage-clothed monster's demise and the survival of its human victim, it is the victim's soul and mind that dies, allowing the demon to move into the person's body and live again, usually with the intention of wreaking even more havoc on mankind. Obviously that's a situation we do our best to prevent, but we don't always succeed.

The second term is "electroplasmic juice." When you stab a ghost or demon, an electric shock is emitted, which is quite painful and after repeated stabbings, can be dangerous as well. (I should note that a powerful enough ghost killer can channel this juice and use it to kill someone, also not good.) Most of us carry something to alleviate this concern...I prefer an unsharpened yellow number two pencil. My ghost-killing partner, Billy Wilkinson, prefers a chopstick. (She used to use her grandmother's antique chopstick, but more often than not, a powerful demon's juice can reduce our preferred tool to ashes, so she's opted for the cheaper version which you can purchase by the dozen in China Town).

Chapter 1

"Uh, George, a little help here," Pete said. His voice was low, but the strain and fear came through loud and clear.

"Damn it, we need Billy!" I hissed in frustration. The man standing in front of me was thin and pale, with sallow skin that bore the scabs and scars of a longtime drug user. He gave me a wicked grin that showed a mouth full of rotted teeth, giving him a haunted look, which made sense…after all, he *was* being haunted. A short time ago, his wasted and abused body probably couldn't have hurt anything bigger than a fly, but since he'd been possessed by a demon from the 1880s, he could do all sorts of things, like trying to kill yours truly. He held a piece of rebar he'd picked up at the mouth of the alley when he and his two companions chased us into it. Now he was rushing me, wielding the deadly metal bar like a sword.

His demon was smiling viciously behind him and I threw myself to the left, kicking up the alley wall and somersaulting back toward him, with my trusty number two pencil leading the way. The demon was powerful and my pencil disintegrated when I stabbed him, but so did he. My body fell through the dissipating grey mist as the previously possessed man slumped to the ground, the rebar clanging loudly on the asphalt. I hit the other side of the alley wall with a solid thud that would definitely leave a few bruises to match the ones I'd already received from the other possessed man I'd relieved of his demon just a few short minutes ago.

"Yeah, well, she didn't get her bell rung on purpose. Now get over—" There was a loud thump and Pete's voice was suddenly cut off as all the air audibly rushed out of his body. The last I'd seen of him, he was being cornered at the end of the alley by a third possessed man using a two-by-four like a baseball bat, and from the sound of it, the demon and his victim were winning. I jumped up and ran to his rescue, coming upon the demon from behind. Pete was slumped against the brick wall and the demon was commanding its victim to pulverize Pete's head with the length of wood. Grabbing another pencil from my back pocket, I stabbed the demon, causing it to disintegrate; his victim fell forward onto Pete, the two-by-four banging loudly as it hit the ground.

Pete groaned, shoved the unconscious man off to the side, and looked up at me. His complexion was ashen and there was a trickle of blood at the corner of his mouth, but otherwise he looked okay. I put my hand out to help him up, and he took it, grabbing his stomach and groaning some more.

"You gonna be okay?" I asked as he staggered to his feet.

"Yeah, just another day at the office," he said sarcastically. "Did we get 'em all?"

"We got 'em. Let's get out of here."

I pulled Pete's arm up and over my shoulder and did a walk-stagger towards the mouth of the alley, leaving the three unconscious men where they'd fallen. They were mostly unhurt and would wake up soon, having no idea what had happened to them...probably a regular occurrence considering their drug habits. By the time we reached the opening, Pete was pushing away from me and looking cautiously up and down the sidewalk and street. It didn't look like anyone had paid any attention to the two clean-cut guys that had been chased into the alley by three not-so-clean cut demon-possessed ruffians. We were in San Francisco's Tenderloin District, and the neighborhood watch generally consisted of watching for the cops, not the bad guys doing bad things to good guys.

As Pete and I walked to the public garage in Union Square where we'd left his car, he said, "Man, I hate seeing that."

"Seeing what?" I asked. I knew he couldn't be talking about ghosts and demons; he'd been fighting them for years, and although it wasn't pleasant by any means, it was what we did.

He nudged his chin toward the other side of the street where a teenage kid stood. "Kids on the street. I mean, look at him...he can't be more than fifteen or sixteen."

I looked at the teenager. Lightly soiled clothes hung on a gangly five-ten frame, and although his hair wasn't long, it was dirty and unkempt. A lost and confused expression covered his face. He was looking our way, probably because even though we'd just battled three strong demons in a disgustingly dirty alley, we were still the best dressed and most likely the cleanest people in the neighborhood. The Tenderloin is the armpit of San Francisco and unfortunately it's also where many of the city's homeless spend their days and nights, including runaway teens, which he probably was.

It was sad, and all I could muster in response was, "Me too." When I turned back to look at the kid again, he was gone.

* * *

On a typical day of ghost and demon eradication I worked with Billy Wilkinson. However, she'd been benched for the last few days due to a concussion. Although she had a generally caustic personality, she was also incredibly compassionate when it came to people and their wellbeing. A few days before, she'd been on her daily run and was jogging in place while waiting for a green light. A woman in her twenties approached the corner, texting furiously and oblivious to her surroundings, and walked right into the intersection, never looking up from her phone and almost getting herself killed by an oncoming car. I say almost, because Billy saw it coming and jumped to her rescue, pushing the stupid woman to safety but landing hard on the curb herself, knocking her noggin viciously. Thus the concussion.

Billy was adamant that she didn't need medical attention, but we got her some anyway and the doctor declared her condition severe enough to insist on at least a week of in-home bed rest, or hospitalization. Under protest, Billy agreed to the former. Fortunately for Billy (and anyone who had to deal with her during her recuperation), she's a ghost killer, which means she heals damn fast, making her forced down time a few days instead of a week.

Our little corner of the world had been experiencing some rather nasty ghost/demon possessions recently, and Aris, our fearless leader, didn't think it would be a good idea to send me in alone when the call came in about the current situation in the Tenderloin, so he assigned Pete Cowell to lend me a hand. Pete's ex-military (Special Forces to be exact), tall and strong, with the same high-and-tight haircut he'd been wearing since his service days. He discovered his ghost killing power while stationed overseas. He'd been injured during a training exercise and was taken to the base hospital, where he saw his first ghost. Like most of us, when we see the first one, we're not really sure what it is we're seeing, but some sort of instinct kicks in and we're driven to kill it. Now Pete was one of Aris's right-hand men, and a formable ghost killer to boot, but not nearly as powerful as Billy and me.

Aris and the Watchers employed a variety of people to keep their eyes open for unusual behavior by our fellow citizens, specifically something that might indicate someone was being haunted or possessed. The man who'd called it in was a long-time resident of the Tenderloin, who'd been receiving a stipend for years from the Watchers to…well, watch. When he observed the three men—regulars in the neighborhood, but generally harmless—harassing people and violently acting out, he called Aris. Of course the three longtime drug users could simply have been on a bad "trip", but Aris decided their behavior warranted a closer look and called Pete and me. As it turned out, drugs were the least of their problems. They were being haunted and possessed by three demons from the late 19th century.

My ghost killing career started off with a bang. I encountered several new people, some good and some bad. One of them wanted to harness my power, and when I refused, he attempted to unleash a torrent of demons on the city. His name was Frederick Vokkel, and he was Billy's estranged grandfather. He's dead now…she killed him. Afterwards, I agreed to work with the Watchers and things got pretty quiet. Occasionally the Watchers would get a report about some badass demons that needed killing by some badass ghost killers, and Aris would send Billy and me off to slay the ghouls. Usually these were exotic locales like Boca or Toledo…for some reason, the really bad demons didn't like to go to mundane places like NYC or Honolulu. For a while there, I was actually getting bored.

That all changed a little over a week ago. Suddenly every demonic monster on the planet seemed to descend on our little corner of terra-firma, and things were elevating at an alarming pace. We were nearing Halloween, and I had to wonder if there was a connection. Several assaults had been perpetrated by powerful demons, and the sheer frequency prevented Billy and I from handling them all, which meant we needed to call in less powerful ghost killers to assist. So far we hadn't had any fatalities, but some of our people had ended up in the hospital. There were a few commonalities as well; first, the demons were not just haunting their victims, but possessing them and forcing them to hurt others, and once we arrived, the demons directed their human weapons on us. In addition to all of that, as if *that* wasn't enough, there was the sighting of a 17th century musketeer at almost every incident. However, this fiend wasn't doing any damage or possessing anyone, just making himself seen, and we believed he might have been instigating the attacks. The question was, why?

Chapter 2

The following morning I went over to see Billy. She lived with my much beloved elderly neighbor, Justine Wilkinson. Justine was Billy's grandmother's cousin, but it was much easier to refer to her as Billy's aunt. We share the sixth floor of an Art Deco apartment building in Pacific Heights that was converted to condos back in the '50s. Each floor originally had five one-bedroom apartments with formal living and dining spaces, a den, and a good size kitchen. I have one of those, but when Justine's very wealthy father purchased her unit, he bought three and combined them, making Justine's the largest in the building, and by far the nicest.

Margie, Justine's new companion, chef, and sometimes chauffeur—and a retired ghost killer—answered after my first knock. She had a slight scowl on her face when she opened the door, but smiled when she realized it was me.

Margie was hired to replace Anne, who was Justine's previous companion. Anne turned out to be a spy for Vokkel and the half-sister of Vokkel's closest minion, Edgar; she subsequently died for those relationships, right along with Vokkel. Margie came highly recommended by Aris and the Watchers, and Justine seemed to be quite fond of her, so that made her A-Okay in my book. She was a tall, sturdy woman with salt and pepper shoulder length hair that was always neatly pulled back into a ponytail, and she had an endless supply of khaki pants and polo shirts that she wore like uniforms.

"Hello, George. I'm so glad you're here!" Margie was a good-natured woman and almost always in an upbeat mood, but she seemed a little distressed this morning, and I was pretty sure I knew the source. Billy.

Billy, like me, was one of the most powerful ghost killers to have been born in quite some time. In fact, the last two that were as powerful as us were my mother and Billy's grandmother, Wilhelmina Wilkinson (also known as Billy), who were both dead now. Billy was also one of the most brazen, obnoxious, and generally difficult people I'd ever met. She had piercing green eyes and a wicked ability to use those optical beauties like a weapon—an especially focused glare usually meant impending danger to the recipient. It was unsettling, and had sent many a stronger man into a state of panic. But, much to my surprise, she'd become one of my closest friends.

Reluctantly, I asked, "What's wrong?"

Margie sighed. "Nothing…no snide remarks, no eye-rolls. She's been positively pleasant and polite! I can't take it anymore; if I don't get one of those devastating glares from her soon, I'll lose my mind! But thankfully, she's also much better, and with a hope and a prayer," Margie made the sign of the cross and looked upward toward Heaven, "you can get her out of my sight for a while."

I looked down at her in surprise, "She's been nice?" This was new…and a bit disturbing. I would have thought that being locked in the house for the last few days would have ramped up Billy's obnoxiousness tenfold.

Margie gave a hint of a smile, "Yes, even Justine is worried."

"Where is she?" I asked, still stunned by this strange behavior.

"She's in the living room. Go, I'll bring some coffee," Margie said as she pushed me toward the entrance of the room.

Billy was sitting on the couch, her legs curled underneath her, reading something on her iPad. She was wearing flannel pajamas, her hair loosely pulled back. The large lump that had graced her forehead a few days before had entered the final stages of healing and was hardly noticeable now. Ghost killers come with a slew of fun skills; seeing and killing ghosts, exceptional speed, strength and agility, and the *crème de la crème*, we heal very quickly. That last one was my favorite, as it came in handy whether it was a nasty paper cut or a nasty fight with a possessed victim. Either way, it was a winner.

"How ya feeling?" I asked, trying to shake the shock of Margie's complaint from my voice.

"Better...what's wrong?" she asked, almost politely. Who was this woman?

"I...ah...well, Margie says you've been acting strange and she's concerned."

Her faced hardened and her eyes flashed, her signature dagger-like stare attempting to cut me in half. She said, "I've been trying to be nice to the woman who's been waiting on me hand and foot so I could get better and *help* you!" she chuffed. "And obviously the sooner the better; what happened to your face?"

I'd come out of last night's Tenderloin fray with a few cuts and bruises, but nothing too bad. I smiled broadly at her less than pleasant attitude...my detestable Billy hadn't gone anywhere after all. Margie had come in with the coffee tray just as Billy finished berating me, and as she passed me, she winked and said, "I knew I could count on you to bring out her shining personality."

I sat in the armchair nearest Billy and asked, "Seriously, how are you feeling? You look pretty good."

"I'm fine," she said amicably enough. She poured two cups of coffee and handed me one. In a not-so-amicable tone, she asked, "So what happened? Why are you all beat up?"

I regaled her with the previous night's exploits and she cocked her head to the side and asked, "No musketeer sighting this time?"

I frowned. "Now that you mention it, no, I didn't see it. But it happened pretty fast and we got backed into an alley, so it could have been around."

"Someone has to be pulling the strings, right? I mean, ghosts and demons don't work in groups, not without someone encouraging them to do it. It's like they're trying to lure us to them. . . ."

She was right, it did feel like that. Normally the ghosts and demons hunted on a solitary basis, and aside from the surges that Vokkel had called in, we didn't see multiple demons or ghosts working together. Not only that, but most demons weren't able to possess their victims for more than a minute or two at a time. However, in the last week or so, we'd encountered attacks that were clearly organized, and more importantly, the demons were in full possession of their victims for ten minutes or more; in many of the recent cases, much longer, depending on how long it took us to eradicate the demons. In our world, there are levels of both ghosts and demons and ghost killers. It couldn't be a coincidence that powerful demon attacks were happening in the backyard of two of the most powerful ghost killers.

"Yeah, I don't know what to make of that. They were pretty damn strong, and Pete had a lot of trouble keeping up. . . he almost got his head bashed in. I'm glad you're feeling better, because I *obviously* could use your help," I said with a sarcastic grin. She glared at me and I laughed in return, causing her eyes to take on a threatening hue. "Come on, you need to get out for a bit; go get dressed." My tone didn't invite argument, and for once, she didn't put one up.

It was almost lunch time, so I thought I'd drive her down to Louis' Restaurant out by the Sutro Baths and the Cliff House.

After lunch I thought we'd go find some ghosts to kill. What better way to spend a sunny San Francisco afternoon?

I loved Louis'; not only did it have a spectacular view of the Pacific, but it had a friendly ghost in residence. I didn't know her name, but based on her apparel, she died in the 1940s. She's featured in one of the many old pictures hanging on the wall, too. I asked the waitress about her once (referencing the photo on the wall, not the actual ghost), but all she could tell me was that she thought she worked there many years ago. I think she hangs around to keep an eye on the place, to make sure they continue to run it like they have for the last eighty-plus years.

Although most ghosts are bad, some are not... they just didn't manage to keep going when they died. Many good ghosts gesture to us (ghost killers) to send them on, but some don't want to go. Louis' 1940s ghost is one of those.

After lunch I gave Billy the option of hitting the San Francisco Veterans Hospital or the large private hospital closer to home. Hospitals (along with unsavory neighborhoods like the Tenderloin) tend to have more than their share of ghosts, either looking for victims or already haunting victims. She was feeling patriotic, so we hit the SFVA and visited the various outpatient and ambulatory clinics, as well as portions of the hospital, managing to take out several ghosts. Some vets went home wondering why they'd been there in the first place, (once a victim is relieved of their ghost or demon, they don't remember being sick or disabled).

Chapter 3

The following evening....

From somewhere to my left came Billy's scream of frustration and anger, but there wasn't much I could do about it. I'd spent the last ten minutes getting pummeled by a possessed man; he was about my age, but much bigger and much stronger. Linebacker comes to mind. I had managed a few well-placed round-house kicks and a series of body-blows, but he just kept coming. As big and strong as he was, he was also pale and sickly. I'd seen him vomiting earlier, but none of that mattered because his illness was caused by the demon that had complete control of him, and that demon would force the unwitting man's body to fight to the death.

I hated having to physically hurt these poor possessed souls, but at that point, it was me or him—his demon was so adept at keeping the man between us that I hadn't had a single opportunity to vanquish him with my trusty yellow friend. I was even willing to risk the ultimate shock and jab him bare-fingered, but I just couldn't get close enough. This was an incredibly powerful demon, and he was making his already strong victim that much stronger.

They'd been backing me down the lawn toward a four-foot wall, which bordered a seaside cliff. The wall was the only barrier between me and a thirty foot drop into the frigid Pacific

Ocean. I thought I could survive a dunk in the water, but not if I hit the jagged rocks that made up the shoreline instead.

I decided to charge him, if only to get some distance from that wall. I held my pencil out in front of me and crouched into a run, and so did the man. He was so much bigger than me, and when our tired and battered bodies met, he caught me off guard by grabbing ahold of my shoulder with one huge hand and my thigh with the other, essentially lifting me up off the ground. His momentum kept us going all the way to the wall, and suddenly I was flying through the air.

When I hit the water, all of the fogginess from my recent beating evaporated. I was terrified, and survival was my only concern. Fortunately, I landed about fifteen feet out from the rocky beach, but the waves were pushing me toward the rough shoreline at an alarming pace, and if I didn't get control, I'd end up pulverized by the rugged rocks.

On the drive up from San Francisco, I'd used my phone to look up the property on Google Earth, and recalled seeing a small pier at the base of the cliff. If my internal compass was working—and I had doubts due to the recent blows my head had taken—the dock should be close by. I turned in the direction I thought it was, took a sea swell to the face that felt like a sharp slap, and went under for a minute. When I surfaced, choking out salt water, I saw white safety lights and realized it was the dock. Before another wave rushed me closer to the shore—and what would surely be my death, or at least extreme disfigurement—I swam like my life depended on it...and of course, it did. I hit the pier piling with my forehead, causing a bright flash across my vision, but still managed to grab at the barnacle and oyster encrusted wood and hold tight. Although they were sharp and cutting into my hands, the sea life attached to the piling was keeping me from slipping on the otherwise slimy surface and back into the rushing ocean waters. I pulled myself along the wooden cross supports until I reached a ladder that descended into the water, and climbed to relative safety.

I needed to catch my breath, but more importantly, I knew Billy was in trouble back up at the hotel that sat near the cliff. The sound of Billy's voice yelling down at me spurred me into action, and I scrambled up the cliff-side staircase. I was halfway to the top when I realized that she wasn't yelling in distress—at least not her own distress—but yelling at me to, and I quote, "Stop screwing around, George, and get your ass up here!"

I laughed. It hurt like hell, but I couldn't help it. The earlier pounding I'd taken had included several upper-cuts to the lip and chin, and even more body blows to my ribs and stomach. Not only that, but my hands were chopped liver from the sharp barnacles and oysters that I'd recently clung to. I was a mess...but still, I kept going.

When I reached the top, Billy was fending off a tall, athletically built woman in a lovely silver evening dress. The woman had a large carving knife in her hand and a nasty demon at her back. The women lunged, knife aimed directly at Billy's chest. Fortunately, Billy was damn fast and quickly leapt to the side, then darted back with lightning speed and stabbed the woman's demon with her chopstick, vanquishing it into a swirling grey mist. The woman, who had no idea what was happening to her, promptly fainted.

The wide expanse of lawn, which spanned from the hotel to the cliff wall, was brightly and beautifully lit by the full moon. Unfortunately, that beauty was spoiled by the macabre scene before me. In addition to the woman Billy had just saved, two other people were sprawled unnaturally on the lawn, and I was pretty sure they were dead. A teenage boy stood off to the side, nearest the path to the parking lot, with our new archenemy, the 17th century musketeer, at his side. I didn't think the boy was possessed, but based on what I'd seen of him earlier, there was plainly something wrong. They were observing the mayhem, and I thought I saw pleasure in their expressions. Two more demons and their victims remained...Billy was in pursuit of one, and the other was my linebacker nemesis and his oh-so-powerful demon.

Billy was now at the top of the lawn by the hotel terrace with a female demon and her victim. The demon was wearing a graceful 18th century evening dress in a dark chiffon fabric that flowed elegantly around her as she moved, and of course she wore round-rimmed glasses. The lights from the terrace lit her face, and I could see that she'd probably been quite beautiful in her more corporeal days, but death had changed that. I'd become quite adept at identifying the fashion of the last several centuries...it was a necessary tool in order to determine the strength of the demons we faced—the older the clothes, the older *and* more powerful the ghost or demon. Aside from the demon who'd been standing next to the boy, these final two were the oldest we'd come across on this particular ghost killing adventure, which was probably why they had been walloping us with such ease.

The 18th century ghost's victim was a man; not a very tall one, but broad with an athletic build. He was swinging a croquet mallet with demon-fueled force at Billy, keeping her from killing his demon and saving his life. I heard her cuss loudly as the unwilling man connected with her leg. I could see her out of the corner of my eye...she went down, and the man, with his demon at the helm, grabbed her by the arm and tried to drag her towards the parking lot, *and* the musketeer. I started after them; however, my cliff-tossing foe and his demon had other plans.

The linebacker's demon was decked out in the traditional uniform of a British regular...or if you prefer the more colloquial term, he was a redcoat. His uniform was dusty and dirty and his pants were stained in what I thought was probably the blood of his centuries-old enemies. Even his round-rimmed glasses seemed to be coated in dust.

The man, who'd been quite ill from the demon's haunting over the last several hours, looked less formidable than he had just a short time ago. But I knew that no matter how sick he was, as long as the demon had control, the man's body would fight viciously. He rushed me, but I wasn't going to be caught again. I went left, then right while simultaneously jabbing the former British soldier. With a sigh of relief, I watched his ghostly form turn to mist and float away as his victim slumped to the ground.

Just before vanquishing the redcoat I'd caught a glimpse of Billy again—she'd managed to separate herself from the man, but he'd recovered and was backing her up toward the terrace. Now that the redcoat was eradicated I headed that way. The terrace was strewn with overturned patio furniture and broken planters and their contents. I heard a low moan and headed in its direction. The man Billy had been battling was slumped against some lounge chairs, covered in dirt and battered flora. Aside from the fact that he was beat up and more or less unconscious, he looked to be okay. I looked around for Billy. A string of expletives rang out from my left and I smiled. *Ah, there she is.*

"Billy, you okay?" I asked, trying to catch sight of her amongst the wreckage.

"No, I'm not okay! What the hell was that?" Billy snarled.

"I don't know…," I said quietly. There are technically three categories of ghosts; low-level, which are the newly dead, meaning they've only been dead for twenty to forty years; mid-level ghosts are older, usually having died forty to eighty years back; and the high-level are the oldest, sometimes hundreds of years dead. Those I considered demons instead of just ghosts, because the longer a ghost haunts and the more victims it kills, the more powerful it becomes. The powerful demons were always a threat, physically, but usually only to their victims. However, as Billy had mentioned the day before, it felt like we were being lured into these battles so the demons could hurt *us* as well as their victims. But the teenager was the most disturbing, because I was positive that he killed two people by using the power of the 17th century demon that seemed to be his companion and not his tormentor. I was also positive that I'd seen him before...unfortunately, my brain was a bit too rattled at that moment to focus on where.

I glanced toward Billy's voice. She'd managed to push most of the debris off herself, and now that I saw her face clearly, it wasn't pretty. She had a gash running across her forehead; the blood that oozed down her face was infused with potting soil, giving it a thick, muddy appearance. She had more cuts on her left cheek and chin, and her shirt-sleeve was ripped and soaked in blood. I checked the man again, and then went to Billy. She pulled away and swatted at me when I tried to assess her wounds.

"Stop that. I need to see how bad this is." I grabbed the back of her neck to hold her still. She said something very unladylike, but very Billy-like, and I smiled painfully. Her injuries looked superficial and her belligerent attitude was spot-on...she was going to be fine.

I slumped down on the terrace floor next to her and tried to take a deep breath. I was pretty sure I had a broken rib or two, and now that the action had stopped and the adrenalin flow had slowed, I began to shiver uncontrollably from my dunk in the very cold ocean.

"What happened to you? Why are you all wet...? Shit, look at your hands, they're wasted!" Billy's tone was gruff, but I heard concern too.

"The redcoat's victim beat the crap out of me and threw me off the cliff." I held my hands up for a better look. "I had to climb up that dock I told you about, it was covered in barnacles and oysters.... I'll be fine." I moaned and promptly passed out.

Chapter 4

I woke up sometime later on a couch in one of the hotel suites. Every single inch of my body hurt, and as dramatic as it sounds, I was sure I was dying. Someone had kindly cleaned and bandaged my hands and covered me with a blanket...I guess they were hoping I was going to live. I glanced around the room. It was empty, but I could hear voices on the other side of a door in the far corner. On the coffee table, sitting in a puddle of condensation, was a crystal glass filled with amber liquid and the remnants of melting ice-cubes. The smell of the sweet Irish whiskey from two feet away gave me hope... if I could smell the whiskey, my nose probably wasn't broken or too badly damaged. I sat up painfully and noticed the aspirin bottle next to the glass, and attempted to smile through my cut lips. Billy might be the most obnoxious woman I knew, but deep down inside she must love me a little to leave these much needed medicinal miracles.

I swallowed two aspirin, drank the whiskey in one long gulp, and leaned back against the couch, closing my eyes. We were at a small resort hotel on the picturesque Marin Coast just north of San Francisco. Aris had received a distressing call from an associate, Robert Grant, who was attending a weekend wedding at the resort. Some of the guests had begun to feel viciously ill, and like most of us in that situation, they sequestered themselves in their rooms in the hopes of feeling better soon. Robert was a retired ghost killer, and one of his friends was among the infirm. When he decided to check on his companion, he was greeted by his deathly ill friend and a nasty demon, which Robert, although in his seventies, vanquished post-haste. Robert was aware of our more recent troubles and became suspicious that the other guests were being haunted as well. Of course, it would have been quite inappropriate to go barging into strangers' rooms to confirm they had unwanted ghosts with them, so he called us.

By the time Billy and I arrived, there was no doubt about the other guests; they were being haunted too, and possessed. In their altered states, they'd garnered their evening wear and come downstairs to the main lounge to join the wedding party, where these unfortunate possessed souls began to torment the other guests, starting both verbal and physical fights. Robert tried his best to get at their demons, but they were faster and very powerful.

As Billy and I began to go after the ghouls—there were probably ten or twelve total—the teenager had grabbed a petite woman by her hair and shoved her to her knees. At that point the musketeer demon appeared and reached out to him, as if to hold hands—not literally of course... ghosts aren't solid, but they did somehow connect—and all at once I could almost see the electroplasmic electricity arc from the demon, through the boy, and into the woman. Billy, realizing what was happening, charged the trio and separated him and his demon from the woman, who fell to the floor in a pile of evening clothes, but she was alive. The boy ran outside through the terrace doors and the musketeer followed. Billy looked a little shell-shocked, like she'd received a jolt of the demon's juice, which she probably had, and I stopped to see if she was okay.

"Forget me! Get that kid!" she seethed. I left her and followed the boy out to the lawn, where I was attacked by the redcoat and his victim. While we fought, the boy and the evil musketeer killed two people and I got thrown off a cliff....

A few minutes later I heard the door open and Billy walked into the room. Considering her injuries were far fewer than mine, I really hoped for a little compassion and sympathy. Instead, she said, very *un*-sympathetically, "Finally, you're awake. We need to get going."

I rubbed my head. "Wait, what happened?"

"The real fighting between the haunted guests and everyone else started a little before we got here. By the time I pulled the kid off that woman, someone had called the sheriff's office; they arrived right after you passed out. Pete got here a few minutes after we did with two of his guys and got the ghosts we left inside, and then helped me get you up here. The room isn't registered to anyone, so they don't know about us, but they will if we don't get out of here."

"What are they going to say happened?"

She let out an impatient sigh. "Pete told the sheriff that he stopped to get a bite to eat at the café across the lobby from the ballroom where the wedding reception was taking place. He told them he heard yelling and screaming and ran to help. A huge fight was in progress, the kid appeared out of nowhere with a stun gun or something, and went nuts and tried to kill that woman I saved, then killed those two other people and tried to zap some of the other guests. Since the ones that were actually being haunted and possessed won't remember anything, Pete persuaded them that that's what happened. All the other guests are too shaken up to give reasonable accounts, so unless we want to explain why we're here, since we're not guests and all...let's go!"

There's a difference between a possession and a haunting. When a ghost haunts a victim, it makes them sick or disabled; but when they possess a victim, the ghost-demon not only makes them ill, but it can control the victim, and most of those times the demon will cause its victim to kill themselves. When a ghost or demon is killed and its victim is cured, the victim doesn't have any memory of being sick, and no one else would remember they'd been sick either. This is just the way it is...we don't know why, we just know that once we kill the ghost that's haunting them, they're cured, like nothing ever happened. Billy explained it to me like this: "*You know when a friend or acquaintance shows up with a new haircut and you're not sure why, but you know there's something different about them, you just can't pinpoint it? It's kind of like that. Their friends and family know something's different, but they don't know what, they just know the person is better for it.*" However, if a person is possessed by a demon and a ghost killer is lucky enough to intervene, the person not only doesn't remember, but they're very suggestible to other explanations because their brains were temporarily scrambled by the demon's presence.

I sighed and started to get up, only to fall back on the couch as my head swam and my vision blurred. I wasn't sure I was going to be able to move as quickly as she'd like. Billy came over and held out her hand, "Come on, George, suck it up, we gotta get out of here." I took her hand and managed to stand, but I was still wobbly.

She led me to the end of the hallway and opened the stairwell door. "Really Billy, stairs...?" I said weakly. She scowled, put her arm around my waist, and walked me one flight down. The door at the bottom opened onto another hallway. At one end was the main lobby, at the other, a side exit that would take us to the parking lot. Billy looked toward the lobby; Pete was standing in view, but away from several sheriff's deputies. He casually walked in our direction. Billy ushered me into an alcove containing an ice and soda machine, out of sight of the lobby.

A minute later, Pete ducked into the alcove, took one look at me, and blew out a long whistle. "Please tell me it was an old one that did that to you."

I said, careful of my lacerated lips, "Redcoat."

Pete's eyebrows shot up, "Really? Never come across one of those before."

"How's it going out there?" Billy asked.

"Fine, I guess. So far they seem to be buying my story." He didn't look all that convinced.

"Do we know who the kid was?" I asked. Something about him, besides his murderous actions, was bugging me. I just couldn't grasp why at the moment.

"Not a clue, but one of my guys saw him leave in a blue four-door...he thought it was a VW. He isn't a hundred-percent sure, but he did get a partial plate. Aris is trying to track it now. So don't go far, we may need you two to help catch this little shit," Pete said viciously.

"I'm not all that sure I have it in me tonight." I turned to Billy. "Where are we headed, back to the city?"

"There's a motel about a mile down the road...get a room. I'll call you when Aris gets back to me," Pete said as he grabbed us by the shoulders and shoved us toward the exit.

Billy and I headed to the guest parking lot where her Mustang GT was parked. She didn't go out the main driveway though; if the sheriff saw us leaving, we'd be detained. She used the service road instead, and within thirty minutes we were huddled in a two star motel room with two double beds, the strong smell of disinfectant, and an ancient TV, tuned to the local news channel, which was already reporting *our* version of the evening's events.

Chapter 5

Ghost killing takes copious amounts of energy, and apparently Billy had used all of hers, so she left me on one of the lumpy beds and went in search of food. I tried to follow the news, but ended up dozing off instead. I woke to the sound of Billy shaking the ice around in her soda cup and slurping loudly through the straw.

"Did you get me anything?" I said, and rolled over to face her. She was sitting Indian style on the other bed, a mostly empty take-out container in front of her and the offending soda cup still in her hand. Without a word, she pointed to a closed take-out container on the nightstand between the beds. I edged into a sitting position and put the container in my lap. She'd brought me a PB&J and french fries. I looked over at her and said, "Really, this is the best you could do?"

"Your lips are swollen and split in two places. It was thin, and the only thing I could think of besides soup that wouldn't make you reopen those wounds." She glanced at me and grimaced. "You look like shit, by the way."

"Thanks...on both counts." Billy was hardly ever considerate of my injuries, but tonight was probably the worst we'd come across, and in her own little way, she was trying to be nice, *and* acknowledge I'd taken the worst beating between the two of us.

"Any word on the teenager?" I asked between bites. She shook her head. "Billy, that kid was doing what you did in Germany, right?"

Billy's mother, Julie, was raised by Justine because her own mother, Wilhelmina Wilkinson (Grandma Billy) wasn't able to handle her ghost killing abilities and for the most part, was quite insane. However, Julie was a spoiled little rich girl, who didn't even bother to attend her mother's funeral, took her inheritance, and disappeared. A few years later she showed back up, broke and with a toddler in tow. Justine agreed to help, but there were rules, which Julie followed, at least for a while. When Julie had reached the point that she no longer wanted to follow the rules, or wanted to be a mother any more, her father approached her with a monetary deal she couldn't refuse. All she had to do was turn custody of her daughter over to the man. That man was Frederick Vokkel, and he wanted his granddaughter so he could study her. He was convinced she'd be like her grandmother, who, despite her mental problems, had been one of the most powerful ghost killers alive.

Vokkel ended up taking Billy away to Germany where he could monitor her more closely and without interference from Justine, who was constantly suing him to regain custody of her beloved Billy. When Billy was a teenager, she knew she had more power than most ghost killers and she knew she could use that power to escape her deranged grandfather. While on a field trip to town with her bodyguard, Billy "communicated" with a demon, and when she held the hand of her bodyguard, the demon "took" Billy's hand and the same type of electroplasmic electricity the teenager had used earlier in the night shot through Billy and into the bodyguard, killing her. Billy hadn't done it again, but she knew she could and knew how dangerous it could be, as evidenced by her willingness to put herself in mortal peril to save the woman earlier in the evening.

"Yeah, that's pretty much it…," she said quietly.

"Something wasn't right about him...I mean, aside from his demon buddy. Did you get the impression he wasn't...all there? Like he wasn't in complete control or something?" I asked.

"He was in control. I watched him kill one of those people, and he knew exactly what he was doing!" she replied fiercely.

"Okay, calm down. I was getting tossed off a cliff, and I missed that part." I tried to sound contrite, but she didn't care. I asked, "So he has to be a ghost killer, right?"

"Yeah, and I'm guessing a pretty powerful one...a lot like I was at that age," she said mournfully. I'd only broached the subject of the German bodyguard's death once, and it hadn't gone over well. The time she was imprisoned by Vokkel were the worst years of her life, and in my opinion, one of the main reasons she was so adversarial all the time. Well, that and what her mother did to her.

"Billy, that last guy tried to grab you, didn't he?"

She nodded. "Yeah...I guess, but I managed to kick him in the family jewels and he went down for a second." She glanced at me...was that fear I saw?

Before I could say anything else, her cell phone rang on the nightstand and she leaned over to get it. Looking at the screen, she said, "It's Pete." She put him on speaker. "Hey, Pete."

"Hey, how are you guys doing?"

She glanced at me and grimaced again. "I'm okay; a few cuts and bruises, but nothing to cry over. George, on the other hand—"

I said, "I'll be fine, Pete...bumps, bruises, and cuts, an ordinary day at the office." Billy chuffed loudly at that. "So, what's the story with the kid?"

"Nothing yet. Aris is running combinations of the partial plate along with blue four-door sedans. The list is long and we need to sort through it to try and determine if a teenager is the registered owner, but it could belong to his parents or it could be stolen, so that makes it harder." Pete sounded tired.

"Pete, we need to find this kid. If the police catch him he'll no doubt just kill whoever he comes in contact with!" Billy said angrily.

The thing that had been bothering me earlier in the night about the kid suddenly broke through. "Pete, it was the kid from the other night, the teenager we saw in the Tenderloin—remember?"

Pete asked, "Yeah? I didn't see him...I mean, not up close. Are you sure?"

"I'm sure. He had on different clothes, but I'm positive it was him. And you know what else?" I glanced at Billy. "I don't think he was in complete charge of the situation...he seemed sort of dazed." Billy gave me a hard glare, but didn't say anything.

Pete said, "Well, he was using that demon to hurt people, so we know he's a ghost killer, but maybe he was on drugs or something. I mean, you'd have to be pretty messed up to do that on purpose, right?" I couldn't have agreed more. "Listen it's late." And it was, almost 2 a.m. "Why don't you two get some sleep and get back to the city in the morning? Hopefully we'll have some leads at that point," he said through a yawn. Then he asked, "Did either of you see Mark when you were leaving the parking lot?" Pete had arrived at the resort with two other ghost killers...Mark was one of them.

"No, why?" Billy asked suspiciously.

"I haven't seen him since we arrived at the hotel. Jason, the other guy I had with me, the one that saw the kid drive off, said he thought he followed you two outside, but...." Pete yawned again. "I don't know. He got there on his own...maybe he saw the kid leave and took off after him. I'll try his cell again."

"Yeah sure," I said. "You sound pretty tired yourself. You headed back tonight?"

Pete laughed wearily. "On the road now, my friend."

"Good, drive safe," Billy said, and disconnected the call.

I looked around the room. It really was a dive and it smelled funny. I wanted to go home. Now.

"I want my own bed…let's go. I'm wide-awake now; I'll drive." I pulled myself up from the bed and headed to the bathroom. She didn't argue.

We cleaned up our dinner trash, dropped the key with the night clerk, and were on the road in less than fifteen minutes. Billy was snoring softly in twenty minutes, and remained that way until we hit the toll booth of the Golden Gate Bridge. From there it was only another ten minutes to our building in Pacific Heights.

Chapter 6

As I unlocked my apartment door, Billy gave me a concerned look and asked, "You going to be okay? You want me to stay with you?" I must have looked pretty bad. The hour-long drive really wore me down, and the shellacking I'd taken the night before was catching up to me again. Billy was in no way the mothering sort, but she knew better than anyone what it was like to get your clock cleaned by a demon, and it was probably the only thing that brought out sympathy in her otherwise callous personality.

"Naw," I said tiredly. "I'll be fine. But don't tell Justine how bad off I am. I'll be better after some sleep."

Justine worried, and although I was sure Billy had texted her the night before to say she wasn't coming home, Justine was an early riser. Even though it was not quite 4 a.m., she would probably hear Billy come in and would want an update on my condition and our evening. My current state would cause Justine a great deal of stress, and I wanted to avoid that in the hopes that I would be in better shape later in the morning. Billy nodded her head and walked the twenty feet to her front door.

I needed painkillers and sleep, and a healthy shot of whiskey would provide the former and help along the latter. I hobbled into the kitchen, put a few ice-cubes into a tumbler, and hobbled back out to the living room bar cabinet to pour myself a good amount of Bushmills. Then I sat on the couch and sipped slowly, all the while thinking about just how lucky I was to be alive.

I'd fallen asleep on the couch sitting up, whiskey glass still in hand and precariously close to spilling it's watered down remnants into my lap. Although it was now approaching 8 a.m., the drapes were closed and the room was shadowed and mostly dark, but I still felt a presence. I wasn't alone. Standing in the furthest corner was GG, my mother's childhood ghost friend. She'd been instrumental in our fight with Vokkel and his demons, but I hadn't seen her since and thought maybe she'd been vanquished in the melee. I smiled at her, ignoring the pain it brought to my mouth.

"I thought we killed you...," I said groggily. GG smiled and shook her head. "Where have you been?" I asked, knowing she couldn't answer with words. She looked around the room. In the past, GG attempted to communicate by finding items and making me guess what the meaning was. This time she moved to the clock that sat on my mantel.

"A clock?" She shook her head and moved her ghostly finger around the dial. "Time?" I asked. She nodded and pointed to her temple and twirled her finger around, then waved her hand absently. I thought for a moment. "Do you mean you have no concept of time?" She nodded vigorously. "Well, you seemed to know when I needed you last time," I said in sleepy confusion. She smiled again and pointed at me, then pointed to herself. "I need you now?" She nodded again, and disappeared. I sighed, pulled myself up, and went to my bed.

When I woke up several hours later, it was to the muffled sound of my cell phone ringing. It took me a minute to realize it was still in my front jeans pocket, which I hadn't bothered to remove when I'd stumbled into bed. Grimacing at the pain that seemed to have worsened since I hit the mattress, I dug my phone out and answered it, not bothering to see who it was—I knew it had to be Billy, Aris, or my good friend, Phil James.

It was Phil. When I answered, he said, "Hey man, you're alive!" I groaned in acknowledgment. "Heard you had a little Revolutionary War reenactment last night." Phil chuckled at his joke, but I couldn't laugh back…it would've hurt entirely too much.

"Yeah—tough night. What's up?" I asked. I could hear the roughness in my voice. Lack of sleep and coughing up salt water hadn't done my usually pleasant baritone any favors.

"Dude, you sound horrible." Phil sounded concerned, so I put him at ease as best I could.

"I'm all right, Phil. But you woke me up. I'm just a little groggy."

"Okay. Well, we might have a lead on the kid and Aris wants to meet, but it sounds like you need a little more sleep. Why don't you text me in a few hours and we can assemble at the old haunt later today." The *old haunt* was really called Seymour's, a Victorian-themed bar where I'd first gotten to know Phil. From that point on, it had become our local watering hole and informal debriefing station. Phil referred to it as the "old haunt", pun intended, because of what we usually discussed there…ghosts and hauntings. It was also the first place I'd laid eyes on GG.

"Yeah, sure, I can do that. I'll let Billy know and we'll see you later on, okay?" We hung up and I rolled over and groaned some more.

When the ghosts first appeared to me, I had needed to find out what was happening and why. My research led me to a ghost tour that was conducted four nights a week in Lower Pacific Heights that guaranteed the patrons they'd see or at least experience a ghost. Phil owned the business, and after the tour we talked. He had figured out what I was, because there was indeed a ghost on his tour and I saw it and he knew it. Although Phil couldn't see ghosts—well, he'd seen one or two, but he couldn't do it regularly—he was well versed on them and what they did. Moreover, he was well aware of the ghost killers and the Watchers. He helped me a great deal back then, and now he helped the Watchers. He'd also become a good friend.

Chapter 7

I stunk—I smelled like salt water and sweat and blood, and I knew that a hot shower would do me a world of good. Instead of getting up though, I rolled over again, closed my eyes, and wallowed in self-pity until I heard a pounding on my front door. That had to be Billy.

Billy had cleaned the blood and dirt off her face back at the motel, but she still hadn't looked much better than me in the wee morning hours when we parted ways; however, I was extremely annoyed at how she looked this morning. She was scrubbed clean, hair hanging in ebony waves down her back, and aside from the butterfly bandage on her forehead, I only saw two minor cuts on her chin that looked more like scratches. Her short-sleeved blouse showed her upper arms, one of which was wrapped in gauze, but she didn't have any bruises anywhere that I could see. She smelled good too, which made my rank disposition all the more difficult to stomach.

"Whew, you need a shower," she said, waving her hand under her nose as she shouldered past me to the kitchen.

"Yeah, good morning to you too—make yourself at home," I replied sarcastically, and headed to the bathroom. She'd make coffee, and if I was really lucky, she'd make breakfast too.

Fifteen gloriously hot and steamy minutes later, I stood in front of my bathroom mirror and assessed the damage. There were large swaths of bruising on my ribcage where I'd taken the body blows, but I no longer thought anything was broken, just bruised. The cuts on my chin and lips looked better too, now that they were clean, but there was some swelling and bruising there as well. My hands, however, still looked like minced meat, and I decided to rewrap the palms, where most of the damage was, in a healthy slathering of antibiotic lotion and gauze.

By the time I was dressed, the strong smell of coffee and sizzling bacon had wafted down the hallway, and I was practically drooling in anticipation. Billy was an excellent cook, and breakfast was her specialty. She was working her culinary magic at the stove when I entered the kitchen, and I moved around her to get at the coffee.

Glancing at me from the corner of her eye, she quipped, "Well you smell better, but you don't look much better."

"If it wasn't for the coffee *and* the breakfast, I'd tell you to leave," I retorted. "How's Justine today?"

"She's fine. She had a charity thing this morning, but she was worried about you and asked me to come over and check on you. I called her while you were in the shower, told her you were fine…an obvious lie," she said as she glanced at me again and frowned. "She wants to know what your dinner plans are for tonight."

It was a little after one in the afternoon and it would be another hour or so before we got to the bar, and depending on what was discussed, we might be tied up for the evening. "I'm free so far, but Phil and Aris want an update, and if they need our help, we might not be available. Oh, and I think I saw GG earlier this morning."

Billy spun around so quickly that the spatula she was holding almost flew from her hand. "Really?" Billy had taken to GG immediately, and she had been just as distraught as I was when GG hadn't reappeared after our fight with Vokkel.

"It was kind of dark and I was pretty sleepy, so I'm not a hundred percent sure it wasn't a dream." My tone was casual and teasing.

She shot an unpleasant green glare in my direction and turned back to her cooking. Once she'd plated the food and slapped it on the table, she sat and stared at me, finally saying, "Well, what did she say?"

"I think...," I started, taking a large bite of my omelet and chewing slowly and methodically, garnering another icy glare. Laughing lightly at her annoyance, I said, "I think she was trying to tell me that she has no concept of time and comes when I need her."

"What the hell does that mean?" Billy said thoughtfully as she shoveled a rather unladylike fork full of food into her mouth. Once she'd chewed and swallowed, she said, almost to herself, "So she's connected to you through your mother, and showed up just in time to help fight Vokkel and his surge of demons." She waved her fork around. "Maybe she's back because of what happened in Marin...to help us with that kid...." Her brow furrowed. "But why wait to show up? These attacks have been going on for more than a week now."

It was a good question...I'd have to try and ask GG. Regardless, GG had displayed extreme power by bringing a surge of good ghosts to fight Vokkel's demons, and God knew we could use that sort of help now.

We finished our late breakfast in silence. After Billy put her dishes in the sink, she turned to face me, leaning against the counter and saying, "I have a few things to do today. Tell Phil we'll meet him at three, and I'll let Justine know that dinner is iffy at best." Then she left.

I spent the next hour cleaning up my apartment, and then walked next door to Justine's to collect Billy and head over to Seymour's.

Chapter 8

As usual, Margie answered the door. "Hello, George." She paused and looked at my face. "Oh my, it looks like you took the brunt of it last night."

"Hi, Margie," I said, smiling lightly. "Yeah, Billy got off easy…," I let out an exaggerated sigh, "as usual."

Margie chuckled. She found the antagonistic banter between Billy and me very amusing.

"Yes, I'm sure she saved all the really bad ones for you," she mocked. "Come, they're waiting on the terrace with bated breath."

I followed Margie through the living room and out onto the terrace. Justine gasped lightly at my condition, and I went to her, kissed her lightly powdered cheek, and said, "Honestly, Justine, it looks much worse than it feels. There's no need to worry." I finished with the biggest smile I could produce… it hurt like hell, but my smiles, big or small, usually put Justine at ease. This time she glanced at Billy and shook her head dismissively; Billy was probably in for a reprimand later on.

"Would you like some coffee, dear?" Justine asked.

"Please. Did Billy fill you in on last night?" I asked.

"She did, and it is very disturbing. Have you learned anything more about this boy… teenager?" Justine asked, concern wrinkling her otherwise smooth brow. Justine was in her early eighties, but she'd aged beautifully and I thought it would be hard to convince most people that she was a day over sixty-five.

"No, but Aris had his people on the kid's trail all night, so hopefully we'll know more when we meet them in an hour," I answered.

"Billy tells me that the devil who did that to you was a Revolutionary War soldier. That is quite old."

"Yeah, it is. But not as old as the kid's demon... that guy was mid-17th century."

Justine's eyes lit up. She was fascinated by the oddity of the age of the ghosts and demons, but even more fascinated with the clothing styles they wore and the fact that they all wore round-rimmed glasses. We frequently discussed the topic. We had spent hours over the last few months poring through websites and books, educating ourselves on men's and women's fashions decade by decade as far back as the 1400s. As far as the glasses were concerned, Justine and I hadn't made any more headway than anyone else. The only reference anyone had found was a dream interpretation: if someone dreamed of glasses, it was supposed to represent a clearer view of a problem or situation—we assumed, as ghost killers, we could see a problem that no one else could. Billy thought it was all a stupid waste of time, and as far as she was concerned, if the clothes looked old and they were wearing round-rimmed glasses, she stabbed them with her chopstick, they swirled away into a grey mist, and that was the end of it. I, on the other hand, liked to know the power of the ghosts and demons, and their clothes were a direct indication of how long they'd been dead, which also gave me an idea of how much power they'd amassed.

"Do tell, dear, what was he wearing?" Justine asked excitedly, and Billy rolled her eyes and moaned audibly, which netted her a slap on the wrist by Justine. "Billy dear, don't be rude. You know that I enjoy learning about these devils, especially their clothing." She winked at me and I described our musketeer-clothed demon.

After I finished my description of the ghostly garments, Justine asked, "What about Frederick's papers? I believe you said that Mr. James has been studying them. Has he found any references to this young man? I would think a ghost killer of this boy's caliber would have been on Frederick's radar." Justine was referring to Phil... as I mentioned earlier, he'd been assisting the Watchers, and one of his new duties was to attempt to decipher Vokkel's notes and journals.

I shrugged. "I know he's been working hard on it, but I'm not sure he's had time to search them for references to the kid. I'll check with him when we talk this afternoon."

A few hours after Frederick Vokkel's death, Aris had sent four men to his house. Since we knew that Vokkel had a home security system and assumed there would be a safe, our guys went prepared, bringing along two professionals—a security systems hacker and a safecracker. The Watchers have an eclectic group of associates who usually don't ask questions as long as the price is right. They were able to infiltrate the house and safe without leaving a trace, unless of course, you counted the absence of Vokkel's papers. Vokkel had dedicated his life to the phenomenon that is our world, and we were hopeful we'd find something useful. They left with a stockpile of boxes containing unorganized research notes and journals. Vokkel was a madman, and his writings were reflective of that. He preferred his own version of code and shorthand, some of which Phil had managed to decipher, but there was still some that he'd made no headway on whatsoever.

Vokkel had started out as a garden variety shrink. At some point he was exposed to several patients experiencing a form of anomalistic psychosis and it fascinated him, so much so that he focused his research on these types of patients and their disease. He discovered that the paranormal delusions weren't delusions at all, nor were they the result of mental illness. These people actually saw ghosts, and they could kill them. It turned out that Vokkel had latent paranormal abilities of his own, but he had no control over them. All of this led him to another discovery; not all ghost killers were alike. Some were more powerful and could communicate with the more powerful ghosts and demons. This discovery prompted him to open a "school" in Switzerland that wasn't much better than an institution, and that was where he met Billy's grandmother and my mother. We knew from the journals that the school started out small and he expanded as he came across more and more people who exhibited paranormal abilities, including two longaevus, Edgar and Anne, half-siblings that became his protégés and did his bidding.

Eventually Vokkel closed the Switzerland school down and moved to San Francisco, primarily to be near Grandma Billy, because she was by far the most powerful ghost killer he'd ever encountered, aside from my mother. Knowing that the type of power Grandma Billy had was mostly due to genetics, he managed to seduce her in the hopes of impregnating her, which worked—although in Billy's mind, it was rape, since Grandma Billy didn't really have the mental capacity to provide proper consent. What didn't work was the child they produced together...Julie, Billy's mother. Julie's only ability was her own self-centeredness, and Vokkel gave up on her, for a while at least. When Julie was all grown up, Vokkel paid her to seduce a powerful ghost killer and get pregnant, with the belief that Grandma Billy's talents had simply skipped a generation and would materialize in her grandchild, which they did. He continued his research and opened a new "school" shortly after Billy was born. He was rightly convinced that she'd be like her grandmother, and he wanted to be prepared. Then he "bought" custody of Billy from Julie when she was just four years old, and eventually moved her to his new school in Germany.

Chapter 9

We arrived at the bar and entered through the double oak doors. Seymour's was located on the bottom floor of a Victorian building that had been beautifully preserved and restored. I'm a huge fan of San Francisco's historic architecture, which was one of the reasons I bought my apartment in an ornate 1920s building, and another reason I was so fond of Seymour's. The bar is loaded with Victorian charm, complete with tufted red velvet booths and chairs, ornately carved dark wood features, and electrified gaslight style fixtures.

The booth in the farthest corner was our regular spot and Billy headed toward it, ignoring the nod of greeting from the bartender, Ed. Although I was positive that Justine taught Billy manners, she rarely used them. I, on the other hand, used mine often. I walked up to the bar and greeted Ed with a smile and asked how he was. We traded pleasantries for a few minutes while he poured our pints. He no longer asked me about my occasionally bruised or cut-up face…I think Phil had told him I was a boxer, and not a very good one.

I took our drinks and sat next to Billy in the booth. She always picked the side against the wall so she could see the bar and the front door and anyone who came through it. Billy had been sullen and quiet on the walk over…sullen wasn't unusual, but quiet was. We sipped in silence, and finally I asked, "What's on your mind, Billy? You're too quiet."

She glanced over at me, and a spark of dread flashed in her eyes. "I'm worried, George."

"We all are, but what's got you *specifically* worried?"

"That kid last night, the demon he was with, the recent attacks... they aren't surges, they're organized, and I have trouble believing it's some teenager that's behind it all. The fact that it's escalated to murder...." She blew out a hard breath, a telltale sign of her frustration.

"I've been thinking about him too, and everything else." I was hesitant to say what was on my mind next because I knew it was too close to home for her, but I had to say it. "Billy, I don't think the kid was playing with a full deck." She started to say something and I held my hand up to shush her. "You know what I mean... sometimes this ability happens to people that can't handle it or just aren't equipped to handle it."

Billy's grandmother had been a person like that. She was a bright and intelligent child and young woman, but emotionally fragile. When she started seeing ghosts and killing them, it drove her insane for the most part, which spurred her father to institutionalize her, even though he was a ghost killer too and probably could have helped her through it. That turned out to be even worse, because it put her in Vokkel's hands, and we knew how that turned out.

"And I don't think it's anything like your grandmother. I think he's probably mentally disabled to some extent, or maybe he was on drugs like Pete suggested. Or maybe he's just a killer at heart and the demon knows it and enjoys the fact that the kid can use its electroplasmic juice."

Billy cringed. She hated that term, but it was the best one I could think of to describe the jolts of electric-like charges the demons emitted when we touched them barehanded, or when they were so powerful they torched my pencils or her chopsticks when we stabbed them.

"As far as the other demons are concerned, I'm not sure what to make of them. But I'm pretty sure that kid deliberately lured us outside so we could get our butts kicked by his demonic friends. Did you notice that almost all the victims were healthy and well built... solid? That's not right... demons pick the weakest in the crowd. They're easier to possess and control, but last night's victims looked like they'd been in pretty good shape before they were haunted and possessed. What are the chances that a band of demons would assess the crowd and pick out the biggest and strongest? Let's not forget, the one guy tried to grab you before you kicked his ass. What was that? Was he trying to kidnap you?"

Her voice was low, almost a whisper. "You think that kid set us up? That he wanted us there, to kill us, or...." She paused and her brow furrowed deeply. "Why would they want to kidnap me?"

"I don't know." I picked up my glass and drained half of my beer.

One of the front doors opened and Phil sauntered into the bar, looked in our direction, and tipped his hat in greeting. Phil was in his early forties, tall, with large, expressive eyes that appeared to protrude from their sockets when he spoke passionately, which was often. His hair hung in frizzy curls almost to his shoulders, and his beard and mustache were neatly trimmed. His apparel consisted of a few constants; he always wore a hat of some sort, and a vest with a silver pocket watch tucked into the left pocket, with the chain attached to a button. He usually paired these items with jeans, biker boots, and if needed, a long wool topcoat. He had an energetic personality that some might mistake for hyperactive, or at the very least enthusiastic about everything—good or bad.

Phil stopped at the bar for a beer, then strolled over to the booth and placed his glass on the table. "Hey, man, how the hell are you?" He reached out to shake my hand, which was still bandaged; he grimaced and thankfully shook lightly.

Leaning past me, he murmured something to Billy, probably a compliment. He was a bit of a suck-up when it came to her, and the only man I'd met, besides myself, that actually enjoyed her abrasive personality. Billy, although she wouldn't openly admit it, liked him quite a bit too.

Phil got settled, took a gulp of his beer, and said, "So, man, I heard that was some show in Marin."

Billy and I nodded at the same time. Phil leaned closer and scrutinized each of us, then said, "Man, you got the lion's share of it, didn't you? Either that or Billy really is a better fighter than you." He winked at her and a slight smirk spread across her lips.

"She didn't have to fight a possessed linebacker, and she didn't get thrown off a cliff," I said defensively.

Phil held his hands up and said, "Just teasing, man." He smiled and winked again. "So Pete said there were about ten or twelve demons, including the kid and the demon he had with him."

I nodded. "Yeah, that was the largest attack so far, and the boldest. I mean, there were a lot of people there that weren't possessed and saw the whole thing. I can't imagine how Pete managed to spin it so the cops bought what he was selling."

Phil nodded, but before he could say anything, the doors opened again and I said, "Aris is here."

We waited quietly as Aris stopped at the bar and ordered his drink. As usual, he was wearing a perfectly tailored suit, a stark white shirt, and silk tie. Aris was about my height and build, but where I was just clean cut and not too hard on the eyes, he was handsome in an elegant and exotic way. He had dark, almost black eyes, olive-toned skin, and jet-black hair with a touch of grey at the temples. His reserved personality and impeccable fashion sense added an air of mystery to him as well. When I first met Aris, I assumed his only employment was simply "head Watcher." Turned out it was a lot more—he was a homicide detective with the SFPD. I wasn't sure how he found the time to be good at both things, but he did, and of course his career with the police department allowed the Watchers access to information that wouldn't be available through legal civilian channels.

Aris slid into the booth next to Phil and placed his drink on the table without saying a word. Once he was situated, he looked Billy and I over carefully and said, "I am told that was one of the worst attacks to date. However, I am very grateful that you both survived with…," he paused, "*minimal* damage."

I felt Billy stiffen and I grabbed her hand to calm her down. She and Aris had been acquainted for years, and Billy believed that Aris and the Watchers could have prevented some of the more unfortunate events in her life. She was partially correct, but Aris respected her a great deal and we agreed to work with him, so she usually kept her ill feelings in check. However, she was tired and frustrated today, and I had no doubt that she was about to say something offensive and obnoxious, and I didn't see any point in getting the meeting off to a bad start.

"Pete and Mr. Grant were kind enough to provide a full report of what they experienced. Is there anything you would like to add?" Aris asked.

"Well, George seems to think the demons we followed outside deliberately picked their victims, because they were healthy and fit, strong…." There was a little attitude in her tone, but I thought it was mostly directed at me. She relaxed a bit. "I guess they were, now that I think about it. He thinks maybe that kid and his demon communicated with the others with the intention of calling us out, using stronger victims so they could hurt us or kill us." She looked at me. "They sure put a hurt on him."

"That they did, no thanks to you," I said mockingly. She elbowed me and I snapped at her, "Damn it, woman, that hurt!" We might heal quickly, but it hadn't even been twenty-four hours yet, and my ribcage was still suffering from last night's assault.

I turned back to Aris and Phil and asked, "Did Pete tell you that I'm positive this kid was in the Tenderloin the other night?"

They both nodded, and Phil said, "Yeah, he did. But I think all that confirms is that the kid is working with the musketeer demon." Phil paused to take a pull off his beer. "But why?"

Not all ghost killers are good; some use their power to communicate and work with powerful ghosts and demons for personal gain. These have historically been seasoned ghost killers though, people who've honed their abilities over many years of practice and experience. So to have a mere teenager, a child really, with enough power to work alongside a demon as old as this musketeer was frightening. How did he learn to do it at such a young age? Who taught him? Based on my companions' pensive expressions, I guessed they were all contemplating the same thing.

"So tell us what you've found out about the kid," I said.

Phil said, "Okay. Well, you know we ran that partial plate, along with a description of the car. We came up with hundreds of matches. We were already checking DMV registrations for owners with teenage drivers, and we found a woman in a town east of here with a seventeen-year-old. The car is a dark-blue Volkswagen Jetta, so that fits. We ran the woman and her name is Gail Brelong…her son's name is Calvin Brelong."

"All right, so what do we know about them?" I asked.

"They live in a small town at the base of the Sierra Foothills in Calaveras County, called Valley Springs. The mother, according to the county assessor, owns a house and has lived there since the kid was five years old. The assessor also shows that she owns another property about twenty-five miles away, up the mountain, near a rural town called Rail Road Flat. Looks like she might have inherited it based on the info on the assessor's website. Carol ran the previous owner's name and discovered that he died in 2013 in a freak accident at his home."

Carol was Aris's niece, a mid-level ghost killer and a damn good hacker/computer geek as well.

"The local newspaper wrote a small story about it, stating that he was found by his sixteen-year-old nephew, who'd been visiting for the weekend. They didn't disclose the kid's name, but the age fits our teenage kid...."

"How did this person die?" I thought I knew the answer, but asked anyway.

"The official cause of death was listed as accidental electrocution," Phil said, his voice laced with suspicion.

"What, you think this kid killed his uncle?" Billy asked impatiently.

Phil wasn't fazed by Billy's frequently unpleasant disposition, so he just gave her a toothy grin and said, "Well, the guy died of electrocution, and we know this kid's playing with that demon, using its juice...." He shrugged. "But maybe it was just an accident."

"What else?" I asked.

"Pete and one of his guys are up there now trying to confirm this is our teenager. The mother isn't home, but they talked with the neighbor, who said that the kid takes the car all the time. In fact, he got home last night around 3 a.m. The neighbor knows this because the stereo was blasting as the kid pulled into the driveway and it woke him up. The neighbor says the kid is strange and the mother lets him run wild most of the time. He said he thought the kid spent most of his time up the hill at his uncle's place. He has a beat-up old motorcycle he uses when he isn't driving her car, and had taken off on the bike an hour or so before Pete got there." Phil paused for a breath. "Pete was headed up the hill to the uncle's ranch to check that out. He said he was going to swing by the mother's house again on the way back...hopefully she'll be home by then."

Phil took a long pull off his beer; his usual enthusiasm had faded, and he seemed hesitant when he spoke again. "There might be a Vokkel connection...I found some references in Vokkel's journals. He'd really pared back on his research after he shut the German school down and moved back to the city. I think that's because he knew he was constantly under surveillance by the Watchers, so he didn't want to draw attention to himself. Plus we know he sort of became a recluse, barely leaving the house. But he didn't stop completely. He did stop dating the entries, but for the most part, I think they're in chronological order because of what he documented." He looked at Billy. "He documented your college years via reports from Caleb." Vokkel had hired a perfidious ghost killer to get close to her and determine the extent of her power and knowledge when she was in college. When Billy discovered Caleb's true purpose, she beat the crap out of him. He had rematerialized a few months ago, again hired by Vokkel, but this time it was to determine *my* power. He was a traitor to our cause and needless to say, an unscrupulous ghost killer.

"I remembered seeing some notations that I believe are from the early 2000s about a subject, a child that he'd located and coded C1, which could fit Calvin Brelong if he's our kid." Vokkel had used a coding system to describe his patients, a first initial and a one, two, or three to describe the ghost killer's level (one being the strongest). He'd used the same system to describe a longaevus, but he used a four or five to reference their level of power.

"Anyway," he splayed his hands on the table, "Vokkel was methodical about his research notes. His entries were concise and chronological, not like his journals, which are a mess." Billy shot him an impatient look. He was constantly complaining about Vokkel's journals and the indecipherable way he wrote in them.

"He also documented Edgar's encounters with other ghost killers, noting what levels they were and if they were amicable to doing his dirty work. Then there's you...." He looked at me. "Those last few weeks of his life, he wrote a lot about you." His eyebrows rose curiously. "He noted that he'd figured out who your mother was. He'd been having you followed not just by Caleb, but others, so he noted your power level and mentioned something else." He stopped again to sip his beer and consult a notebook he'd taken from his pocket. "Okay, I'm going to read these to you in the order they were entered…I'm not sure they relate to each other, though. He wrote, '*My disease is progressing quickly, the demon is too strong for any but the most powerful to eradicate, I had hoped C1 could cure and turn me, he is not ready though.*' The next entry says, '*Discovery of G1 may be the solution*'; then '*They are growing impatient and wish to proceed immediately, G1 can perform the confluence and cure/turn me, although he will need persuading as he is much like B1*'; and '*The time for fulfilling the prophecy grows near, C1 cannot help me until that time, G1 must be convinced.*' And the last one, which I'm guessing he wrote a day or two before his death, says '*I have convinced them that I can persuade G1 to perform the convergence for a few of the more powerful ghosts and cure me of my demon. It will allow the time needed to prepare C1 per the prophecy.*'"

"What the hell, Phil?!" Billy spurted loudly, causing a few patrons at the bar to turn in our direction. She shot them a glare that clearly stated "mind your own business", then lowered her voice and asked, "Why are we just hearing about this now?"

Phil cocked his head, a hint of amusement in his eyes. "Because, *Billy*…." He dragged her name out, netting a frustrated puff of breath from her. "You two already knew all that stuff, and there was no reason to think the C1 references had anything to do with you guys. And I'm still not sure they do." Phil drained his beer and waved at Ed, the bartender, who nodded and looked to the rest of us to see if we wanted refills, which we did. "So there's some more stuff on C1 that's interesting. Vokkel wrote '*I have arranged for C1's care and tutelage, his proximity will allow periodic assessments*'; and '*C1 is the offspring-chamber vault prophecy?*' Don't know what that means, but I'll be checking into it tonight. Either way, we need to consider that C1 could be Calvin Brelong, especially since he's able to work with a demon like that, he's definitely strong."

Aris nodded. "That is certainly plausible. If we assume Vokkel was aware of this boy, he would want to keep him from us. Furthermore, he would want to easily observe him."

"What about the local Marin County Police…do they know about the car?" Billy asked.

Phil said, "Another guest saw a small sedan scream out of the parking lot, but he didn't get a plate or make, just the color. So for now, we're the only ones that know who Calvin is, and we need to keep it that way."

"Anything else?" I was worn-out and wanted to go home and crawl into bed.

Phil looked at Aris with concern, and Aris nodded for him to proceed. "There's one other thing, and again it might not relate, could just be coincidence…." Aris didn't believe in coincidences, so the fact that he wanted Phil to mention it led me to believe it was anything but. "A couple of our nomadic GKs, the ones that came in to help over the last week, are AWOL. So is Pete's guy, Mark, the one that helped in Marin last night."

"What do you mean, AWOL?" I asked.

"Well, the two that came in last week, they're mid-level and tend to show-up, conquer, and split, so we're not all that sure we should be concerned about them just yet. But Pete's been trying to call them to get specific details from the attacks they helped on, and they're not answering their phones, which is unusual. Mark's relatively new to ghost killing, but he's mid-level too and has been pretty dedicated and responsible so far. Pete's other guy is positive he saw him follow you two outside, but they haven't seen him since. Initially Pete thought he'd followed Calvin's car, but Mark's car was still parked up at the resort and he isn't answering his phone either." Phil shrugged. "But maybe the whole scene in Marin freaked him out and he just took off out of fear. Either way, Pete asked Carol to try and locate them just to be sure they're okay."

"So what now?" Billy asked. The irritation that never really left her voice was back in spades, but I knew it was more a product of frustration, exhaustion, and the fact that we really didn't have anything that would help us find the kid yet.

Aris lifted his glass, but instead of drinking, he gave Billy a compassionate look and said, "Julie arrived in the city last night, and is staying at Vokkel's house. Our sources tell us that she is here to settle her father's estate."

"Well, she can have it," Billy said emotionlessly. I knew she'd be fine as long as she didn't lay eyes on the woman, and that shouldn't be a problem since the two of them more or less avoided each other like the plague.

Aris tipped his glass to her and took a shallow drink, then said, "I suggest you both go home and get some rest. Once we locate this boy, we will need the best of our forces, and that is you." He placed the half-empty glass on the table and slid out of the booth.

We watched Aris leave, and once he was out the door Billy said, "Well, he's right about us needing rest. I feel like I haven't slept in days." Last night's exploits on top of recovering from a pretty good concussion appeared to be catching up with her...she did look tired. She glanced at me and said, "And you *look* like you haven't slept in days."

Phil chuckled. "Yeah well...," he rubbed his hands together eagerly, "I need to get to the sanctum. I've got some things I want to follow up on." He winked as Billy rolled her eyes at the word "sanctum".

The sanctum was Phil's term—and only Phil's term—for a room he'd commandeered in a rather large Edwardian house the Watchers had owned since the 1920s. It's located on Lincoln Way and 41st Avenue, directly parallel to the south side of Golden Gate Park. The original purpose of the property was to provide a temporary home for our transient community of ghost killers, and a place to train newly minted ghost killers who didn't otherwise have someone to instruct and teach them. It's still used for both purposes today, although more the latter than the former. The house has one full-time occupant, another GK named Eric Tidbey. He does most of the training and maintains the property. But he only uses three or four rooms on a regular basis, making it a perfect location for Phil's library.

I should mention that the Watchers, as a group, are very wealthy. It's rumored that they used less than ethical means to obtain their initial fortune (meaning they used ghosts and demons), but over the past several centuries, that money has been legitimatized. The secondary source of funds comes from the estates of ghost killers that were heirless. Those estates generally included any journals or diaries they kept. So on top of a vast fortune (that is used to maintain these safe houses and pay the salaries of the transient ghost killers who otherwise don't have incomes), the Watchers have a vast treasure trove of written information that no one has bothered to centralize or organize.

When Phil was first shown the house, he noticed boxes and boxes of documentation, journals, letters, etc. written by visiting ghost killers and left there or sent there after they died, dating back to the purchase of the house. That gave him an idea... why not turn the large and mostly vacant living room into a library and research center, and contact other Watcher groups to have them send what they have to San Francisco, and allow Phil to become the "librarian" of sorts.

He'd spent the last few months doing just that; the collection was monstrous now, and had come from all over the world. Phil spent most days hovering over an antique library table piled high with these tomes, journals, and missives, familiarizing and cataloguing them so they could be properly shelved on the floor to ceiling bookcases he had installed all around the perimeter of the room. I'd heard it was quite impressive, if not a bit chaotic. It was also where Vokkel's papers were housed. Once it was all organized, it would be the largest and most complete collection of information the Watchers have ever had, and it will be a fantastic resource, not just for them, but for ghost killers as well.

"This C1 thing?" I asked. Knowing Phil, he would probably spend all night poring through papers trying to find a connection, if there was one. But he looked tired too. "Phil, when was the last time *you* slept?"

He smiled. "It's been awhile, but don't worry about me. I've survived on less." He drained his beer and tipped the brim of his hat. "See you two later." He left before I could chastise him.

I hailed a cab to get us home—I was too tired to walk six blocks, uphill.

Chapter 10

The cab driver deposited us in front of our apartment building, and Billy and I wearily took the elevator up to the sixth floor. I was suddenly exhausted, but decided to decline Justine's dinner invitation in person.

When we entered the apartment, Billy let out a quiet but vicious expletive and stopped abruptly, causing me to run into her. Mumbling ungentlemanly words of my own, I moved around to face her. She looked angry and I asked, "What's wrong?" Then I heard the voices coming from the living room…one was Justine, the other I didn't recognize.

Billy walked stiffly into the living room with me at her heels. Justine looked up as we entered, a pained smile distorting her otherwise beautiful face. A woman was sitting in the armchair across from Justine, and although I'd never met her, I knew who she was immediately.

She was gorgeous in a glamorous and worldly way. Her ebony hair hung just below her shoulders and her green eyes shone mischievously. She was dressed expensively in a navy-blue silk dress and high-heeled shoes that accentuated her perfect, long legs. I knew that she had to be in her early fifties, but like Justine, this woman was aging very well and could have passed for the same age as Billy. The resemblance between mother and daughter was uncanny, but where Billy was very pretty in a natural way, Julie's beauty was sophisticated and elegant.

"Ah, there you are," Julie exclaimed. Suddenly frowning, she said, "You look positively horrible. What in the world have you been up too?" She didn't wait for a response; instead, she turned to me and said in a flirtatious tone, eyelashes fluttering, "And who might you be?"

I was a hundred different kinds of exhausted, but the good manners my dad spent years pounding into my head took over, and I cordially replied, "Hi, I'm George. You must be Julie." I began to offer my hand in greeting, then remembered the bandages and pulled back. "Sorry, we...," I glanced at Billy, "have been up to all sorts of things." I walked over to Justine and sat next to her, quietly asking, "Are you all right?" She smiled at me and nodded her head.

Julie was on the receiving end of a particularly nasty green-eyed glower from Billy. It would have crumbled most people, but Julie just smiled arrogantly and said, "I heard about your little fight with Daddy...it wasn't very nice, what you did." Her tone was indifferent when she said, "Although I suppose I should probably thank you; after all, he left everything to me."

In an eerily calm tone, Billy said, "Maybe I should remedy that and become the last in his line of heirs."

If the threat had any effect on Julie, she didn't show it. Instead, she smiled and condescendingly said, "It appears that someone has broken into his house and taken some items." Julie's eyes narrowed accusingly. "I'd like them back."

Billy's face began to reveal the hurt and pain Julie had caused her over the years, and I could feel Justine stiffen beside me. Tossing my manners aside, I decided to put an end to it.

"Julie, I can't imagine what anyone would want to steal from that old bastard, but I can assure you that Billy is the very last person who'd enter the house of the man *you* sold her to."

Julie swung her head slowly in my direction, arching it just slightly in surprise.

I continued. "Perhaps it was Edgar who took whatever is missing, or maybe one of Vokkel's little minions…maybe it was the person who misinformed you about your father's death. I heard it was a mugging gone bad."

"George…is that what you said your name is? I don't believe this conversation is any of your business." Her eyes brightened a bit. "Unless of course you're the young man that helped her kill her grandfather." She clapped her hands together in delight. "Of course, I should have guessed. After all, I doubt Billy has any other friends."

"Since you don't know anything about Billy, you wouldn't know about her friends either," I said snidely. Yep, those manners were toast. "But do tell, what was taken?"

Julie stared at me for a moment, one that lasted long enough to make me a little uncomfortable. Finally she broke away and turned to Billy. "Father kept a great many notes and journals of his work, and I've found no such things in his house. You have until tomorrow to return them. If you do not, I'll contact the authorities."

I let out a condescending sigh, one that matched Julie's earlier tone with her daughter, and said, "Julie…." I waved my hand between Justine, Billy, and myself. "We're all sort of tired…it's been a long few days. Why don't you leave your number, and in the unlikely event anyone here wants to talk to you, we'll call." I started to stand, but sat back again, my weariness exasperated by this woman's presence.

"Aren't you the knight in shining armor?" Julie said mockingly.

At that moment Margie appeared, somehow looking twice her normal size and mean as hell. "I'll walk you to the door, miss…." I'd have sworn Margie was going to bite her, and Julie must have thought so too. She stood up, smoothed her dress, and turned to Justine. “It was nice seeing you again, Aunt Justine. I’m glad to see you’re well.” There was sincere affection in her voice and her eyes, which seemed at odds with what I knew of her.

Margie took Julie’s elbow, which Julie immediately retracted as if she’d been stung. Margie smirked and directed Julie to the front door. She was very protective of Justine, and undoubtedly would continue her escort all the way to the street to ensure Julie was out of the building.

Billy said tiredly, “What did she have to say before we got here?”

Justine sighed lightly. “She was quite charming, actually. She spent most of the time inquiring about my health and activities, and appeared genuinely interested. In addition, she asked about you, dear. She wanted to know if you were happy. It was a bit surprising…her past visits, infrequent as they have been, have always focused on herself and her life.”

Billy replied with a simple “humph.” Clearly she wasn’t impressed with her mother’s attempt at reconnecting with her family.

“Ladies, I’m beat. Justine, thanks for the dinner invitation, but I need to decline and become one with my bed for at least twelve hours.” I pecked her cheek and got up from the couch with some effort. Billy walked me to the door.

“You going to be okay?” I asked. She nodded, opened the door, and shoved me through it.

Chapter 11

I was so exhausted, I went straight to bed and slept solidly until 4 a.m., when I woke with a start, sensing someone was in my apartment.

I kept a baseball bat under my bed for protection. Our building was extremely secure, but the habit had rolled over from my first city apartment, where we had a midnight break-in. I started to reach for the bat when I realized my intruder was GG. She was standing near the window, and when she noticed I was awake, a slight smile graced her ghostly face.

As GG had indicated the morning before, she came when I needed her, and God knew we needed her now.

"The boy and his demon?" I asked. She nodded. "We have to find them...can you help?" She frowned. "You're not sure you can find them?" She nodded again. "Do you know if this kid is working with the demon or if the demon is controlling the kid?" She frowned again. It's always difficult talking to someone who can't talk back. I tried another question. "Do you know why he's doing this? Is it to kill ghost killers?"

She nodded vigorously, then changed her mind and shook her head; we were getting nowhere fast.

I exhaled lightly in an attempt to hide my frustration. "Let's try one question at a time. Do you know why he's doing this?" She nodded.

"But he's not trying to kill ghost killers?" She pointed at me. "Okay, he's trying to kill me?" She sort of nodded and shook her head at the same time, and I remembered the night in Marin, when the man tried to grab Billy, so I asked, "Are they trying to kidnap us?" She did that nod/shake thing again and I took a deep breath. "All right, are they trying to kidnap one of us, and maybe kill the other?"

If a ghost could sigh, that's what GG did. I could see her apparitional chest rise with a ghostly inhale and her mouth open slightly as she exhaled nothing at all.

Finally I said, "It's okay, GG. Phil and Aris are working on it, but try and stay close. We may need your help when we find the kid and his demon." She nodded sadly and faded away.

I fell back against my pillow and slept restlessly for the next couple of hours, finally crawling out from under the covers at 6:15. My first instinct was to call Billy and tell her about GG's visit, but Billy wasn't an early riser, and waking her up could be life-threatening to yours truly. I decided to make some breakfast and try and catch a tennis game at Lafayette Park.

Chapter 12

I love early mornings in the city when most people are still at home and the streets are empty, but I especially love Lafayette Park, with its open green spaces and large swaths of trees. It's one of those inner-city treasures...eleven acres atop a hill that allows the visitor to enjoy incredible city and bay views. As if that wasn't enough, it has first come, first serve tennis courts, and I frequent those as often as possible, usually catching a game with my friend Greg, who religiously shows up every morning between six and eight to play. Greg and I had been playing together for years. He always gave me a run for my money, and once in a while I beat him. We played for a little over an hour...he destroyed me as usual, but the workout was good and I was ready to face the day with a clear head.

When I approached the courtyard entrance to my building, I was hit with two things simultaneously, both involving Billy. The first was that she was out of bed and outside...it was almost eight...normal for most people, but an un-Godly hour according to her. The second was a sense of déjà vu.

I saw Billy, not as she was right now, but as she was when I'd first met her. It was several months ago, this ghost killing business was new to me, and at the time I seemed to live in a perpetual state of confusion and fear. That particular day I'd made the mistake of visiting the house of Frederick Vokkel, where I'd had an unpleasant experience with Edgar. In those days, I didn't know that Vokkel was Billy's estranged and insane grandfather; in fact, I didn't know Billy at all.

She was sitting on the bench in our front courtyard, disheveled from the road and wearing lightly tinted round-rimmed glasses, which I initially mistook for the typical glasses the ghosts and demons always wore. When I realized she wasn't a ghost, I asked her why she was there, received a sarcastic reply, and being that I was exhausted from my experience with Edgar, I wasn't in the mood. After a few minutes of not-so-pleasant back and forth, she told me she was there to visit her aunt, Justine Wilkinson. Since Justine had told me she had no family—an omission she later apologized for—things got worse from there, and I almost called the police on Billy.

Billy had always been a loner, and after college she had decided to travel the world solo, killing ghosts. Her personality, in part, was due to that nomadic existence, but now I thought it was more like a habit she couldn't quite shake. She smiled a lot more these days, and she was without a doubt a happier person. Perhaps that was because she finally had a permanent place to call home, and she was surrounded by people that loved her. I smiled at the memory… it sometimes amazed me that we'd become as close as we were in such a short time.

This morning she was sitting on the same bench in the courtyard, wearing calf-length spandex jogging pants and a tank top. Her skin glistened from the sweat she'd worked up on her run. Her forearms were perched on her knees and her head was lowered, her breathing still labored as she cooled down. I sat next to her and leaned back enough to rest against the building.

"How was your run? No inattentive texters to rescue today?" I asked teasingly.

I expected to get a rise out of her, or at least a grouchy response due to the hour of the day, but instead, she quietly said, "Fine."

“GG stopped by last night.” I thought that would perk her up a little...I was wrong.

“And?” she replied blandly. I regaled her with our ghostly conversation. “Figures.” Her tone was apathetic.

The intensity of the last thirty-six hours had dumped quite a bit on us, and the confirmation that someone and something was trying to kill us should have brought on a more impassioned response. Something else was bothering her—I just wasn't sure what it was.

“What's going on, Billy?” I asked tentatively.

Billy's chest hitched slightly as she exhaled, and when I looked over at her, her eyes were moist. Billy didn't bother with too many human emotions, and the only other time I'd seen her cry was after she'd killed her grandfather. Although, I thought those were tears of relief and finality...these tears were full of anguish. Her hands moved to the edge of the bench and tightened to the point that her knuckles whitened, then she released her grip and moved them to her lap.

“She has this power...over me...she can reduce me to nothing, to the sniveling little brat she gave to Vokkel. I...I won't do that again. I won't let *her* do that to me....” A tear ran down her cheek.

Sometimes I felt like Billy's big brother, which was odd since I was an only child and didn't have any brothering experience, but occasionally that's what she invoked in me, and I suddenly had the urge to comfort her. I put my arm around her shoulders and drew her close. She let me, and that bothered me. This wasn't my Billy...it was the one that her mother had left behind all those years ago, and I wanted my brazen, obnoxious green-eyed monster back.

I suddenly felt horrible that I'd been too tired last night to realize the impact Julie's unwelcome visit would have on Billy. I couldn't imagine the life she'd lived, not knowing her father and being traded to an evil man for money. I knew Justine had done everything she could to give Billy the love she didn't get from her parents, but maybe it wasn't enough.

"Well, you don't have to see her again, it's that simple. She'll finish cleaning out his house and his money and she'll move on."

Her chest hitched again but the tears were gone, and I decided to push forward using her annoying version of encouragement. "Come on, Billy, put your big-girl pants on. We've got bigger fish to fry with this kid and his demon!"

She stiffened and began to pull away, but not before she elbowed me in my ribs. My bruising had already reached the final stages of healing and I was hardly sore now, but I doubled over dramatically and said, "Keep that up and you're on your own." When I looked over at her she was smiling…well, more like smirking, but that was good enough for me.

Chapter 13

We went back to our respective apartments with the intention of getting cleaned up from our workouts. As we left the elevator, she said, "When you hear from Phil, call me immediately." I nodded and headed to my front door.

While I was in the shower I made two decisions; call Phil for an update, and Google Julie Wilkinson. The latter was plain old curiosity, the former necessity.

"Hey, Phil," I said when he answered his phone.

"Hey, man, how ya feeling this morning?"

"Much better. How are you?" He sounded amped up, probably on copious amounts of coffee or some other caffeinated beverage. "What's new? Any word on the kid?"

"I'm good, man. Listen, I was just gonna send you and Billy a text. Aris wants us all to meet at Lincoln Way in about two hours. Can you two be there?"

"I guess. What's going on?"

"Pete got back late last night, and he's got some stuff to report. I found some stuff too that I think might tie into all of this."

"Okay. Well, things got interesting last night when Billy and I got home." I told him about Julie's visit, her accusation about the burglary, and the other thing that had been bothering me since our encounter with her.

"How'd she know what really went down? I mean, the only people that survived our little scrimmage, besides our people, were those poor bums we saved, and possibly Edgar...." I let that hang out there for a second.

I'd fantasized that Edgar was fatally injured that day in the abandoned auto garage and had simply found a sewer to crawl into until death took him, but deep down inside, I knew that was just a pipedream. Our people would never mention that day to outsiders, and the bums wouldn't remember enough and didn't really see much anyway, because Vokkel had them drugged almost to the point of unconsciousness. And let's not forget, Julie knew about the papers we'd liberated from Vokkel's house. I didn't think she was close enough to her father to be aware of his work, but I could be wrong.

Phil sighed. "Sorry, man, but we all knew that Edgar probably survived, and I don't think we should discount him as Julie's source of information."

"Yeah, I know, but there's another possibility we need to consider. I think we need to see if Caleb is around. He could have known about the notes and journals, and he sure as hell knew things were going from bad to worse between me, Billy, and Vokkel. He could have easily told Julie we killed him, or at least had something to do with it."

"Yeah, not a bad idea. I'll run it past Aris."

"Good idea, Phil. Ah...one more thing." I hesitated. "GG made an appearance last night, and when I asked if she knew why the kid was doing this...." I paused again. "She thinks he's out to kidnap one of us and kill the other...at least that's what I think she was trying to say."

Phil moaned loudly and said, "Not good, my friend. I'll let Aris know about that too. But you two need to be careful, more so than usual, okay?"

"We will, I promise. See you in a couple of hours," I said, and hung up.

After I texted Billy, I got started on Julie. I entered her name into my search engine, using both Wilkinson and Vokkel. I had no idea where Julie had been living or under what name, so I wasn't that hopeful.

Much to my surprise, there were more hits than I expected...she wasn't keeping a low profile in the least. They were all society page updates about who attended what and with whom. Most of these events were held in the UK and European cities, but a few were in the US, and particularly in San Francisco. So she had been here as recently as last year. One hit caught my eye...a party at a London socialite's house in December of 2014. Julie was in one of the pictures, arm-in-arm with a handsome man. The caption read, "Miss Julie Vokkel, San Francisco shipping heiress and her current love interest, famed Italian attorney, Matteo Surtos." There was nothing else, but at least now I knew how she was referenced and could narrow down the search perimeters. I typed in "Julie Vokkel" and "San Francisco" and her boyfriend's name.

A few other mentions came up, mostly just noting who she was and that she attended such-and-such event. One picture was interesting though; it was from a Paris tabloid and paparazzi-like in style, and she clearly hadn't known her picture was being taken. The caption read "San Francisco socialite having an intimate coffee with an unknown man, no sign of Surtos". Julie was sitting at a café table, a serious yet tender look on her face, her body close to the man next to her. The man wore a similar expression, but his posture was stiff and reserved. The picture was dated a few weeks ago. I zoomed in on his face and heard, more than felt, the air leave my lungs in a long whistling breath.

There was no doubt about Billy's resemblance to her mother—the hair color, eyes, and nose, not to mention the body-shape and height, were all from Julie—but there were some things she'd picked up from her unknown father, and I was looking right at them. The sharpness of the chin, the shape of her hairline, even the ears were his.

I leaned back in my chair, not sure what to do. Honestly, I didn't think now was a good time to drop this on Billy, not with everything else going on.

It was pretty easy for me to find Julie on the Internet, and I wondered if Billy had done her own searches. If she had, was it recently, and did she know or at least have her own suspicions as to the identity of the man in the café picture?

Chapter 14

When I knocked on Justine's door to collect Billy, I could tell her mood hadn't improved, so I decided to take the scenic route to Lincoln Way. I headed west to the Great Highway and then south until I hit Lincoln Way. I thought a drive along the Pacific Ocean might cheer her up a bit; it didn't, but I enjoyed it. Unfortunately, the parking gods weren't with us and it took a few circles around the block before we found a spot. By the time we got to the front door, Billy was moody *and* slightly agitated. Of course, that was nothing new...she was generally in a perpetual state of moody agitation, so I chastised her teasingly and ordered her to perk up, which almost got me socked. I was saved by the bright and dynamic smile of our host, Eric, as he opened the front door.

Eric was just shy of six-feet tall and well-muscled. He favored dark colors in his wardrobe, which, combined with his deep ebony skin and well-developed physique, created an intimidating appearance. However, when the guy smiled, he could charm the socks off anyone, which was fortunate for me, because the minute Billy caught sight of him, she relaxed and went in for a hug. I shook Eric's hand and followed him into the house.

The main floor consisted of Phil's library, which was at the front of the house. There was also a good size den, and in the back, a kitchen/dining room, which was where Eric was headed.

The room was probably the only real upgrade the house had seen. The wall between the two rooms had been removed to make it an open space, and the kitchen itself had been upgraded with all the modern conveniences. Pete, Aris, Phil, and Carol were all seated at the table.

Phil was fidgeting with a pile of leather-bound books and loose sheets of paper, and he smiled enthusiastically when we entered. "Awesome, you guys made it! Grab some coffee and have a seat."

We did as instructed, and Aris asked, "Mr. Cowell, would you care to begin?"

There was a touch of anger in Pete's voice. "I drove up to the ranch after I talked to the neighbor." He frowned lightly. "I'm not sure I'd qualify it as a ranch, though…it's more like several overgrown acres and some ramshackle buildings that consist of a house, a barn, a pump house, and a dilapidated shed. The power is still on and there was food in the fridge that was still relatively fresh, so I'm guessing someone was there recently and maybe plans to come back. Two of the three bedrooms were furnished and there were linens on the beds. Calvin, or his house guest, was pretty tidy…hardly any dust on the furniture or floors, so they haven't been away for that long. I found a shopping bag under the bathroom sink with most of the items still in it, including a three-month old receipt from a pharmacy in Valley Springs. The receipt listed antibiotic lotion, bandages, a suture kit, an eight-inch surgical clamp, and a five-inch Kelly clamp…the sorts of things you might need to remove a bullet and dress the wound." He looked around the room expectantly.

"When I searched the barn, I found a Honda 750 motorcycle with blood on the seat and splattered around the neutral and shoe stand switches. Initially I thought it was the one the neighbor had mentioned, but I had Aris run the plate anyway; it belongs to a guy here in the city. He reported it stolen the day we killed Vokkel. He was in an alley about two blocks from the garage we fought in. Said he was parking the bike when a bald black guy approached him, walloped him over the head, and took the bike and his helmet. By the time he came to, it was over an hour later." Well, at least that explained how Edgar had gotten away. I'd always wondered how he'd managed to disappear so quickly, especially since we knew he was injured.

Phil glanced over at me and mumbled, "Speak of the devil and the devil doth appear...."

A heavy silence filled the room as all hope that Edgar was dead vanished.

"So we think Edgar is in cahoots with the kid?" I asked, not waiting for an answer. "I guess that would make sense...he'd be pretty pissed that we killed his master and his sister, and based on what we saw of the kid's power and what he's been doing with that demon, Edgar could be using him to exact his revenge." There were nods all around. "Do we think he's the one that told Julie about what really happened? Or could it have been Caleb?"

Aris answered, "It is certainly possible that Edgar had been in contact with Ms. Vokkel. As of yet, we do not have a cell number for her, so we cannot track her recent calls. As far as Caleb is concerned, Vokkel's acolytes went underground when word of his death spread. We have known his cell phone number for some time and I asked Carol to trace the activity and check his call log. The phone is in Vancouver, and has been since shortly after Vokkel's death. In addition, we have confirmed with our local sources there that Caleb has been seen with much regularity around the city for some time, and we can identify all the numbers he's called or texted in the past three months."

I glanced at Billy, then back to Aris. "Why would Julie want her father's papers and journals though? I thought she kept her distance from all this stuff."

"We know that she visited her father a few times a year, but what was said between them, or what knowledge she had of his work, is unknown. Perhaps she feels they have monetary value... after all, there are others out there like Vokkel."

Billy grunted. "That's probably it. She's greedy, so if she thinks they're worth something, she'd want them." Her shoulders sagged a bit. "That, and I think she just likes to make me miserable, and the missing papers were a good excuse to stop by and grace me with her noxious presence." Billy did look miserable, so I'd say Julie was succeeding swimmingly.

Carol said, "I did an extensive search on Gail Brelong. She owns the house outright, only works part time but had a decent income, according to her bank account. She's been getting a monthly deposit from an out-of-state corporation since she's lived in Valley Springs, but the deposits stopped a few weeks after Vokkel died." She punctuated the last statement with raised eyebrows. "Not only that, but the vesting deed for her house shows the same corporation as the grantor... the sale price was a dollar. I was able to peel back the ownership layers of the corporation, and eventually traced it to one of Vokkel's shell companies."

"Right," Pete said. "We headed back down the hill to see if the mother was home yet... she wasn't, but we did get a chance to talk to the neighbor some more. He said that the mother pulled Calvin from school after the first grade because he had trouble keeping up and he didn't play nice with the other kids. The neighbor thinks the kid has some sort of intellectual disability. Around the same time, a guy named Sam Smith moved in with the Brelongs. The mother told the neighbor he was an old family friend and she was giving him a room in exchange for tutoring the kid. He thought maybe this Sam guy and the mom had a thing, but he couldn't say for sure. Sam disappeared last year, shortly after the uncle died, but when the neighbor asked the mom about it, she just said he moved out of town. I think we need to figure out who this Sam guy is."

Pete paused to sip his coffee, and then said, "We waited around for another hour or so. Just as we we're getting ready to call it quits the mother arrived, but she wasn't very cooperative. She said she hasn't seen Calvin in almost a week, but that yes, he could have used her car the other day. She said she's been out of town with friends for the last several days. She did confirm that he spends most of his time at the uncle's property, and does odd jobs up on the mountain to earn money. She was sort of nervous, like she knew something was wrong. I asked her if she had a cell phone number for him... she said she's tried calling it over the last week and just got voicemail, but she gave it to me." He looked to Carol. "Any luck tracking the phone?"

Carol shook her head. "No go. It's either turned off or the battery is dead. I hacked into the account though. In the last several months he's only made or received calls from his mother."

Phil was practically bouncing out of his chair, his excitement palpable. Aris nodded at him and he dived in. "Okay," he said, rubbing his hands together, "so we can definitely connect this Calvin kid to Vokkel. Carol, show them the picture." She tapped on her tablet and shoved it in our direction. It was a CDL photo of Calvin Brelong, the same kid from the Tenderloin and Marin. I nodded, as did Billy and Pete.

"As you know, I found references in Vokkel's research about a subject that fit Calvin's description, and he noted that he'd arranged for the kid's 'tutelage.' So this Sam guy that Pete mentioned might have been hired by Vokkel to keep tabs on the kid and teach him, but I haven't had a chance to see if Vokkel mentions Sam by name yet. Anyway, I did attempt to find references in Vokkel's journals." A scowl replaced his earlier enthusiasm. "Vokkel's research notes are pretty straightforward, but the journals are a different story entirely. It's almost as if he had dissociative identity disorder... although there's no evidence he actually did have DID...." He paused to take a breath. Phil tended to talk fast and furiously, especially when he was excited. "Regardless, we do know the man was as mad as a hatter, so why not add DID into the mix? The journal entries are like a mish-mash of information jotted down in no particular order…like he had a stack of identical blank books lying around, and grabbed the closest one, filling it with random stuff. There doesn't appear to be any chronology to the entries either. The only way we can even tell that he made the entries on separate occasions is because he tended to use whatever was handy to write with; a red, black, or blue pen, a pencil…he even used a crayon in one entry. There's also varying differences in his handwriting. Sometimes it appears manic, other times it's crisp and methodical, and others, it's printed instead of cursive. And there's one journal that's filled with weird writing and drawings. I think the writing is some form of Latin, but not one I've ever seen. I sent a few pages to a buddy of mine who specializes in languages, especially odd ones and dead ones, but he hasn't gotten back to me yet."

Billy was very impatient and clearly uninterested in Phil's difficulties in deciphering Vokkel's journals—not that she didn't appreciate his efforts, she just didn't care about the details. She rolled her hand in mid-air, her way of saying "move it along".

He winked at her and said, "Don't get yourself in a bind there, Billy; I'm getting there."

Turning to the rest of us, he said, "So here's what I did find. In the research notes, Vokkel refers to 'C1,' 'offspring,' and 'chamber' together. He also mentioned the word 'prophecy.' I remembered seeing those words used in the journals, so I went back and checked them and found an entry that said…," he grabbed one of the leather-bound books and opened it to a page he had tabbed, "'*G has appeared to C, the offspring and father are together per the prophecy!*'" He paused to sip his coffee. "But I can't figure out what the G reference is."

He shoved the journal aside and picked up another. "In this one he wrote, '*The chamber has been located at the edge of the cemetery.'*" He flipped to another tab. "And here he wrote '*G/C to become one.*' The problem is, I have no idea what order any of this was written in, so for all I know, there's another C somewhere in his earlier research and this pertains to that person."

Pete asked, "So basically what you're saying is that this may or may not have something to do with the kid, right?"

Phil's shoulders sagged a bit. "Well yeah, that's what I'm saying, but…," he shrugged, "he uses C in reference to this stuff, so we can't discount it as important."

"Perhaps you could continue your research into Vokkel's papers," Aris said. "In the meantime, I have issued a BOLO for the boy and his motorcycle. I have also issued a BOLO for Edgar, although his ability to sense danger will make him difficult to find, and since he has not been seen since Vokkel's death, I assume he's keeping a very low profile."

Billy, Phil, and I looked at Aris quizzically, but it was Pete who spoke. "BOLO…it's an acronym for 'be on the lookout.'"

Billy asked, "Any word on the missing ghost killers?"

Carol replied, "Nothing yet. I checked their phones…they're either dead or off. I put a post on G&G to see if anyone has seen or heard from them." Ghosts and Ghouls, aka G&G, was a game site designed for thousands of simultaneous players. The Watchers and the ghost killers use it to communicate with each other using a designated message board. What appears as game banter to most is usually some sort of message about what is needed from, or general information to, the ghost killing community.

"All right, so what now?" I asked.

Pete looked at Carol. "Can you try and run this Sam guy down? He might be able to help us find the kid, or at least provide some additional information on him."

Carol nodded. "I'll get right on it."

Pete smiled tiredly and stifled a yawn. "I say we take the remainder of the day off and get some rest. We can meet again tomorrow with any updates."

“Not for this guy,” Phil said heartily. “I’m hitting the sanctum to scour those journals and notes.” A wink. “After all, you’re the ghost killing warriors, and you need to be on your best game. I’m just the research dude.”

Eric looked to Phil. “I’ll give you a hand if you want. I’ve got nothing going on today.”

Aris said, “Thank you both.” Turning to Pete, Billy, and me, he continued, “Pete is correct. Please take the remainder of the day and night to rest and relax; the next few days could be quite trying.” And he was right, they would be *very* trying.

Chapter 15

The idea of resting and relaxing was a good one, but I was feeling anxious and antsy, and needed a distraction. Luckily for me, I got one just as Billy and I pulled into our garage in the form of a text from my college roommate, Mike. After college I didn't really have any career prospects, so Mike had talked me into moving to San Francisco and working for his father, who was a real estate tycoon, so to speak. I finally decided I hated it and moved on to another job, but Mike and I were still close and got together as often as we could.

Another thing Mike had talked me into was joining the Presidio Softball League with him. I used to play regularly, but these days I'd been relegated to a back-up player. Ghost killing can kill your social life. The games last up to six innings or one hour, whichever comes first, and the league follows the ASA Slow Pitch Softball rules, although the umpire has a lot of discretion. Generally it's more of a social gathering than a competitive sport, especially since each team always shows up with a cooler of beer. One rule, however, is strictly enforced, and that's the men to women ratio. Our team has four "full time" women, but two of them travel often for work, so our team captain finds himself scrambling at least twice a month for back-ups. According to Mike's text, that was the case this week, and he wanted to know if I was in for tonight's game and if I knew of any eligible young ladies that wanted to drink beer and play softball at the foggy fields of the Presidio. Before I could respond he sent another text.

Sorry George, I forgot, you don't spend time with the ladies, LoL so how could you know anyone. ☺

I wasn't amused, especially since he was more or less right. I would date if I had time and if I thought I could explain my odd hours and departures to a woman, but I wasn't ready to tackle that hurdle yet.

I texted him back and told him that I might know someone and would get back to him soon. He replied with *????really?????*

I still wasn't amused.

Billy needed a distraction as much as I did, and maybe a team sport would help to dispel her bad mood. I'd asked her to play before but she'd adamantly refused, saying she'd never played softball and knew nothing about it. She may not have been an athlete, but she had the physique and stamina of a well-trained tri-athlete, and nowhere in the rule book did it say she needed to know how to play—she just needs to be a *she.*

As we got off the elevator, I told Billy I wanted to stop in and say hello to Justine and Margie. She gave me an odd look, but didn't argue. When we entered Justine's apartment, Margie was vacuuming the front hallway. I motioned to her and whispered, "I might need your help…is Justine here?" She pointed toward the living room where Billy had disappeared, Margie nodded and followed me into the room.

Justine was seated on the couch and greeted me affectionately. "George, dear, what a lovely surprise." Then she frowned. "Is everything all right?"

"So far. We haven't found the kid, but we've identified him." I gave her a run down on what we knew, the Vokkel and Edgar connection, and briefly mentioned Phil's mysterious journal findings, which she thought interesting. I finished up with, "So basically, we're in a holding pattern, and I thought Billy and I could use a nice little outing...you know, something to distract us." I smiled ingratiatingly. Billy scowled; she was on to me.

I hurried through my next statement, "My softball league plays tonight and we're short a woman, so I think Billy ought to gear up and come play." Billy's scowl deepened and she started shaking her head negatively.

Justine clapped her hands, "That is a wonderful idea." She turned to Billy, who was seated next to her. "Dear, I think you should go. It will be a fun experience for you, and perhaps you will meet some new people."

Billy was still shaking her head when she said, "I don't know the first thing about softball...hell, I don't even know much about baseball in general." Green-eyed lasers were attempting to destroy me, but Margie came to my rescue.

"I'll teach you the general rules and give you some pointers. I know how these games go. George has told me all about them. You'll be fine, and you'll have fun too!" Margie was a big baseball fan and we frequently talked about the game, and I usually told her all about the softball games when I got a chance to play. I'd even thought of inviting her to play on occasion.

Billy was outnumbered and she knew if she didn't acquiesce, she'd never hear the end of it. With a dramatically belligerent sigh, she said, "Fine!" and huffed out of the room.

Justine was smiling and Margie asked, "What time is the game?"

"Seven—at the Presidio fields."

"Okay, that's good; I can get her up to speed in that timeframe. Do you have a glove she can use, or should I loan her mine?"

My eyebrows shot up. "You have a softball glove, Margie?"

"Of course," she replied, her tone clearly implying that I should have known better than to ask.

I beamed at her. "Maybe you should play instead."

"Some other time. Today its little Miss Grump's turn." She winked devilishly.

I called Mike as soon as I got home. "Hey, Mike, my friend Billy is going to play with us tonight. She's never played, but I'll give her a quick tutorial and we can put her in right field."

"Great! Who is she?" Mike asked bluntly. He thought I had gynophobia since the only real female friend I ever talked about was Justine.

"She's Justine's niece…we work together." It wasn't a complete lie. When I decided to take on ghost killing full time, I had to resign my career with the development firm I'd been with for almost ten years. But I had no plans of resigning my friendships, and those friends would need an explanation as to how I could still afford my lifestyle. Justine, much to my surprise, had set up a trust fund for me. She was excessively wealthy, and I used it to pay my mortgage and other expenses. But I also used her wealth to explain my career change. All my friends were aware of my friendship with her and they knew she was loaded, so I told them she'd asked me to run her charitable fund, a full-time job that required a great deal of travel. They bought it hook, line, and sinker.

"Right, okay, see you at 6:45. I gotta go," Mike said and hung up.

Chapter 16

I knocked on Justine's door at 6:20. I wanted to get to the field a little early so that I could do some warm up with Billy before the game. Billy answered the door, and the glower on her face told me this might not have been a good idea after all. She had her hair pulled back in a braid, the glossy ebony plait competing with the sheen on her black long-sleeved sport T. She was also wearing her calf-length running pants. All of it showed off her figure nicely…she looked good. If she wasn't any good on the field, at least she'd be a distraction to the opposing team's male players. She held Margie's softball glove in one hand and a pair of cleats in the other. I pointed down to them questioningly.

"Apparently Margie and I wear the same size shoe." She pushed past me and headed toward the elevator.

"So, how did your softball lesson go?" I asked, trying not to let the amusement in my voice show through.

"Fine. She made me go to the batting cages. I can now bat, toss, and catch." Billy grumbled, but I detected a bit of satisfaction in her voice.

"And?"

"I did okay. It's just hand-eye coordination…I don't get why people think it's so hard," she said with more than a little condescension.

"It's more than that! Did she run the rules down with you?" I was trying to match her tone and failing.

Billy nodded her head, but said nothing else. On the ride over I began to doubt the sanity of my decision to ask her to play. I didn't have very many friends, and the last thing I needed was for her to alienate the ones I did have.

When we arrived at the south field, most of my team was already there—drinking beer and watching the six o'clock team finish up. I introduced Billy to everyone and much to my relief, she was pleasantly polite. Mike was hovering over a picnic table with our team captain working out the line-up. When he finished he strolled over, eyeing Billy curiously.

"Hey, George, you made it!" He turned to Billy. "And who is this lovely lady?" Mike had everything going for him; he was handsome, rich, and very likable, and was a serial dater. I'd never known him to stick with one woman for more than a month or so.

"Hey, Mike," I said, trying to catch his eye to let him know that Billy wasn't his type, but he was too busy staring at her, so I made the introductions. "This is Billy…Billy, Mike."

Mike thrust his hand forward and Billy took it. The shake lingered far longer than I thought necessary and eventually Billy broke it, a very slight blush spreading across her face.

We did a little warming up; Billy had a surprisingly good arm and made some powerfully accurate throws. She also caught everything I threw at her. I was beginning to wonder just how truthful her claim was of never having played before.

The game got started and I played second base while Billy played right field. There weren't many balls heading in her direction and I could tell she was getting a little bored. I threw her a bone and traded places with her in inning three. She caught two fly balls, retiring the batters, and she hit two homeruns, surprising the hell out me; the last one was the go-ahead game winner. When the game ended Mike and our team captain were adamant we celebrate by going to the Final-Final Sports Bar on Baker Street in the Marina District.

I didn't think Billy would want to go, but her performance on the field had elevated her to celebrity status with my teammates and they were insistent that we join them for at least one beer. Resistance was futile.

When we arrived, Mike and I went to order while Billy hit the restroom. "So, what's the story with her?" Mike asked.

"Story?" I replied, knowing exactly what he meant.

"You know what I mean. You two…got a thing?"

I laughed insincerely at him. "No, Mike, we're just friends…co-workers, that's all."

"Mind if I ask her out?"

I'd known this was coming, but I wasn't sure how to respond. My big-brother instinct was trying to kick in for the second time that day, but I also knew I didn't have any right to make decisions for Billy.

"Nope, but I'll warn you, she's not much for socializing. It was like pulling teeth to get her to come tonight." I was hoping my discouraging tone would deter him—the flicker of determination in his eyes told me otherwise.

Billy came out of the restroom with another player, smiling at something the woman had said. Billy said something to her and they both laughed. I had no idea who this Billy was, and for a minute I wondered if she'd been possessed. A quick scan of the bar told me it was just us mortals…damn ghosts were never around when you needed one.

Mike was talking to me again. "So what happened to your face?" Billy's cuts had faded to the point where she dabbed a little makeup on them and they virtually disappeared; mine were fading, but still noticeable. The first thing that came to mind was Phil's explanation to Ed, the bartender at Seymour's.

"Oh, that, it's nothing. I decided to try out boxing at my gym, it didn't go so well," I said, but Mike was no longer interested in me or my injuries. Billy had joined us and all of his attention was suddenly on her.

Mike and Billy spent the entire time together, ignoring everyone else. She seemed flattered and a little flustered at the attention, but she didn't shy away. A few beers later, I told Billy that we should get going, early morning and all.

As we were crossing the street toward the car, Billy stopped abruptly. Our teenage demon-befriending killer was leaning against my driver's side door.

Calvin nodded lightly in our direction, looking a little frightened and unsure of himself. Billy began walking again at a leisurely pace. Her body language, which was normally guarded, was now relaxed and non-threatening.

I started to walk too, but then I heard Mike call out my name. I turned to find him outside the bar, walking towards me.

"Hey." He tossed his head toward Billy and my car. "Who's that?"

"I don't know," I lied, "but Billy seems to know him. What's up?"

"Uh, well, I wanted to get her phone number... to ask her out." Mike was suddenly shy, very unlike him—clearly Billy had made an unusual impression. I gave him her number, said goodbye again, and walked over to the car where Billy and Calvin were in quiet conversation.

Billy introduced us in a tone I'd never heard her use... soft, almost nurturing. I wasn't sure what she was playing at; this kid was a killer, with his own personal demon in his arsenal. I looked around. No musketeer in sight... that was good.

I nodded my acknowledgment. The kid had a black eye and a bruised cheek; someone had thrown a couple of solid punches at him. He was pale and shaking lightly. It wasn't cold out, but he could have been hungry—who knew where he'd been or what he'd been living on for the last two days. I didn't sense any animosity in him either; if anything, he just looked nervous and a little scared. After another moment, I said, "You hungry? Why don't we get something to eat?"

Calvin looked nervously at Billy and she nodded. Using that soft tone that seemed so alien coming from her, she said, "Come on, you can ride in front. I'll take the back seat." She led him over to the passenger side while I unlocked the car, and once he was seated in the front, she moved to the back. I looked over my shoulder at her and she nodded her head slightly.

I drove over to Lombard Street looking for an open diner and spotted the 24-hour IHOP. My passengers nodded in silent acknowledgment when I asked if it was suitable. Once inside and seated, Calvin said he needed the bathroom and left the table. I gave Billy a questioning look.

"He said GG directed him to us. He's scared and he wants our help."

I smiled lightly. She'd found him...that was good, and perhaps it also meant she could help us find the demonic musketeer too. Maybe even Edgar, if we were really lucky.

"That's good, but how?" I asked. Some ghosts can and will communicate with us, but it's not verbal, so how did he get specific instructions from GG?

She said, "He didn't say...we can ask him later."

I intended to do just that. I didn't like the idea that he'd found us when we didn't even know we were going to be at the bar in the first place.

Calvin returned a few minutes later, having washed his face and hands and run water through his hair, giving it a semi-combed look. His nervousness hadn't subsided much, but that didn't seem to affect his appetite. When the waiter arrived he ordered the Big Steak Omelet with a side of blueberry pancakes and an English muffin. Billy and I ordered more modest dishes of bacon, eggs, and toast.

After the waiter left, Calvin laid his hands on the table and began to pick at his fingers. Despite his recent attempt to clean up, the nails were black with dirt, and the cuticles and surrounding tissue were ragged and red with irritation. He worked at his fingers with a fidgety tension that cemented my earlier impression of a scared and nervous kid.

"Calvin, what happened in Marin? Why were you there?" Billy asked gently.

"To find you," he said quietly.

"Why were you looking for us?" she asked.

"'Cause, they told me to find you...."

I asked, "Who told you?"

He didn't answer. Instead, he began to sway back and forth at a mild pace and his complexion turned waxen. He looked completely exhausted, and I thought he was going to faint.

Billy asked, "Calvin, when was the last time you slept?"

He shrugged. "'Dunno. A few days, I guess."

So he was exhausted and on the verge of collapse. *Great*, I thought...we weren't going to get much out of him tonight. I excused myself and left the table, pulling my cell phone out of my pocket as I headed toward the restrooms.

Aris answered on the second ring. "Aris, Calvin Brelong is with Billy and me. He's a wreck, but I think he'll cooperate if we can get him some rest and make him feel safe. There's no sign of the demon so far." I finished up by briefly explaining how we came together and where we were.

I wasn't really that concerned about the musketeer demon showing up while the kid was with us. It had to know who we were by now, and I didn't think it would risk materializing in our presence since we'd happily relieve it of its current existence.

There was an interminable silence, and finally I said, "You still there?"

"Yes, I am. Will he come away with you?"

"I think so. I mean, he came to us in the first place, so I'm guessing he wants our help."

"Good. Bring him to Lincoln Way as soon as possible. We will be able to protect him there."

I disconnected the call and went back to the table. The food had arrived and Calvin was digging into it like a starved animal.

Billy looked at me curiously, and I said, "Calvin, we're going to take you to a safe place for the night. Is that okay?"

He glanced up at me. His eyes were green, much like Billy's, but the fiery intelligent passion that often weaponized her eyes wasn't there...his were blank and lost. It seemed to confirm what I'd sensed in Marin—this kid wasn't dealing with a full deck.

"Don't worry, Calvin. You'll be safe, I promise." Billy's tone was soothing, almost motherly. I'd ask her where that came from later—it was so counterintuitive to her normal demeanor, and it was freaking me out a little.

Chapter 17

I took Lombard west toward Golden Gate Bridge, then cut through the Presidio, the Richmond District, and Golden Gate Park until I reached Lincoln Way, from there it was just a few blocks further. The drive took twenty minutes, but Calvin was clearly exhausted and had dozed off minutes after we got in the car.

As I pulled into the driveway, the garage door opened—obviously Eric was on watch, yet again, for our arrival. I drove into the deep cavernous space and parked. Eric's bright smile caught the meager light as Billy and Calvin came around from the passenger side. He shot his hand out in greeting. Calvin stepped back, but then timidly reached out and limply shook his hand.

Eric said, "Listen, kid, I hear you need some downtime. I've got a room all set for you...clean sheets and towels and a TV with three-hundred channels of nothing but crap to watch." He winked at Calvin and his smile broadened. Calvin smiled back, *sort of*, but he did relax, and that was the important part.

Eric led us up a narrow stairwell that opened into a large hallway; from there we walked to the front of the house, where the main staircase was located. He waved his hand upwards. "Your room is the first door on the left...there's a bathroom right next to it. You hungry or thirsty or anything? I can make something up for you."

Calvin shook his head and Billy said, "Thanks, Eric, we just ate. But if you've got any bottled water he can take up with him...."

"You bet, be right back. Go on up and make yourself at home, Calvin." He headed to the kitchen and Billy took Calvin by the arm and steered him up the staircase while I waited for Eric. He returned a minute later and glanced up the stairs, quietly saying, "So that's the killer kid? He doesn't look like he's got it in him."

"Yeah, I know."

"You think that demon is anywhere nearby?"

"Honestly, Eric, that monster would be crazy to show up here; we'd take him out in a second. But we do need it to show up at some point. It's clearly one of the strongest and most dangerous we've come across, and it needs to go," I said tiredly. "I'll take those up and be back down in a few minutes. Will you still be awake?"

He laughed lightly. "Not sure I'm going to be able to sleep with that kid in the house. From what I've heard, he's got some serious skills—using that demon's juice and all. I don't want to get caught off guard, know what I mean?"

I patted his shoulder. "Yeah, I do."

I took the water and followed Billy and Calvin's path up the stairs. The door to the room Eric indicated was slightly ajar and light seeped out around it. As I approached, I could hear Billy and Calvin speaking in quiet tones. I knocked lightly and entered the room.

Calvin was standing next to the bed, staring down at the coverlet longingly.

"Here's your water, Calvin. You need anything else?" He shook his head. "Calvin, I know you're tired, but I need to ask you something, okay?"

Billy was now standing next to me and he looked at her for approval. She nodded and Calvin tilted his head in my direction.

"How did you find us tonight?"

His gaze darted between us, and finally he said, "A ghost, she came to me and told me you could help. She told me where you were."

Billy and I exchanged glances, and she walked closer to Calvin and said, "When did she tell you this, Calvin?"

He shrugged absently and sat down on the bed…more like slumped onto the bed. "'Dunno, this morning I guess…she said to come to the city and she'd find me. And when I did she sent me to that street and showed me your car." His words were beginning to slur and I decided we should let him sleep—we could interrogate him in the morning. I took Billy by the arm and led her to the door.

"You get some sleep, Calvin. We'll be downstairs if you need us, okay?" I said, trying to mimic Billy's gentle tone.

Out in the hallway, Billy said, "I don't want to leave him alone. What if that demon shows up?"

"I think he'll be okay…I think GG's around and watching over him." I wanted to believe that was true, and then Billy smiled and pointed to Calvin's door.

GG stood like a sentry, her expression hard and firm. "Is everything okay?" I asked. She nodded and waved us away.

Billy and I found Eric downstairs in the large and comfortably furnished den, talking quietly on his cell phone. We both took a seat on one of the couches and waited for him to finish up his call.

When he was done, he sat on the couch opposite ours and said, "That was Aris. He wanted me to let him know when you guys got here, and he wanted to know what the kid's condition was." He tilted his head upward and asked, "Is he asleep?"

I said, "Probably. He seemed pretty wiped out. Listen, Eric, you should know, we're not the only ones in the house. There's a ghost up there watching out for the kid." Eric's eyes widened and I held my hand up. "She's a good ghost...she helped my mom when she was at Vokkel's institution, and she helped us fight Vokkel's surge a few months back."

Eric relaxed. "Right, I heard about her...." He paused. "So did you call her here?"

I shook my head. "No, but she came to me the other day and more or less told me that she was here to help us with the kid...and according to Calvin, she came to him too, and convinced him to come and find us."

Billy was nodding off beside me, and I looked at Eric and said, "Why don't you get some sleep? We'll stay down here and keep our ears open for the kid."

Eric smiled and said, "Uh-uh, I'm staying right here with you two. That way if that demon shows up or the kid goes berserk, we'll be able to fight together." He winked and pulled a throw blanket from the back of the couch, kicked his shoes off, and laid down; he was snoring lightly in a matter of minutes. So much for not being able to sleep with the kid in the house.

By now Billy had moved to the end of our sofa and curled into a fetal position, snoring softly too. There was another blanket on the couch behind me and I covered her with it, then put my feet on the coffee table and leaned my head back. I didn't think I'd sleep, but woke almost seven hours later to a stiff neck, the smell of coffee, and the sound of voices from somewhere in the house.

Chapter 18

Rubbing the sleep from my eyes, I made my way to the kitchen. Billy was seated at the table with Phil, Aris, and Carol. Eric and Pete were standing at the large island counter.

"Hey, man, you're awake," Phil said cheerfully. "I brought some bagels and Eric made coffee…help yourself."

"Morning everyone." I took Phil's suggestion and sat next to Billy. "Is he awake yet?" I asked. Billy shook her head. "Is GG still here?" She shrugged. Another one of GG's talents—actually, any super strong ghost or demon could do this—was deciding who saw her and who didn't. Billy may not have seen her this morning, but that didn't mean she wasn't here.

Aris turned to me and asked, "George, from what you've told me regarding your communication with GG, she uses a form of hand signals and encourages you to guess her meaning, is that correct?"

"Yeah, and I know where you're going with this. How was GG able to give the kid such specific directions?"

Aris nodded.

Billy said, "Look, we don't know much about him and his power, aside from what we saw in Marin." She paused to sip her coffee. "For all we know, he can talk to ghosts on a higher level than any of us have experienced before."

Eric cleared his throat and said, "Hey, Calvin, how'd you sleep?"

We all turned to find a somnolent Calvin standing in the doorway. Billy stood up and walked over to him, gently placing her hand on his shoulder.

"Come on in and have some breakfast." She guided him over to the table and into a chair next to hers. "Calvin, this is Aris, Carol, and Phil." She nodded towards Pete, who was still standing at the counter. "And that's Pete. They're here to ask you some questions, okay?" He nodded.

Eric asked, "You want some coffee or juice? We have bagels too."

Calvin nodded timidly and Eric went about arranging the proffered items and setting them in front of Calvin. Much like last night, he dug in with enthusiasm, eating two bagels and downing both beverages. When he was done, Aris asked if he would mind talking for a bit. The boy shrugged in response.

"Calvin, you told Billy and George that the ghost, GG, spoke with you; can you tell me about your encounters with her?" Aris had adjusted his customary monotone for something more soothing.

Calvin glanced at Billy, then at me—he looked scared and insecure. I said, "He means the ghost from last night…her name's GG. She's the one who told you to come to us, right?"

"I know her name…," he said, his tone slightly defensive.

"You do? How?" Billy asked. GG may have managed to get the message across about us, but I couldn't see how she would have been able to tell him her name—which wasn't her real name anyway. GG was a moniker that Phil had given her. It stood for Guardian Ghost, and she didn't try and correct or direct us otherwise.

"She told me…she said you call her GG." Now Calvin's tone had softened.

"Calvin, how does GG talk to you?" I asked.

His brow furrowed. "I guess she's like… in my head, but I just talk to her regular, like we're talking now."

Aris asked, "Have you always been able to speak with ghosts in this form, Calvin?"

He shrugged. "I guess, I been doing it since I was a little kid… don't remember not being able to do it."

"Did you always know they were ghosts?" Phil asked.

"I s'pose." Calvin started to chew on his nails. They were still filthy and I looked away in disgust.

"Do you speak to the musketeer ghost in this form?" Aris asked.

Calvin nodded. We'd suspected the kid must be pretty strong, and Vokkel had him labeled as a '1,' which meant he thought the same. But to speak to the ghosts and demons on this level was unheard of, and I was beginning to worry we were dealing with a power level we hadn't seen before.

Before Aris could pursue this line of questioning—which was definitely important, but not as important as his connection to Edgar and why he decided to come to us—I asked, "Calvin, we need to understand some things. Why did you come to us last night?"

"I was scared and she said you could help."

"What were you scared of?"

"This man, he… he was hurt, and once he got better he said that you hurt him and needed to pay, and that me and Gilles could make you pay. But it didn't go right in Marin and he beat me up, said it was my fault."

"Okay, Calvin, slow down…," I said soothingly. "Was the man Edgar?" He nodded. "Who's Gilles?"

Calvin frowned, "He's my friend… he's a ghost."

"You mean the musketeer?" He nodded again and I looked around the room. I could tell everyone else was concerned about his use of "friend" in connection with the musketeer demon.

"Calvin, I want to know more about him...Gilles...in a minute, but right now, tell us about Edgar and what he wanted you to do."

His nervousness hadn't subsided, but he'd stopped chewing his nails. "He came to my house a while ago. He was bleeding pretty bad, and said he needed a place to stay and some stuff. He gave me a list and I went and bought what he needed. I told him to go up to the ranch, 'cause my mom didn't like him and she'd be freaked out that he was bleeding like that and stuff. So I helped him fix himself up and took care of him. When he was better he said that he needed Gilles and me to find some other mean ghosts and do stuff to make you guys come, but I don't exactly remember what we were supposed to do." His shoulders sagged a bit. "I get kind of fuzzy in the head when they're both around."

"How does your mom know him?" Billy asked.

"I'm not sure...he and this other guy came to our house a bunch of times when I was growing up."

"How does Edgar know about Gilles? Can he see Gilles?" she asked.

He shrugged. "Yeah, he can see him. I showed him to him a long time ago and he's been able to see him ever since."

We knew Edgar could see ghosts if he was touching a ghost killer with the ability to share his or her sight. Billy and I could share our sight, but I wasn't sure that's what Calvin meant.

"Calvin, can Edgar talk to Gilles without you around? Doesn't Edgar have to be touching you to see Gilles?"

He shrugged again. "Yeah, at first, but now they just talk on their own." Another glance around the room told me what I immediately feared; either Edgar had somehow gotten stronger in his abilities, or this demon was exceptionally powerful and able to make itself appear and communicate with someone other than a ghost killer. That wasn't unheard of, but it was pretty rare.

"Calvin, the other man, was his name Frederick Vokkel?" Aris asked, which elicited another nod from Calvin, who seemed more comfortable nodding and shrugging than actually speaking in response to most questions. Aris continued. "What did Vokkel want when he came to see you?"

The kid's face had taken on a look of concentration, like he couldn't quite remember what Vokkel was doing there. Finally he said, "He asked me stuff about the ghosts I could see and talk to mostly; he didn't come that much."

"Calvin, do you know where Edgar is?" I asked.

He shook his head. "I went home after the last time and got my bike and took off. I haven't seen him since then."

I was confused, and I asked, "When did Edgar hit you, Calvin? Does he have his own car, or were you sharing your car?"

"He...I don't know, I can't remember. It's all fuzzy and stuff...." Calvin slumped into his chair.

Billy asked, "Are you all right, Calvin?"

"Yeah, I'm really tired."

Aris said, "Of course, you have been through a great deal. However, we must ask you a few more questions. Afterwards, you may go back to your room and rest. Is that acceptable?" Another nodded response, and Aris smiled. "Thank you, Calvin. Please, tell me everything you can about Gilles."

He took a deep breath. "His name's Gilles d'Aubray."

"How did you meet him?" Aris's voice took on a hypnotic tone that Calvin seemed to focus on.

Calvin said, "He started hanging out at my uncle's house."

"Could your uncle see him too?"

Calvin shook his head. "Naw."

"How come he started hanging out at your uncle's?" Phil asked.

Calvin shrugged...again. "I don't know, he never told me."

"What else did Gilles say to you?" Aris again.

"He said he could make my uncle strong." Calvin started to pick at his nails now, but at least he wasn't chewing on them.

"Why did your uncle need to be strong?"

"I don't know. My mom always said he wasn't very smart, but he was loyal or something like that. I figured Gilles meant he could make him strong in the brain."

"How did Gilles plan to do that?"

"He said he could get into Uncle Leo sometimes, and when he did that, Uncle Leo was stronger. But only, you know, like muscles and stuff... he wasn't much smarter in the head." Calvin pointed to his temple. "But he said that if he lived in Uncle Leo all the time, then he'd be really strong *and* smart."

Aris asked, "Calvin, did Gilles tell you how to make him live in your Uncle Leo permanently?"

"He tried to explain it, but I didn't really understand." He shrugged again, "But it didn't matter, 'cause Uncle Leo did that stupid thing and he got electrocuted."

"What stupid thing was that, Calvin?"

"He had this old hot tub... he said it needed new wiring and I couldn't use it. But then I came up one weekend and he was in it, dead. They said he was drunk too, and the wires in the underwater lights were bad or something like that. He got shocked to death or something."

"What does Gilles want now?"

"He wants to be human again. Edgar said he could make one of you do that if we helped him," Calvin said as he looked from Billy to me.

"Thank you, Calvin," Aris said softly. "Billy will walk you to your room. If you'd like, I will arrange for new clothes to be brought in for you. Would that be acceptable?"

Again with the shrugging, Calvin said, "Yeah, sure, that'd be okay."

Chapter 19

Pete had remained quiet through the entire interview, but I could tell something was on his mind. When Billy returned, he took a seat at the table with the rest of us and asked, "Anything on this Sam Smith guy?"

Carol cleared her throat lightly. "I ran Sam Smith and naturally came up with a million hits. I decided to try something else since we know this kid is dangerous, at least when the demon is around. I combined Sam Smith and electrocution and found an article in the crime section of the Amador County paper—Amador is one county over from Calaveras County, where Calvin grew up. From there I hacked the sheriff department's data base. The body of a man was found, electrocuted, in a seedy motel room in Ione, which is not that far from Valley Springs. It was last year, about the time the neighbor says Sam took off. He was found in the bathtub; the clock radio that normally sat on the dresser was plugged in near the sink and submerged in the tub with him. But the coroner stated that Smith was probably dead before he was put into the water. So the case was classified as 'unresolved—death at the hands of another.' The only ID on Smith was a forged out of state driver's license. The neighbor had given Pete a description of Smith and this victim fits that. A maid they interviewed at the scene said she saw a teenage kid go into the room a few hours before the body was discovered.

She gave a description, too, and it loosely fits our kid, but no one was ever questioned."

That didn't tell us much about Smith, but it did tell us that he was dead and that the coroner believed he was electrocuted, which is exactly how it would look if Calvin used the demon's juice to kill Smith.

I said to no one in particular, "I wonder why he'd kill Smith, especially if he was just the kid's tutor."

"We don't know that he did. We just know a guy fitting Smith's description is dead," Carol said.

Phil said, "I think the neighbor might be right; you notice how he talks—almost as if he's twelve instead of seventeen."

"Yeah, I noticed that too, but maybe it's shock. I mean, if he's been under Edgar and Gilles's spell for the last few months…or years…maybe his brain is sort of scrambled." I said, remembering my encounter with Edgar a few months back. "When Edgar got to me, I was pretty shocked and dazed for a good while." I turned to Billy and asked, "Do you think he knows that he can kill the ghosts—that he should be killing them?"

"Oh, man, I didn't think of that!" Phil said, his eyes jutting out to the point of rupturing. "I mean, if Vokkel wanted to train this kid to control demons and stuff, I guess he'd discourage that inherent desire, or need, or whatever you all call it, to kill ghosts and demons."

Billy nodded solemnly. "I don't think he knows he can do it. Honestly, I don't think he knows much of anything. But I'm going to wait for him to get cleaned up, and then we're going to have a long one-on-one chat."

Aris agreed. "I think that is an excellent idea, Billy. You seem to have established a rapport with him, and I am hopeful he will open up to you." He rose from his chair. "I am needed at the precinct. Perhaps we can reconvene here this evening." Turning to Billy and me, he continued. "I would appreciate it if you would stay here with the boy until we get this situation resolved. I am very concerned about this 17th century demon and Edgar… they both appear to have their own agenda, neither of which would be in our favor, and I do not want them taking us by surprise."

Billy and I nodded in unison.

"George, do you believe GG will remain to help us?" Aris asked.

"I think so, but I can't be sure." GG was unpredictable and I had no way of knowing if she'd stick around or just make periodic appearances.

"Understood. Do you feel the need for additional ghost killers in attendance?"

I looked to Billy and Eric, and she answered, "No, I think we'll be okay with me, Eric, and George."

Pete said, "Whether you think you need them or not, I'm going to bring in some extra guys…not just for inside the house, but also to patrol the area. I don't want to get caught with our pants down if Edgar and the musketeer decide to call in a demon storm."

Aris agreed. Before leaving, he asked Eric to go shopping for Calvin, then he left the room. Thirty seconds later we heard the front door open and close. Eric left to go shopping and Pete said, "I'm out of here too; see you both tonight."

I turned to Phil and Carol. "What do you two have planned for the day?"

Carol stood and started toward the door, saying, "I've got things to do, so I'll see you all later."

Phil said, "Still going through Vokkel's stuff. I want to make sure I find all the references I can on this kid, and see if a Sam Smith is referenced. And I'm pretty sure the 'G' I found in Vokkel's notes is this Gilles demon, so I want to search more for him too." He stood and stretched, then said, "I've got a few things to do also, but I'll be back this afternoon." He gave us a two fingered salute and left the room.

I leaned back in my chair and ran my hands down my face. "We never got to the part about how GG told him exactly where we were last night. We didn't even know we'd be there...or why he's doing all of this crap in the first place!"

Billy looked at me. "Well, GG seems to know how to find you, so maybe that's it. As far as why he's doing this, he said Gilles and Edgar wanted to attract our attention." She angled her head. "You don't believe him?"

"No, I don't think I do. Gilles is very old; he's been around long enough to know that most ghost killers are good, especially the ones that respond to the sort of the things they did in Marin and the other attacks. I think there's more to all of this, and I think Calvin has an idea of what that is." She was pensive and I decided to lighten the mood a little. "So tell me, when did you become so kind and nurturing?" Playful sarcasm seeped into my voice. "I didn't even know you knew the definition of those words."

Her response came in the form of a pernicious glare, and I laughed outright. She pushed her chair back loudly and stomped out of the room. I laughed again.

Chapter 20

I wandered around the house for the next forty-five minutes, snooping around like a curious child. I'd been there once before, but only on the main level, and prior to Phil's renovations. The main living room, which was at the front of the house and ridiculously huge, was sparsely furnished on my first visit. Now the walls were lined with bookcases and filing cabinets, with the exception of one section that housed a long, narrow table loaded with computer monitors and CPUs. A large library table was centered at one end, and a low round table with four comfortable club chairs at the other end in front of the fireplace. The library table was piled high with papers and books, some of which I recognized as Vokkel's journals. A desk chair flanked one side, and I assumed Phil used this as his desk area. There were also stacks and stacks of boxes taking up most of the remaining floor space. A few of the bookcases were occupied with neat little labels beneath the contents, but otherwise it didn't appear that Phil was making much of a dent in what he'd accumulated.

I climbed up to the second floor. Calvin's door was closed, but I found three other guest bedrooms and two bathrooms, as well as a master suite with its own en-suite bath. Based on the clothes strewn around the room, I figured that was the one Eric occupied. The top floor, which was a wide open space, contained a variety of workout equipment at one end and a large dojo mat at the other. The mat was flanked by racks containing an assortment of wooden bokkens, tantos, nunchakus, and a box filled with smaller items similar in size to my trusty yellow number two pencils and Billy's chopsticks. The Watchers probably used this space to get the newbies up to speed and learn the best techniques.

I headed back downstairs toward the kitchen, and as I passed the den, I saw Billy sitting on one of the couches. She was texting with someone...I assumed it was Margie or Justine, but when I looked more closely at her, I noticed a slight blush creeping up her cheeks and the corners of her mouth were upturned in a smile. I moved into the room to see who she was texting—I admit, I was being rude, but her mother wasn't wrong...she didn't have many friends, and curiosity was killing me. When she noticed me, she quickly turned the phone away, but I still caught most of the number, and I was pretty sure it belonged to my friend Mike. I smiled knowingly, but before I could say anything, we heard the rumble of the garage door from the ground level below us. She scowled and shouldered past me.

I followed Billy out and was greeted by Eric coming up the stairs from the garage. He handed the bag of clothes to Billy, who took them without comment and headed up to Calvin's room.

Eric went to the kitchen and I padded along behind him, sat at the table, and asked, "So, what's the story with mission control in the living room?"

He looked at me quizzically and smiled. "That's all Carol's stuff; she monitors our activities around the world, and she keeps Ghosts and Ghouls running from there. She also communicates, *clandestinely*," he said with a wink, "with our other Watcher groups around the world." The Watchers and the ghost killers like *and* need to keep a low profile. Vokkel wasn't the only jerk out there that knew about us and what we could do, and what the ghosts and demons could do. There's always someone lurking around that wants to harness these powers, and it's the Watchers' job to keep us all safe. Had today's technology been available when Vokkel was running his institutions, the Watchers could have intervened much sooner than they had. I'd heard Carol mention algorithms and programs that monitor general communications in search of keywords that might pertain to us and what we do. If she came across something, she could send someone to investigate. It was all very high-tech *and* big-brother like, but I was glad it existed.

"Does she live here?" I didn't see any indication that she was occupying one of the bedrooms, and wondered how she monitored things if she wasn't here all the time.

"She used to, but now she's got it all tied into her smart phone and she gets alerts or something if things go weird or whatever. And she's got that crotch-rocket she rides around on, so if she needs to get here fast," he smiled, "she can." Carol drove a Ducati 1199 Panigale R. I made the mistake of asking for a ride home once. The woman had no concept of speed limits...she swerved in and out of traffic like a Frogger game on steroids, and didn't really care that her passengers were screaming in terror while holding on for dear life. But Eric was right; she could probably get from one end of the city to the other in no time.

"Why is it all here and not at her own house?"

"Carol likes her downtime; she doesn't want to look at a bank of computers when she gets home from whatever it is she does all day long." Carol was a freelance programmer when she wasn't doing work for the Watchers or off killing ghosts, so I knew she had to have some equipment at her house. But I understood her reasons, because like most of us, I didn't have much of a life outside of ghost killing, and my apartment was my sanctuary.

"What about you; does it bug you living here all the time?"

"Not really. It's rent free, and to be honest, aside from Phil and Carol dropping in all the time, we only get a few visitors a month. Of course, if it's a newbie, I'm pretty busy training and they usually stay with us for a while, but we haven't had one in a few months. I'm thinking of getting a cat, though," he said offhandedly.

Billy appeared in the doorway and said, rather matter-of-factly, "I'll be with Calvin in the den for a while." That was Billy-speak for "Stay away while I grill the kid".

I decided I wanted to run home to get a change of clothes and grab a shower. Before she could disappear, I said, "I want to run home. You want to call Margie and ask her to put a bag together for you?" She nodded and headed back down the hallway.

I turned to Eric. "You okay with me leaving for an hour or so?"

"Go, we'll be fine. Pete's guys will be here any minute, and I've seen Billy in action. If she can't take out that bastard demon, we're all screwed anyway." There was a twinkle in his eyes when he said her name; I'd seen something similar the night before from Mike. I thought maybe he had a little crush on her, which would be the second man in two days to show interest in Billy. Wonders never ceased.

Chapter 21

After I showered and put a bag together, I stopped at Justine's to pick up Billy's overnight bag. As usual, Margie answered the door. She wasn't her normal cheerful self though, and I assumed our current situation was causing her concern. If it bothered her, I figured it must really be bothering Justine...and I was right.

"Come in, Justine wants a quick chat. There's Billy's bag." She pointed to a duffle on the floor of the hallway. "Grab it on your way out." She disappeared down the hall and I went to the living room where I assumed Justine was.

"Oh, George dear, how are you?" she asked sweetly. She always asked sweetly and I loved her for it. I kissed her cheek, said I was fine, and took the armchair nearest her.

"And the boy, how is he?" she asked.

"Honestly, I don't know. He's pretty messed up, and get this...he says it was GG who convinced him to find us."

"She has been tried and true to you and your mother, and I am relieved to know she is involved. However, I am very concerned about your safety, and of course, Billy's. This teenager and the demon he is associating with, killing people with...I discussed it at length with Margie last night and we are both of the conclusion that this is a terribly unusual situation. Does the boy understand what he has done...what he is doing?"

"I'm not sure. He said he doesn't remember killing those people. But I get the impression he's not telling the truth, at least the whole truth. You were right, by the way… there's definitely a connection to Vokkel. Phil's trying to find more information on that, and Billy's having a little chat with the kid now, so hopefully she'll get something from him too."

She sighed gracefully…Justine did everything gracefully. "Are you sure that you are strong enough to face it, to kill it?" Her beautiful eyes were pleading that I would say yes, so I did, and I did it with conviction. She reached over and patted my hand. "Good… now go. I do not like the idea of Billy being alone with this boy any longer than necessary."

I smiled at her, rose from my chair, and gave her another kiss on the cheek. As I crossed the living room toward the front hall, she said, "George, I expect that one or both of you will update us regularly." This wasn't a question or request… it was a mandate. I gave her a sloppy salute and nodded.

The rest of the day was about as exciting as watching paint dry. Billy spent hours on and off with Calvin—he seemed to need quite a few breaks, especially for snacks. At one point, she was even giving him a tour of the house. When they finally parted for good she was quietly solemn. I spent a few minutes badgering her in an attempt to find out what they'd discussed, which ended in a sharp refusal on her part to share their conversation—she'd rather wait until this evening so she didn't have to repeat herself. At that point she stormed off, probably to the top floor where she'd hopefully work off some of the mood she was in. I asked Eric if I could use one of the computers in the living room so I could run the name Gilles d'Aubray.

We don't know who the demons were before death, so having an actual name was a little exciting. Finding the person in the annals of history—via the Internet, of course—was another thing all together. When I typed in Gilles's name, I found a couple of hits, and one was our demon.

Gilles d'Aubray, born in Nice, France in 1622, was the youngest son of a moderately noble French family. He became a musketeer at the age of eighteen, and soon gained a reputation as a boisterous and spirited fighter. His reputation put him on the fast track for advancement until 1642, when his family was disgraced and their nobility status was stripped. Although d'Aubray was able to remain a musketeer, his position was now stagnant and he was often considered unworthy of advancement due to his family's disgrace. In 1645 a series of gruesome murders plagued the upper wealthy classes, and the investigation eventually led them to d'Aubray, who just prior to his execution, admitted that he killed to avenge his family's name. Because of the sensationalism of d'Aubray's crimes, many were still familiar with him decades after his death, and claimed to have seen his ghost wandering the streets of Nice in search of more victims.

Along with the article was a portrait of d'Aubray. He stood with one leg pulled up and perched on a low stone wall. He was wearing a ruffled long-sleeve shirt, waistcoat, petticoat with stockings, and leather square-toed shoes tied with a wide ribbon closure. Topping the ensemble off was a wide-brimmed hat with one side pinned up, and an elaborate feather tucked into the other side. I was staring at our demon in all his 17th century finery. I printed out the article and the portrait and laid them both on Phil's library table so he'd see them when he arrived later in the day.

Feeling satisfied with my search on our evil musketeer, I decided a nap was in order and retired to the den for the remainder of the afternoon. I woke up a couple of hours later just as everyone was arriving.

Chapter 22

Eric was doling out beverages as our group began to congregate in the dining area. Carol and Phil were the last to arrive. I grabbed a beer and planted myself in a chair, then I looked around the room. Pete and Billy wore matching stony expressions—that usually meant bad news—and Phil's normal enthusiasm seemed to be on a break tonight, which I took to mean he hadn't found anything new. Aris was his usual impassive self and Carol was looking around curiously, much like I was.

I looked at Billy. "Where's Calvin?"

"Upstairs,"

"Alone?" I hadn't seen GG all day and didn't like the idea that Calvin was unmonitored.

Eric answered, "No, he's with Jonas." I frowned. I didn't know anyone named Jonas. Eric smiled. "He's one of our younger members and just turned nineteen. I thought Calvin would be more comfortable with someone closer to his own age. They're playing video games in Calvin's room."

I turned back to Billy. "Are we hoping Jonas can get something out of the kid, or did you get everything we need?"

Billy sneered at me. I wasn't being sarcastic, so I didn't think I warranted her wrath. Her mood clearly hadn't improved since our little chat earlier in the day, and I let out an exasperated breath.

Aris said, "Billy, were you able to extract any additional information from Calvin?"

Her tone was flat and tense. "Calvin said that for most of the time Edgar was there, he doesn't really remember much. He said on a couple of occasions he'd find himself far from home with Edgar and Gilles and neither of them would tell him how he got there or why. He said it's happened several times in the last couple of weeks. I think Edgar used that voodoo-brain shit on Calvin, and with Calvin's help he was able to talk to the demon and they put together the attacks... or...," she paused and looked around, "the demon was possessing Calvin."

"Is that even possible? I thought you guys couldn't be possessed," Phil said incredulously. He shook his head like he was trying to dislodge an ugly thought, which I suppose he was.

Aris replied, "As far as I am aware, there have been two documented occasions of a demon possessing a ghost killer. The first occurred sometime in the early 1720s in a small village in Northern Ireland. The ghost killer was of the lowest level, an orphan and essentially homeless, relying on the kindness of the villagers for food and shelter. He was considered at the time to be witless, and his constant ramblings about apparitions and their misdeeds seemed to confirm that. Our network was small in those days, but word of the boy made it to England, and a higher level ghost killer was dispatched to determine if the boy was one of us. Upon arrival, the Englishman discovered that a rather nasty demon was haunting the boy, and possessing him rather frequently, causing the boy to commit atrocious crimes against his fellow villagers. The ghost killer was able to vanquish the demon, but unfortunately the villagers had had enough and attacked the boy out of fear; he died soon after. The second occurrence was in 1956 in Alberta. This ghost killer was not quite of the highest level, but very close to it. He was not a favorable man and frequently used his ability to coerce the ghosts and demons to do his bidding. He befriended, so to speak, a rather nasty demon and eventually allowed the demon to possess him. He and his demon were killed by our people."

Phil said, "So we have three possibilities; the kid's mental... *shortcomings*... are allowing the demon to possess him, or he's just allowing it to possess him... or Edgar's making him do it." His expression was dismal. "Man, this ain't good."

Billy said, "I think if it is possessing him, he's not allowing it." There was empathy in her tone. She seemed to be developing some sort of attachment to the kid, which was understandable considering what she'd been through at that age, but it worried me too. We needed her to be objective about the kid and our current situation.

She continued, "He said Gilles has been around for years, since he was at least ten. I asked about Sam Smith. Calvin said that his mom hired him to tutor Calvin, which Sam did until last year when he quit and left town. I asked if Sam could see the ghosts and Calvin said he could, and they talked about it sometimes, but he wouldn't elaborate, so I moved on to Vokkel. Apparently Vokkel and Edgar visited a couple of times a year for as long as Calvin can remember. They talked to him about his studies and a little bit about the ghosts he could see, but not much else."

"So, I'm guessing this Sam Smith guy was a ghost killer too. Do we know anything more about him?" I asked, looking to Phil and Carol.

Phil's hangdog expression screamed guilt. "I'm sorry, I got caught up in business stuff today, and didn't get a chance to look into anything." Phil tended to think he should drop everything for us, but he had a regular business and we all understood it required his time too. Aris gave him a quick nod, his way of saying "it's okay".

"So we suspect he killed his tutor, and Phil thinks he killed his uncle, and we all know he killed two people in Marin the other day. . . ." I raked my hands through my hair. "What are we dealing with?"

Carol shrugged. "It could have been Vokkel or Edgar who killed Smith. . . like I said, it's unresolved, and that particular motel has a reputation as a druggy hangout, so the kid the maid saw could have been anyone. Anyway, I posted a notice with Smith's license picture on Ghosts and Ghouls just to see if anything popped, and got a hit about an hour ago." She looked down at her tablet. "It says, '*That's Samuel, don't know last name. Freelancer, known to work for both sides, has connections to V and others like him.*'" She looked up and around, her eyes settling on Aris, and asked, "Should I try and find out more about him, or is this enough?"

Aris steepled his fingers, his brow furrowed in contemplation. "Yes, please try and find out where he originates from and if possible, who he has worked for in the past." I didn't think this request had anything to do with our current situation; it was just part of Aris's job to know everything he could about the bad guys, and it was Carol's job to help him. Sam was dead and couldn't do any more harm, so he was no longer part of the equation as far as I was concerned.

Pete said, "I know all of this is important, but I think we need to switch gears and come up with a plan to get this demon *and* Edgar eradicated." He turned to Billy. "Did the kid say if he knows how to get in touch with Edgar?"

She blew out an exasperated breath. "They were staying in touch with pre-paid cell phones, but Calvin said he ditched his after he took off on his bike. He doesn't remember where, and he said he never wrote the number down."

Chapter 23

We broke up for a few minutes so people could use the bathroom and stretch. We still had to put a plan together to find the demon and Edgar. Billy disappeared upstairs, I assumed to check on Calvin. I walked to the front of the house and peeked out the windows, which faced Golden Gate Park. The fog had started to move in and was swirling in ghostly gusts between the street and the forested perimeter of the park. For all I knew Edgar could be standing right across the street and we wouldn't be able to see him. When I turned away from the windows I was faced with another ghostly image, only this time it was GG.

"Hi," I said, smiling a little. "Have you been here the whole time?" She smiled faintly and nodded. I asked, "GG, you can talk to Calvin, with words?" She tilted her head, incomprehension in her eyes. "He said you told him to come to us, and where to find us last night." Her brow furrowed and she shook her head. "Did you tell him to come to us? That we could help him?" She nodded. "But you didn't tell him where we were last night?" She nodded again. Almost to myself, I said, "Then how did he know where to find us...?" She gave me a blank stare. I'd suspected the kid was lying, and now I knew for sure. "Do you think he knows where Edgar is?" She cringed at his name, then shrugged. "What about the musketeer demon...can you help us find him?" She shook her head furiously, a terrified look on her face. "Are you afraid of him?" I asked. She frowned and disappeared. I really hated it when she did that.

* * *

When we reconvened, Jonas had joined us and introductions were made. He was the same height as Calvin, but instead of a thin and lanky frame, he had a solid build. His eyes were bright and intelligent and his curly brown hair was neatly trimmed.

Billy said, "Calvin was tired and wanted to go to bed."

Jonas expanded. "The kid's pretty wiped out and confused, but I got him to open up a bit. I couldn't get him to talk about the demon, but he did tell me some stuff about his childhood. He said he never knew his dad and he doesn't remember living anywhere but Valley Springs. I asked him if he ever talked to his mom about seeing the ghosts. He said she didn't like to talk about it, but she didn't seem to mind if he talked to Sam about it." Much like Billy, Jonas seemed to be growing sympathetic towards Calvin, but based on what GG had just told me, it was probably misplaced. Although I had previously suspected he was lying, or at least holding stuff back, now I knew, at the very least, he lied about how he'd found us at the bar. But I couldn't deny that the kid was probably being used by both the musketeer demon and Edgar, which did warrant some sympathy. They were clearly taking advantage of his low intelligence and naiveté regarding his power.

Aris asked, "Did Calvin tell you anything else, Jonas?"

Jonas nodded. "Yeah, but it was kind of weird; he's obviously not all that bright." He paused, looking a little embarrassed. "I mean, he seems kind of slow, if you know what I mean." Aris nodded. "That's what was weird, he started asking me really focused questions…quite a few." Jonas's brow wrinkled. "He seemed really interested in the library that Phil's building. He said Billy had shown him the house earlier today and he thought that room was really cool. At first I thought it was Carol's computers that had caught his eye, but he kept asking about the books and journals and what they contained. It was a strange line of questioning coming from a kid who's clearly not that smart."

"What sort of questions did he ask about the contents, specifically?" Aris asked, angling his head curiously.

"He asked how far back the information went. I told him I wasn't sure, that Phil had been collecting whatever he could from everywhere, and some of it was probably pretty old. Then he asked if we had journals and stuff from Vokkel. I told him we probably didn't, that Vokkel wasn't exactly on our side and wouldn't have shared his papers with us. He let that drop and asked if we had information on where the demons were buried." Jonas paused, as if trying to recall the exact wording Calvin used. "He said, 'chamber maps' or something like that. I sort of laughed and told him we didn't know who these monsters were, dead or alive, so we couldn't know where they came from or where they were buried. He got sort of annoyed and clammed up." Jonas looked at Aris with concern. "It was okay to tell him that, right?"

Aris nodded, but there was suspicion in his eyes.

Billy looked at Aris. "Do you know what he meant?"

Aris frowned. "I do not." He looked to Phil. "Have you come across any references to chamber maps?"

Phil shook his head. "Nope. I came across references to 'chamber,' but not 'maps.' But I'll see what I can find."

"I saw GG in the living room while we were taking a break. She said she didn't tell Calvin where we were last night." I glanced at Billy. She wasn't surprised, which told me she'd come to agree with me that he'd been lying to us. "I asked her if Calvin knew where Edgar was, and she wasn't sure. I also asked if she could help us get to Gilles...based on her response, I think she's terrified of him." I turned to Phil. "I did an Internet search on

Gilles. Turns out he was a bit of a celebrity back in his corporeal days...he was a serial killer." I heard Billy grumble "figures" under her breath, but ignored her. "I left the printout on your table. Maybe you could check to see if anyone's come across him before."

"I'll try, my man, but most of that stuff is still uncategorized." He didn't sound hopeful.

"So now what?" Billy asked. Her voice was strained and I could tell she was tired.

"I'd like to think about our next move, tactically, and meet again tomorrow if that's okay?" Pete asked.

"I want to drive up and see the mother tomorrow...maybe she'll talk to me," I said.

Billy's tone was cool. "Why would she talk to you and not Pete?"

I gave her a lofty look. "Because I'm a nice guy and people like me. Pete's a nice guy too once you get to know him, but he looks and acts like a soldier, and that can be intimidating." I looked to Pete and said, "No offense."

He shot me a tight salute and said, "None taken."

Carol said, "I want to set up a sensor on Calvin's bedroom door." She had an unsettled expression on her face as she looked from Billy to Eric to me. "We don't know what's going on yet. If that demon is possessing him, and if he did kill Sam, it means he's capable of killing another ghost killer...." She was right and I nodded. Carol winked at me and said, "Good, you can have tonight's watch." Apparently my nod of agreement meant I'd volunteered to monitor Calvin's sensor for the night. If the kid got up to take a leak, I'd know all about it. So much for a decent night's rest.

Aris and Pete left and Carol went about setting up her alarm. Phil spent a few minutes gathering some papers and journals from the library, then he left too. When Carol was done she showed me how the alarm monitor worked. If Calvin opened his door during the night, a bell-like ding would go off and hopefully it would wake me up before he went on a demon-fueled rampage. Eric directed Billy and I to our new guest quarters and retired to his room. I was hoping for a nice quiet night.

Chapter 24

I'm not a big fan of dreams, the kind the sandman brings that is. The aspiring kind are just fine and everyone should have them, but my nighttime dreams are usually freakishly strange and unusual, and I prefer not to remember them. It was a preference I was denied when I woke up in the Lincoln Way guest room at exactly 3 a.m., the witching hour (for those of you who aren't familiar with the term, it's the time of night when ghosts, demons, and other unpleasant things are said to be the most powerful).

Calvin's sensor hadn't activated in reality, but it did in my dreams—in the dream I was startled out of sleep by an obnoxious ding-ding-ding sound, and realizing what it was, I rushed out to the hallway to find Calvin, but he wasn't alone. Gilles was holding Calvin's hand and I could see the electroplasmic juice flowing between them. It got brighter and brighter and I realized they were trying to converge, but without the help of another ghost killer. As I watched in horror, Gilles and Calvin moved closer and closer, and before my dreamy eyes, the two became one. Suddenly Calvin seemed to glow with all the evil of Gilles. Even though Calvin was simple-minded, he was a powerful ghost killer, whether he knew it or not, and I knew they'd become a monster we'd never be able to kill. I screamed. Thankfully my shriek didn't permeate reality or I'm sure I would have caused quite a stir with my housemates.

I slept restlessly for the remainder of the night, and when the real sensor went off at 6 a.m., I was hesitant to investigate...and maybe a bit scared. Calvin was standing in the doorway of his bedroom, rubbing sleep from his eyes. When he finally noticed me in the shadows a few feet away, he said, "Hey."

"Hey yourself. You okay?" I asked.

He shrugged. "Yeah, I'm hungry."

"Me too." I wasn't, not really, but it occurred to me that this was my opportunity to do some questioning of my own, "Let's go find something to eat."

I didn't want to make too much noise with pots and pans because I didn't want Billy or Eric to wake up and interrupt our little tête-à-tête, so I offered to make Calvin a fully loaded turkey sandwich with some chips on the side. Calvin watched in quiet anticipation as I prepared our unconventional breakfast, and when I placed his plate in front of him, he attacked it. Since I wasn't really hungry in the first place, I pushed mine to the side.

"Calvin, I know you don't know much about what's going on." He looked up from his sandwich, but didn't appear to be all that interested in what I was saying. "When I was a kid I started seeing ghosts. I couldn't talk to them like you, not yet anyway. When my mom found out, she had some stuff done to me so I wouldn't see them anymore. She was scared I would be like her. She was really, really strong, and this thing, seeing ghosts, it's hereditary. Anyway, she didn't want the bad people, like Vokkel, to find out about me and take me away like they did with her when she was a kid."

Now Calvin was paying attention. He put his sandwich down and shifted uncomfortably, "What'd they do to her?"

"They kidnapped her and killed her parents...they tried to get her to do bad things, like Gilles and Edgar did with you."

"What'd she do to you?" he asked. It was interesting that he didn't acknowledge my insinuation that both Edgar and Gilles were using him for nefarious purposes.

"She had me hypnotized so I wouldn't remember them. Every time I saw a ghost, my mind would erase it right away and I'd just go on like nothing happened."

"When'd you start seeing 'em again?" He picked his sandwich up and took a large bite.

"A while ago." I didn't think telling him I'd only been at this for six or so months was a good idea... it might lessen any credibility I was attempting to build with him. "We're special people, Calvin. We can see the ghosts because most of them are bad and they're hurting people, and it's our job, *our legacy*, to kill them. Have you ever killed one?"

His head dipped to one side, perplexity in his expression. I rephrased the question. "Did you ever notice that when you see the ghosts, someone nearby is sick or disfigured or something? If you were to kill the ghost, that person, that *suffering* person, would be cured."

"They told me to stay away from them, that they'd hurt me and my mom." He shrugged. "I saw them hurt other people and I believed them."

"But you're not afraid of GG, are you?"

He shook his head and took another bite, after he swallowed he said, "She's a nice one... I can tell."

"How can you tell?"

"I know about the sick people... I mean, I'm not stupid or anything. I figured that out a while ago, so I knew that the other ghosts would hurt my mom. But GG's different." Another shrug. "She doesn't have a sick person around her, so I know she isn't bad."

That was true... she didn't haunt people. There are others out there like her, ghosts that aren't bad. Most of them just want to move on, and I try and help them when I can.

"Calvin, you don't seem to be afraid of Gilles either. How come?"

He stiffened. "He…I was in the beginning, sort of. I mean, he didn't hurt anyone I knew."

"Calvin, did Gilles hurt your uncle?"

Something flashed in his eyes, and he quickly, but not all that convincingly, said, "No. That was an accident…my uncle was being stupid and drunk and it got him killed!"

That reaction was interesting. As if he sensed my misgivings, his eyes began to fill with tears and he said, "I miss him a lot."

"Calvin, Gilles is going to keep on hurting people if we don't stop him. What he did in Marin, do you understand what happened there?"

He nodded slowly. "We told those other ghosts to hurt people, but I don't really remember killing people. I didn't mean to…."

I decided to switch gears. "Calvin, how come Gilles isn't haunting anyone?"

Calvin angled his head. "He just wants to be human again. Edgar said he'd help."

"How was Edgar going to help?"

Another shrug. "He said he would get you or Billy to do it."

"Calvin, Edgar knows we'd never do that."

Calvin was shaking his head. "He said to get lots of ghosts to make people do things, and when you guys were trying to fight them, we'd take one of you and then whoever we didn't take would do what we said to get the other back. But…." His eyes misted again and his speech sped up. "You guys were too good, and we couldn't control the other ghosts enough to grab one of you and it didn't work, and Edgar got really mad and hit me…." He fell back into his chair and lowered his head.

"So Edgar didn't really want to kill us in Marin, he wanted to capture one of us? That's a little different from what you told us earlier." I looked at him expectantly.

He looked up and I caught another sudden flash of…what? Intelligence? Menace? I wasn't sure, but it lit Calvin's eyes for a split second and sent a chill down my spine. Then it was gone and that lost little boy look returned. He shrugged and ashamedly said, "Edgar's mean. He really scares me... that's... that's why I came to you guys. But I thought if I told you everything the other day, you wouldn't help me...." His eyes filled with tears again and he wiped them away.

"It's okay, I get that, and you're right... Edgar is one scary, mean guy." I didn't believe him... something was very off here. "Calvin, how do you and Gilles get all those demons to come to you, to do those bad things?"

"I don't call 'em, Gilles does. He goes away, and when he comes back they're with him. Then my head gets all fuzzy and I don't remember stuff."

I assumed this was similar to the surges Vokkel had unleashed. He had one of his GKs communicate with the ghosts and demons to get them to do his bidding, with the understanding that he'd arrange for a powerful ghost killer to converge them. What Vokkel forgot to mention to his ghoulish army was that the ghost killer he had in mind to do the convergences was none other than myself. But I'm a good guy, and even though he had kidnapped my dad and planned on using him as leverage against me, I had Billy, the Watchers, and a whole gaggle of good ghosts (thanks to GG) on my side, and we kicked their asses.

"Calvin, when your head gets fuzzy, has Edgar been around every time that's happened?"

"Sometimes...." Calvin began fidgeting, reminding me of a child who desperately wanted to be dismissed from the dinner table.

"Okay, Calvin, one more question. Can your mom and dad see ghosts and demons too?" Generally ghost killers inherit their ability from one side of the family, but if both sides have it, they tend to be more powerful, like Billy and like me. My grandfather was adopted, and neither he nor my dad ever showed any ghost killing ability, but based on my power level, someone in that gene pool was a ghost killer too. I thought it was safe to assume that both of Calvin's parents came from a long line of GKs, and that might be important.

He was staring down at his nails when he suddenly shot me a suspicious look from under his lashes…it was quick, but I caught it. He shrugged and said, "'Dunno. My mom never said nothing about seeing 'em, and my dad was a one-night stand thing."

Billy shuffled sleepily into the kitchen and mumbled, "'Morning," as she headed to the cold, empty coffee pot.

"I'm going to my room," Calvin said while pushing away from the table, leaving his crumb filled plate behind. I got up and put it in the sink, then sat back down heavily.

After she finished making the coffee, Billy sat next to me, crossed her arms on the table, and rested her head on them as she looked at me. "What's up?" she asked as she stifled a yawn.

"You look tired, Billy. You should go back to sleep," I said.

"I wasn't the one screaming in the middle of the night."

A flush of embarrassment crept up my face. "Bad dream; sorry if I woke you."

"You didn't…I was coming back from the bathroom. It wasn't loud, but I checked on you anyway. Looked like you were asleep, and there wasn't anyone in your room murdering you." She yawned again. "So I figured it was a dream." I tried to smile. She said, "So…," and nodded her head in the direction that Calvin took. "What'd he say?"

"What makes you think he said anything?"

She pulled my uneaten sandwich toward her, looked at it, and took a bite. After swallowing, she said, "I heard you guys come down, and I know you've been dying to talk to him alone. So what did he say?" The coffee maker beeped and she got up to attend to her caffeine needs. When she returned to the table, I still hadn't answered her question and she was showing signs of irritation; lack of patience, lack of caffeine, and lack of sleep weren't helping either. She said curtly, "Spill it George."

I got up to get my own cup of coffee while I filled her in on the basics of our conversation. I ended with, "I think it's likely that Gilles was possessing Calvin…I'm just not sure if it was with or without Calvin's permission, or how much of Edgar's influence was involved."

She closed her eyes, and with a slight sigh, she asked, "And?"

"Well, he's lying to us. There are quite a few inconsistencies with his version of what's happened." She looked at me curiously. "Okay, well one minute he can't remember the details of his last encounter with Edgar or what happened in Marin, the next minute he can, and when I call him on it, he falls back to the 'my head gets fuzzy' bit, or the 'Edgar scares me' bit. And, I don't know, I just get this weird feeling from him, like the whole simple-minded thing isn't right either." Maybe I was being too hard on the kid. I said, "The question is, is he doing it deliberately, or is he just confused about what's been happening to him? So maybe you and Jonas can try and find out."

Billy nodded unenthusiastically and started back on my sandwich. I left her there and headed to my room. It was a long drive to Valley Springs and I wanted to get on the road.

Chapter 25

Forty-five minutes later I was out of the city, across the Bay Bridge, and onto I-580 headed east towards Tracy and Stockton, where I'd catch the I-205 freeway until I reached a series of smaller interchanges that would eventually put me in Valley Springs. By the time I reached Tracy, my stomach was painfully reminding me that I'd skipped breakfast. I was saved by the looming golden boomerang shaped arrow of the In-N-Out sign—originally a Southern California restaurant I frequented as a child and missed dearly as an adult. They'd eventually opened up shop in Northern California, but the city only had one and it was in Fisherman's Wharf, a place I tended to avoid, not just because it was a tourist mecca, but also because it's the place I'd gone to prove to myself that ghosts weren't real and I was just going crazy. Turned out I was wrong on the former, and the jury is still out on the latter. I used the drive-thru and took my lunch on the road. According to my GPS, I was another hour-and-a-half from Valley Springs, and it was almost noon.

After getting off the freeway, I found myself on a two-lane road that wound its way through several small farming towns full of orchards, vineyards, and produce fields. I headed further into the hill country, past parched rolling hills dotted with large California Oaks and the occasional herd of cows and horses, eventually finding myself in Valley Springs. My GPS spit out a few more turns, and finally I found myself in a quaint little neighborhood. My destination was on the left and I pulled to the curb and parked. The house was a small one-story cottage, nicely maintained, much like its neighbors. The lawn was neatly trimmed, but brown in deference to our latest California drought. However, her deference was only towards the lawn, as there were colorful and overflowing flower boxes flanking the porch. The front door was hidden behind a heavy-duty security screen with an equally heavy-duty deadbolt. The neighborhood looked nice; what was she afraid of that warranted such an enforced entry?

The woman who opened the front door—but not the deadbolted metal screen door—was average height with deep worry lines edged upon her face. Her shoulder-length hair, once dark brown like her son's, was now salt and pepper and loosely pulled back. I knew she was only two years older than me, but her thirty-six years had clearly been harder on her than my thirty-four years had been on me. She had on jeans, a button-up blouse, and flip-flops.

Her eyes narrowed and she suspiciously asked, "Can I help you?"

"Hi, Ms. Brelong, my name's George Sinclair. I'm like Calvin…I can see them, and I really need your help."

Her expression hardened and she began to pick at her nails, clearly a habit she'd passed on to her son. Finally she said, "I told that man the other day that I don't know where he is."

"I know. Could we talk for a bit, on the porch?" I asked, putting on my most ingratiating, and hopefully disarming, smile.

She hesitantly opened the door and waved to the café set on the left side of the front door. I walked over and took a seat while she took the other.

"Ms. Brelong, you know about the ghosts and demons and the ghost killers, right?" She nodded. "I don't know if you're aware of this, but Calvin's been hanging out with some pretty bad people...and things. He's befriended a demon, a dangerous one, and together they killed two people the other day." I waited for her reaction, but she lowered her head and started in on her nails again, picking viciously.

"There's a man too, you've met him—his name is Edgar. He came to Calvin a few months ago. He's been staying up in Rail Road Flat, at your brother's ranch. He's extremely dangerous, and we believe that he, with a demon's help, put Calvin up to killing those people and severely injuring others." She wouldn't look at me, so I kept going.

"Calvin came to me...us. He wants our help." She was shaking her head and I held my hand up to her. "Please, let me explain who we are." She stared at me, eventually nodding.

"You know about the ghosts and demons and the ghost killers, but do you know who the Watchers are?" She sort of shrugged. I wasn't sure if that meant she knew who they were or not, so I explained. "They've been around for a long time. They protect ghost killers from bad people like Edgar, like Vokkel." She flinched at the mention of his name. "We help kids like Calvin learn about their abilities and how to use them to help people. We've been fighting people like Vokkel for years. I guess you know he's dead, right?"

She looked up and swallowed hard. "I figured something happened to him."

"Because the money stopped coming?" She nodded. "Okay, well Edgar had a part in his death and that's why he came up here...he needed to hide for a while."

She started to cry. After a minute she wiped her hand across her face, smearing tears and snot across her cheek. Her voice faltered when she finally spoke. "I didn't know what else to do. He said that people would come after us...if they found us, they'd take Calvin away. He said he'd arrange for us to be protected, for us to be taken care of. He sent Sam, to teach him and make sure he was safe."

I assumed she meant Vokkel, but I needed to be sure, "Ms. Brelong, who do you mean when you say 'he'?

"Mr. Vokkel." She looked up at me. Another tear spilled over the rim of one eye and ran down her cheek, eventually dropping onto her pant leg.

I asked, "Can you see them too?" She shook her head. "But Calvin's father could?"

She took a deep breath. "Yes. My father said he was one of the strongest ghost killers he'd ever encountered." Her voice hitched. "He said he was extremely dangerous, unstable…I should have listened to him."

It was just after three in the afternoon when I finally got back on the road. Gail Brelong had started talking and didn't stop for almost two hours.

Chapter 26

The drive home took much longer than the drive there due to pockets of rush hour traffic, and it was almost seven when I finally made it back to Lincoln Way. The streets were littered with ghosts, ghouls, princesses, Marvel Comics characters, and a variety of other costumed children…it was Halloween night, after all. When I walked up the front steps, I noticed carved jack-o-lanterns on each side of the steps. I was greeted at the door by one of Pete's extra security, a mid-level GK named Dave, holding a large bowl of candy. He smiled as we exchanged pleasantries, and I headed to the kitchen to find the usual suspects assembled and chatting aimlessly.

Phil smiled broadly and said, "Finally, you made it, man! I was beginning to think you ditched us and went back to your place."

"It was a long drive, just hit some traffic." I pointed behind me. "We're giving out candy?"

Eric smiled mischievously and said, "It's the best holiday of the year. Besides, it gives Dave something to do," he said with a wink.

Turning to Billy, I asked, "How's our boy today?"

She looked unsure, but settled on, "He's…complicated." I didn't know what that meant, but I assumed she'd fill us in. Eric offered me a beer, and I took a seat next to Billy.

Aris cleared his throat, "George, please tell us about your visit with Ms. Brelong."

"Gail's father was a ghost killer, and a pretty strong one at that. Gail was the apple of her father's eye and the mother apparently couldn't take it. She took off with little brother Leo when Gail was ten and Gail never saw her again, but she managed to reconnect with Leo…obviously. Anyway, the father/daughter duo traveled around this country and Canada killing ghosts. She can't see them, but she knows all about it. When she was seventeen she met a man who went by the name Drew Adler. He was handsome and charming and quite a bit older than her. They kept their relationship a secret for about six months, but then she turned up pregnant and decided it was time to introduce Drew to Daddy…it didn't go well. Gail's father immediately recognized Drew because his likeness and a list of his bad deeds had been circulating through the ghost killer community in the Ontario Province where they were living. Gail's father tried to convince her to cut off ties with Drew, but she wouldn't do it. So her dad went to the other GKs in the area with the intention of forming a posse to hunt Drew down and take him out. When Drew found out, he killed her father. Gail freaked out and left town.

"She'd never mentioned having a brother to Drew, so she decided to go hide out with Leo in Rail Road Flat. When Calvin was five, Vokkel appeared at the ranch, claiming to be Drew's adoptive father, and also claiming that Drew was dead. He said if people found out that Drew had a son, they'd come looking for him and they'd take Calvin away. Vokkel said he'd help Gail out by giving her a house and a monthly allowance if she kept a low profile and allowed him access to Calvin. She was scared, broke, and hated living up in the hill country, so she agreed to his terms.

"Vokkel and Edgar made monthly visits until Calvin was about seven. After Sam arrived…or was sent to her…the visits petered down to about four a year. Then picked up again right after her brother died, and continued about every other month or so." I paused for a long pull off my beer. "So Calvin obviously lied about how often he met with Vokkel. She also said that during the more recent visits, Vokkel spent tons of one-on-one time with Calvin. She overheard them once, and said it sounded like Vokkel was teaching Calvin a prayer of some sort. She said when Calvin recited it, it sounded like chanting or something. Oh, and she's pretty sure he killed Sam and Leo."

"Why?" Phil asked incredulously. I wasn't sure why he was so surprised...we already suspected this.

"Despite the fact that Sam worked for Vokkel, he apparently wasn't all that bad, he was just greedy. Vokkel was paying him quite a bit to tutor the kid and monitor and report on his progress. The kid was very fond of Leo and spent plenty of weekends up there. One particular weekend Gail asked Sam to drive the kid up to the ranch, and that's when he saw Gilles for the first time. Gilles wasn't haunting Leo and Calvin told Sam that they were friends, so Sam decided to watch and see what unfolded." I looked around. "We all know some ghosts befriend us.

"Not too long after that, Gilles abandoned his new home in Rail Road Flat and came down the hill to Valley Springs. According to what Sam told Gail, that's when Gilles started to do some pretty hardcore haunting and killing, which really bothered Sam because he was going after easy pickings, like the old and infirm and sick kids. Then one day Calvin told Sam all about Gilles's plans to converge with Leo, and asked Sam to teach him how to do it. That really freaked Sam out, especially since it was the kid's own uncle he planned on converging Gilles into. Sam told Calvin he didn't know how to do it and left it at that.

"Gail said that Leo wasn't the smartest tool in the shed, but he wasn't a complete idiot either. He was pretty handy when it came to home improvement stuff, like basic electrical, but more importantly, he was extremely safety conscious, to the point that he'd barely change a light bulb without killing the power at the main. The idea that he'd fill up that hot tub, knowing it had faulty electrical, then get drunk and soak in it, was incomprehensible. She shared this with Sam after Leo died. At that point Sam confessed to her that he thought the kid had killed Leo while trying to converge Gilles, and when it went bad, Calvin staged the hot tub scene. Apparently Sam told Gail he was terrified of not just the musketeer, but of Calvin and of Vokkel. Not long after his confession to Gail, Sam decided he couldn't take it and said he was leaving the following day. He went out that night to say goodbye to some friends he'd made over the years and never returned. Gail was pretty upset that Sam was leaving, because they were a couple, sort of. Anyway, she said she railed on Calvin when he came home the same day Sam announced his departure. She blamed it all on him and he stormed out of the house. Calvin didn't return until the next morning.

"Since Sam had planned on coming back later that night, he left all his stuff at Gail's house. When he didn't return, she figured something had happened to him, probably at the hands of Calvin. I told her what we knew about Sam's death and asked to look at his stuff. There were two thick diaries, which she let me take." I glanced at Phil…this was his department. "I'll give them to you when we're done here." I hadn't had time to look at the diaries and I was too tired to do it tonight, but I knew Phil would go over them thoroughly and report anything of interest.

I drained the remainder of my beer and remembered something else. "When I asked her about Calvin's intellectual disability, she laughed. She said the kid is smart and conniving, could lie at the drop of a hat, and apparently he pulls the 'stupid' act when he needs to manipulate people, like when he gets in trouble. She said if he's acting dumb with us, he's up to something and it isn't good. I think she's terrified of her son, and I think she's relieved that he's out of her hair and in ours."

I nodded to Aris, signaling the end of my report. He said, "Thank you, George. There were other discoveries in your absence." Turning to Billy, he asked, "Billy, would you care to elaborate?"

"Well," there was a bit of annoyance in her voice, "obviously George was right. Calvin is lying to us." She shot those green eyes in my direction, but it was harmless enough. She just hated it when I was right. I did my best not to smirk, but failed miserably.

She ignored me and continued. "I searched his room while he was showering this morning, and found a cell phone tucked between the mattress and box spring. There's no way to know if it's the one he mentioned before, or if that was just a lie to begin with. It was password protected so I wasn't able to access it right away, but as soon as he was done in the bathroom, I rushed him out of the house for a walk in the park. Fortunately, he left the phone behind and I'd already told Aris and Carol, so she was here when we left and she managed to get into it." She finished and nodded to Carol.

Carol said, "He texted someone the night he got here and said, '*365 Linc Way.*' There wasn't a return message until the next morning, which just said, '*and?*' Then nothing until last night, after he told Jonas he was tired. The return text said, '*they're here.*' I tried tracing the receiving phone, but it's a prepaid cell and the GPS is disabled. I can tell you that it pinged off a few local towers, so whoever it is—Edgar, I assume—he's in the city and he's been in the vicinity of this house since yesterday. Regardless, I'm tapped into Calvin's phone now, so if he sends or receives any more texts, I'll know." When Carol was done, she looked to Billy.

"So he texted the address, I assume to let Edgar know where he was, but I'm not sure about the last text. Initially I thought he was confirming that you and I are here." Billy looked at me. "But that doesn't make sense, because I'm pretty sure they planned this." She sighed angrily. "He couldn't kidnap one of us the other night, so they decided to have Calvin play the scared kid and come to us pleading asylum or whatever. If that is Edgar's cell phone, he is undoubtedly watching this place and already knows we're here." There was a definite air of hurt in her tone and I felt bad for her. She really had been getting attached to the little-boy-lost. However, now she was pissed, and that was good... she was damn mean when she was mad.

I turned to Phil. "Did you find out anything new in all your research?"

Phil rubbed his hands together excitedly. "Okay, when I started collecting documents for the sanctum, I was put in touch with an elder Watcher in Berlin... nice old fella." Phil smiled. "He runs a sort of safe house like this one and became the local dumping spot for journals and notebooks and stuff that the ghost killers kept. And, since he's getting up there in age, he was happy to pass it all along to me, but he said to call anytime I had a question, so I called him about Gilles. Since he's been around so long, I figured he might have heard some stuff. He had.

"Apparently there have been stories about a musketeer demon for years, but every time one of you guys gets close enough, the dude manages to get away. The old fella directed me to some diaries he sent over, because he recalled there might be some added details. Luckily I figured out which one it was and was able to read it." He frowned. "Not all this stuff is in English. Anyway, this ghost killer, M. Frankel, who was apparently pretty darn powerful himself, wrote about a musketeer that he pursued throughout Europe during the 1950s. He was quite the artist too, and filled his diaries with sketches of his more formidable adversaries. There's one of a musketeer that sure looks a lot like the picture George downloaded." Phil sobered. "The last sighting he had of this musketeer was in Switzerland." He looked at Billy and me. "Close to the location of Vokkel's school. He doesn't say outright, but he implies that maybe it took refuge at

Vokkel's compound. That's all there was, but if we assume this musketeer was Gilles, it sort of gives us an idea of how strong this demon is, right?"

I knew it was strong just by virtue of its age, but to evade powerful ghost killers—especially ones that were actively pursuing it—meant it was probably stronger than we'd thought. The idea that it might have been associated with Vokkel a half-century before it met Calvin was even scarier.

"Well, we already knew it was strong. Was there anything else to tie it to Vokkel?" Billy asked with unwarranted obnoxiousness. I knew her attitude had to do with Calvin's betrayal, or at least what she interpreted as his betrayal, but it wasn't Phil's fault the kid was a liar, a murderer, and God only knew what else. I kicked her lightly under the table, which got me one of those nasty green-eyed glares, but it also dislodged a mumbled apology to Phil.

Phil winked at her, lightly touched the brim of his hat (today, it was a newsboy cap), and said, "There was, m' lady." He followed that with a big smile, which she almost reciprocated.

"This particular musketeer-hunting ghost killer mentioned a comrade-in-arms that he'd worked with on his pursuits, a guy named Alexander DuPont. He said DuPont had moved on to America, and I recalled seeing the name on some other stuff." Phil pointed toward the ceiling, I assume to punctuate his victory. "And, I remembered what box it was in!" He was very pleased with himself, but Billy twirled her finger around, another one of her less-than-polite ways to say "move it along." Phil smiled in response to her. "Okay, don't get yourself all worked up there, Billy." Another wink.

"So in the mid-1960s, this DuPont fella wrote about seeing a musketeer demon in New York, and apparently he wrote to Frankel asking for descriptions and what not. The reply letter from Frankel was in DuPont's papers. Frankel pretty much described our musketeer. DuPont spent years trying to track him down, finally getting a lead on him in the early-1970s, but before he could actually find him, he heard rumors that it had managed to get converged by another ghost killer of ill repute. The rumors led DuPont to a man that had been arrested in connection with a string of murders in Albany. DuPont notes that he's positive this man was none other than the reincarnated Gilles." Phil's eyes had become so large I was concerned about imminent escape from their sockets.

"I did a search on serial killings for that timeframe and location, and sure enough, there was a guy that meets the description DuPont noted in his papers. The man was arrested, but after a few weeks in jail, the district attorney couldn't make the case and they had to release him. But the DA did an interview a while later saying they had new evidence that this guy was the killer, but he'd disappeared and no one seemed to know where he was. In early 1999, there was a newspaper article about a man that had been found, burned to a crisp, but with two of his finger pads still intact, so they were able to identify the body. It was the aforementioned missing serial killer. But there's one weird thing... the coroner emphatically stated that the burned up man in his morgue was no older than thirty-five, and the serial killer would have been almost thirty years older than the body. However, the fingerprints were legit, so that was that." Phil let his statement permeate. Was he trying to say our musketeer had lived twice—and if the coroner was right, he probably would have been a longaevus the second time around—died twice, and was back again, haunting in his original form?

All eyes turned to Aris. He was the oldest and most knowledgeable amongst us. If this was possible, he'd know. The unasked question appeared to weigh on him, and he finally replied, "If this is true, this demon has incredible power. There are a few unsubstantiated accounts of this happening, but we believe they are accurate. If a powerful demon is able to converge and live again, and is killed and rematerializes as a ghost yet again, it retains its original power, and from what we understand, it gains a great deal more. If this second life is through someone of our nature, a ghost killer or a longaevus, then that power would be exponential." He paused and looked around the room. "It is possible that he could possess our most powerful ghost killers. He would then be in possession of your strength and speed in addition to the strength a possession brings on, it would turn you into an almost invincible weapon."

"Well, the coroner noted that the dead guy should have been much older, so I'm guessing the second coming of Gilles was a longaevus. He might have been known in the ghost killing community. Do you have a picture we can circulate?" Pete asked.

Phil shook his head. "Not yet. The online articles didn't have pictures, but I ordered copies of all the print articles relating to this guy from the newspaper's archives, and hopefully there will be a picture. I should have them by tomorrow morning. There might be something in Vokkel's papers though, since Frankel believed that Gilles was hiding at Vokkel's school, but I just haven't had time to go through it all." He looked embarrassed, like he was letting us down. His next statement was hurried. "I'll be staying up all night until I find it," he finished with an apologetic smile. Phil was incredible at this stuff, and we all knew he was doing the best he could. I started to tell him that he'd done good when Carol came to his rescue.

"I'll help; two sets of eyes are better than one." She smiled sympathetically at him. Eric, Billy, and I all agreed to help too, although I thought it might end up being a case of too many cooks in the kitchen. But at least Phil didn't feel like he'd let us down anymore.

Aris looked around. "Thank you, everyone." Turning to Billy, he asked, "Were you or Jonas able to get anything additional from Calvin?"

She shook her head. "No, he wasn't in a talkative mood most of the day, even on our little walk. But Jonas is up there now, so maybe he's having some luck."

"What's our next move, aside from an all-nighter in the 'sanctum'?" I gave Phil a quick smile and turned to Aris for the answer, who looked to Carol.

Carol spoke. "I got some replies on G&G about our missing ghost killers." She looked around the room. "No one has heard from them. But there were some interesting additional posts." She had an uneasy look in her eyes. "We've got a few more guys that haven't checked-in for a while. They were most recently seen in Northern California, and thought to be headed to us for an assist, but all attempts to contact them since early last week have gone unanswered."

"Are you saying we have more missing GKs?" Billy asked.

Carol looked directly at her. "Well... you know how it is, Billy, you used to travel all over the place. Sometimes you didn't always check-in, or just went off the grid for a bit." She smiled, but there was no humor in it. "These guys are all nomadic like you used to be, so maybe that's what's going on."

Billy's eyes narrowed suspiciously. "But you don't believe that, do you?"

Carol sighed. "No, not really. These days everyone has a smart phone, and they're able to check-in on G&G pretty often. These particular guys depend on us for income, so generally, they're pretty diligent about staying in touch."

"How many is that total?" Pete asked. Now he was suspicious.

"Six."

Pete looked over at Aris. "What are we doing about this?"

"At the moment, there is not much more we can do. Carol has posted a plea of sorts, asking them to check-in right away. In addition, she has asked anyone with information on their whereabouts to alert us."

Without thinking, I stretched out my arms and yawned audibly. Suddenly all eyes were on me, and in an amused tone, Phil said, "Dude, we boring you or something?"

I smiled, a little embarrassed, and said, "Sorry. I didn't sleep well last night, and that drive to the Sierras really wore me out."

Aris looked around the room, stopping ever so briefly on each of us, as if to impress the importance of what he was about to say. "I know you are all aware of the dangers Calvin, Edgar, and the musketeer present, but I would be remiss if I did not remind you all to be very careful and diligent in observance of your surroundings, both in this building and outside of it." He rose from his chair and said, "Billy, George, while it is greatly appreciated that you want to assist in Phil's research, I do not think having our two most powerful ghost killers on the verge of exhaustion is a good idea. Perhaps one of you could decline to help and get some rest tonight instead, so you will be in top condition tomorrow while the others sleep. I believe the next few days will be quite trying, and we will all need to be at our best."

Aris stood, making ready to take his leave, but before he got too far, I said, "Aris, we need to be sure Justine and my dad have extra protection." Vokkel had put them both in harm's way before, and there was no doubt in my mind that Edgar would get a great deal of pleasure out of hurting them now. Aris nodded and left. Pete said he was going to check in with his men, and then head home for some sleep.

Phil smiled and said to me, "Since I'll be here all night, I guess I'm your new roomy... if we ever get to bed, that is." The room Eric had put me in had two double beds, one of which I was dying to get in to. Phil got up and left the room with Carol and Eric following, leaving Billy and I to decide who would help Phil and who would hit the sack.

I asked her, "You okay?"

"I guess. Why wouldn't I be?"

"Because, I could tell you were hoping to get through to Calvin, that you were starting to get close to him, and now you know he was just using us. I want to be sure you're okay."

She waved her hand aimlessly. "I'm pretty sure you were right about the possession thing. While we were in the park I asked him again how often Edgar controlled him, and he started to say that it wasn't Edgar, then he backtracked. I pushed him on it, and finally he just blurted out that Gilles was his protector, like a father."

"That's not good. But why would he let the demon possess him? It doesn't make any sense to me."

Her tone had turned brusque. "I don't know, George. Maybe Edgar got in his head and programmed him to think it was a good idea. I mean, we don't know the full extent of Edgar's power in that regard." She was tired and further conversation would probably exasperate her less than shining personality, and I was too tired to defend myself at that point. But I needed to get her to back down a bit too...she'd been entirely too bitchy with everyone.

We were still sitting next to each other, and I grabbed her shoulders and turned her so she was facing me. "Look, I know you're stressed, I know all of this is pissing you off, but biting everyone's head off isn't going to make things better." She scowled at me. "Come on, Billy, stop that. We're your friends...treat us respectfully."

She slumped a little, then looked up at me and smiled, a very pretty, genuine smile at that. "You're right, sorry."

Getting up from my chair, I said, with deliberate exhaustion in my voice, "I'll work with Phil tonight; you go to bed."

She shook her head. "No, I may not be in a good mood tonight." My eyebrows shot up—a good mood was a rarity for her on any night—she punched me lightly in the arm and said, "Go to bed, you're obviously exhausted and therefore useless." With a sly smile she continued, "I promise to be on my best behavior and do what I'm told, and I'll only stay for a few hours. That way I can get some sleep too."

Chapter 27

Fortunately for all of us, it was a quiet night; no nightmares and no demons, just the way I liked it. At some point Phil made it to bed, but I was so wiped out I never heard him come in. Calvin's alarm went off around 8 a.m., and like the morning before, I intercepted him in the hallway and we made our way to the kitchen together.

I made coffee and Calvin poured himself a bowl of cereal and took a seat at the table. Coffee in hand, I sat opposite him while he loudly shoveled spoonful after spoonful of cereal into his mouth. He might be really smart, but he hadn't mastered manners as far as I could tell.

"Calvin, what do Gilles and Edgar really have planned?"

He shrugged, ate more cereal, and glared at me until he swallowed his food. "Gilles wants to be human. I don't care about Edgar anymore, he scares me."

There's an optical phenomena known as the green flash. If the conditions are just right, it will occur right before sunrise or right after sunset. A bright green spot—or flash—becomes visible just above the upper rim of the sun as it sets or rises and usually lasts for no more than a second or two. I realized when Calvin was lying; the green in his eyes, dull and lost most of the time, flashed quickly, then dimmed again, reminding me of the green flash. However, in his case it wasn't the result of a luminous heavenly-body, but instead, a bright spark of intelligent deception. I saw it just then, when he said he didn't care about Edgar.

"So how do you plan to help Gilles?"

"'Dunno yet." Another flash, then he said, "You or Billy could do it, right?"

"Yeah, probably, but we won't. Gilles kills people Calvin...I think you know that. If we converged him, someone else would essentially need to die in the process, and God only knows what sort of person Gilles would be if he could walk the earth again. Has he ever told you about his previous life, or lives?"

"Whadda ya mean?" he asked, eyes flashing again, and even though his expression feigned ignorance, I was pretty sure he knew all about Gilles's history.

I cocked my head to the side and narrowed my eyes. I wanted him to know I was onto him. "Calvin, I think you *do* know, but in case I'm wrong, here's what *we* know; Gilles died in the 1600s in France, he was put to death for killing several people, he was a serial killer, he reemerged as a ghost many years later and started haunting people. At some point he got his ghostly self to America, and by then he was well-seasoned as a powerful and nasty demon." Still no reaction from Calvin. "He somehow managed to get converged back to human form and he was even more evil...another serial killer. Do you really want to make him human again? A tiger doesn't change its stripes. If he's walking the earth again, he'll be killing people again! Do you want that on your conscience?" I wasn't sure what conscience, if any, Calvin had, so the question was probably moot.

"You're wrong. He just wants to be human again. He isn't going to hurt anyone." The deadpan manner in which he said this was frightening. It was clear now that he wasn't bothering to deceive me anymore, and didn't care if I believed him or not.

I leaned toward him, my jaw tight with annoyance. "Calvin, we're going to get Edgar and we're going to get Gilles, with or without your help."

He stood up and left the room, and I got up and watched him head down the hallway and up the stairs. A few minutes later, Carol came into the kitchen carrying her tablet and cell phone.

She stopped at the table long enough to smile at me and drop off her electronics before heading to the coffee pot. Carol had a Goth sort of thing going on. Her hair was shoulder length and dyed a deep purple that bordered on black. She tended to wear similar colors in her clothes and makeup, although she maintained her attractive olive complexion, as opposed to the ghoulish white that seemed to be favored by many in the Goth community. She was wearing the same clothes from the night before—black jeans and a long-sleeved black T-shirt with a silver skull etched across its front—but her feet were bare and her studded jewelry was missing. When she sat down she rubbed her eyes, spreading the remnants of yesterday's mascara around.

"You get any sleep?" I asked.

"Yeah. I called it quits a little before one, so I logged a few hours," she said between sips.

"Did you guys find anything in all that paper?"

"Phil started with Sam's diaries and had Billy and Eric going through boxes of stuff we brought back from Vokkel's house. I spent some time running Drew Adler, and then helped Eric and Billy for a little while. Phil was mumbling incoherently and writing notes down the whole time. They were all still going at it when I finally went to bed."

"What did you find on Drew?"

"Well, it's not an uncommon name, so there were plenty of hits, but I didn't find anyone that fit our assumed profile of Calvin's father." She shrugged. "Not that we have much of a profile to begin with. I posted on G&G too, and asked if anyone knew him. Since we know he was in the Ontario Province in the mid to late '90s, I specified that timeframe and mentioned that he was involved with a young woman whose father was a GK. I haven't checked yet to see if there's been any responses."

Eric and Phil wandered into the kitchen, apparently with the same goal as Carol…coffee. All three of them looked exhausted, and I felt a pang of guilt for crashing on them last night. A few minutes later, Billy groggily joined us. Phil jovially said, "Hail, hail the gangs all here!" Phil's cheerful demeanor tended to be contagious, even when the recipients were exhausted, Carol and Eric smiled in response, and much to my surprise, so did Billy. A spark of pride swept through me…our little chat the night before had actually taken root in our darling green-eyed vixen.

As everyone settled at the table, coffee in hand, Phil looked around and said, "Sam's diaries were very interesting."

"Yeah?" I asked.

Phil got up. "Hold on, I'll be right back." He scampered out of the room and returned a minute later with Sam's diaries and some loose sheets of paper.

"Okay, well, combined they contain about thirty-five years of entries. The first diary starts in the mid-1970s, when he was a teenager, and finishes off in mid '98, the second one is from mid '98 until he disappeared. His entries are pretty sparse…he documented where he was for the most part, and some of the things he was involved in, but just the basic facts and whether or not it paid well. The response Carol got from the G&G site seems pretty accurate if Sam's entries are to be believed. Based on what he documented and his level of involvement, I'd say he was more than a mid-level GK. He'd been employed to help in some nasty infestations, and had killed some nasty demons. And he's done a lot of work for Vokkel over the years. I guess that's what the G&G responder meant by 'playing both sides.' His work with Vokkel seems to have been mild for the most part, mostly reporting on other ghost killers that he encountered and what their power levels were, and if they were open to coming over to the dark side. Luckily, he didn't come across too many that would betray us, but he did come across a few. He only lists their first names and where and when he found them. I'll pass that on to Aris so he can try and track them.

"There are a few significant and detailed entries though. One is about a job he did in 1997, and the rest relate to his time with Calvin. So, in early 1997, Vokkel had hired another GK to hunt someone down, and in turn this GK subcontracted some of the work to Sam. The guy Vokkel was looking for was a powerful ghost killer. Vokkel gave few details; a general description, the name Aaron, but no last name. Sam was told that the guy was very dangerous, extremely unstable, and he was only to be located, but not approached. Vokkel had told the other GK that Aaron was last seen in the Toronto area, but he was long gone by the time Sam got there. It took Sam and this other guy more than six months to get another solid lead on Aaron. They used a combination of online forums and personal networks, and each piece of information sent them to the next city, and the next, and so on. Some of his notations mention what he learned about Aaron along the way." Phil rummaged through one of Sam's diaries…he'd put sticky tabs on various pages and thumbed through until he found what he was looking for.

"Listen to this. '*Sources say Aaron was a patient of Vokkel's in Switzerland. Description for Aaron is that of a young man. Is he also a longaevus? Also told that he's mentally unstable.*' Next he writes, '*Found Aaron. Local contacts say he had betrayed Vokkel and there was a bounty on his head, but not even the most powerful GKs were willing to go after him, very interesting.*'" He paused to flip to another tab. "This is a later notation, '*Observed him for several days. He's been seeing a woman, she's pregnant. His? Witnessed him kill a man last night, tore him from limb to limb like a crazed animal. Will report, but no more.*'

"Apparently, Vokkel was desperate to know who the woman was, but Sam told his contact that he never got a good look at her face and didn't know who she was. Vokkel wanted them to pursue it, but he refused. He made a side note in 1999 stating that another GK had told him that Aaron was dead, and that it was rumored that Edgar had killed him at Vokkel's behest." Phil looked up, eyes bright and large. "Pretty ominous stuff."

"I suppose, but what does it have to do with Calvin?" I asked.

"I'm getting to that." He smiled. "All right, so in 2004, Vokkel hired Sam for '*an extremely sensitive and important project.*' He wanted Sam to become Calvin's tutor/bodyguard. Sam wanted to know what was so important about the kid, and Vokkel told him the boy's father was one of the most gifted and powerful ghost killers that ever lived and the boy had the potential to be the same, if not more. But it was imperative they keep the kid's existence a secret. He also told Sam that he wasn't to teach Calvin about ghost killing…he was only to observe and document what Calvin did in relation to ghosts, and what the boy's instincts were when he encountered them. Sam figured that Vokkel didn't want the Watchers or other GKs to know about the kid, and Vokkel was paying him an obscene amount of money, so he agreed to take on the job without further questions.

"For the first few years Sam notes that the kid is learning his reading, writing, arithmetic, etc. without any issues, but he notes the kid is sort of strange, introverted, and doesn't want to hang out with other kids, but likes to go up and see Uncle Leo. On one occasion Gail asked Sam to drive the kid up to Leo's for the weekend, and that's when he sees Gilles for the first time. The kid's about eleven years old at this point. He notes that Gilles isn't haunting Leo and he asks the kid about him. The kid says that Gilles is his friend and has been hanging out at Leo's for at least a year. This sort of alarms Sam, because he realizes that Gilles is a really old ghost, and he can sense that he isn't a good one. So he tells Vokkel, and apparently Vokkel is thrilled about it and comes up right away to see Calvin, and

Sam overhears the conversation. Vokkel tells Calvin that Gilles has come to guide him, that it's all written in the prophecy, and Calvin's destiny is intertwined with Gilles's. He said that one day, they will join as one and their power will be immense. He explains to Calvin that now that Gilles has arrived, the prophecy is being fulfilled.

"Like Gail told you, Vokkel and Edgar visited a few times a year up until the last couple of years. In the more recent years, Vokkel and Calvin would retreat to Calvin's room and talk for hours. Sometimes Sam would just leave for the day, but other times he'd stay in his own room. The two bedrooms shared a heater vent, and for the most part, Sam could hear what was being said. Vokkel had started to teach Calvin a foreign language that he didn't recognize. Sometimes, when Calvin repeated the phrases that Vokkel was teaching him, they sounded like chanting or prayers or something."

Phil paused long enough to ensure he had our rapt attention, then smiled and continued. "When Vokkel heard about Leo's death, he made a special trip up to see Calvin. Sam was in his room and overheard the conversation clearly because Vokkel was pissed and sort of yelling. He assumed that Calvin had tried to perform the convergence with Gilles and Leo and he was scolding Calvin, telling him that Gilles was not to be converged until the specified time, and that time was almost two years away. Calvin lowered his voice in response and Sam didn't hear what else was said.

"So, the kid's pretty upset after this visit and Sam goes to him later that night to try and comfort him, but the window is open and the kid's gone. Laying on his bed is a notebook that Sam recognizes as the one Calvin used to take notes when Vokkel was teaching him. Calvin had always kept it hidden from Sam and Gail, so naturally Sam had to peek. Most of the writing was in a foreign language, but there was one paragraph in English, which said…." Phil paused and flipped to another tabbed page in Sam's diary. "I'll read it to you, '*Prophecy: he says that a child of great power, born to the risen dead = me. He said when the time comes, we'll become one and release them, and my father will be reborn.*' There were some other things too. '*Chamber is at edge of cemetery, but he won't tell me where. He thinks I'm stupid and will go without him, but I heard him tell Edgar something about a park. If he keeps treating me this way, Gilles and I will find it on our own!*'

"Some of that is going to make more sense in a minute, but let me finish with the diaries first. So one day..." Phil looked thoughtful for a moment. "In late 2013, I think, on one of Vokkel's visits, Sam got home before Vokkel and Edgar had left, so he came in through the back, intending to hide out in his room until they'd gone. Anyway, he overhead Vokkel and Gail. She was upset because she thought something was wrong with Calvin. She said she knew he had a ghost friend, and she thought they were hurting small animals together, killing them. Sam wrote that Vokkel was firm with her, telling her that her son was very important, and if she wanted to continue her lifestyle, she'd do as she was told.

"The day after Gail's tantrum, Vokkel called Sam and told him to keep a closer watch on Gail and the boy and anyone that might be interested in the boy. But Sam's worried too, because he's seen some strange stuff from the kid, and he told Vokkel he thought Gilles was getting in the kid's head. He told Vokkel that Gilles had been preying on, and killing, frail sick people, and he thought Gilles was trying to build more strength and power for something big, something that might have to do with Calvin—something that could hurt or even kill Calvin."

A demon as old as Gilles would be able to expedite a victim's death, especially if his victims were already frail or sick. If Gilles wanted to stack the deck of power, that would be the quickest route.

"Instead of being concerned for the kid's wellbeing, Vokkel is excited about this information and instructs Sam not to interfere with Calvin's relationship with Gilles. Sam's really suspicious now, because this isn't the sort of reaction he was expecting. Vokkel had always treated Calvin in a caring, grandfatherly way. Sam's scared of Vokkel and Edgar though, so he decides to just do as he's told, and does that for another year. But then in early 2014, he has a conversation with Gail regarding Calvin's father. She told him that the father's name was Drew Adler, they met in Canada in late 1996, and that he was dead. She even showed him a picture of Drew, which Sam copied." Phil's eyes had become engorged at this point. He pulled the second diary toward him and flipped to the back.

Laying the diary flat, Phil said, "Here's the picture that Gail gave him."

It was a black-and-white photocopy, and even though the picture it was taken from was almost twenty years old, it was crisp and clear. An unknown cityscape was in the background. The foreground showed a smiling younger and happier version of Gail Brelong, standing next to a handsome but stone-faced man about fifteen years her senior.

Phil grabbed the loose sheets and shuffled through them. "The newspaper folks in Albany came through and I got this by email right before I went to bed last night…this morning, I mean." It was a newspaper article with a photograph of a man in handcuffs being escorted up an exterior staircase, probably the jail or the courthouse in Albany where he was arrested. Phil had enlarged it so that the photograph took up most of the page. Although it was taken in the 1970s and was a bit grainy, the man's face was clearly captured. Both photos were of the man Gail called Drew Adler.

"Sam writes that it's not just Calvin's father, it's also the guy he was sub-contracted to find for Vokkel in 1997, and he suddenly realizes that it was Gail he saw with Aaron all those years ago. Now he's really worried, because he remembers all the details about Drew/Aaron, and the apple doesn't fall far from the tree. Plus, if the rumors he heard are true, Edgar killed Aaron, most likely by Vokkel's orders. But there's more! The next significant entry is in mid-2014, and it's the last one. Sam says that he's sure the boy is a monster and Gilles is making things worse, *with* Vokkel's blessing. He's decided that whatever plans Vokkel and Gilles have for Calvin, they aren't good, and he can't allow it, so he was going to San Francisco the next day, where he knew there was a Watcher group who could help."

I leaned back in my chair and said, "Wow, so what are you thinking? That Drew and Aaron are the same person, meaning Aaron was a longaevus that got converged with Gilles, and then Edgar—for some reason—killed Aaron? Well, if he was Calvin's father, I guess he was going by Drew at that point."

Phil said, "Well yeah, it's all making sense now."

Billy frowned. "It is?"

Phil shook his head and laughed. "Damn. Sorry, I forgot the other part, hold on." He rushed out of the room again, returning with a few more sheets of paper. "Okay, I told you guys about the journal with the weird writing and pictures in it?" We nodded in unison. "And I mentioned that I sent some of the pages to my buddy, Boyd?" He didn't wait for our reply. "He specializes in languages, and as a hobby, he's really into supernatural literature, and I figured this might fall into that. So he shot me an email around 3 a.m. this morning, saying he'd analyzed part of the stuff I gave him.

"Here's what he wrote. '*Some of the writings are a combo—well, more like a bastardization—of Enochian and prisca Latinitas, (Enochian is the magical language used in satanic rituals, and prisca Latinitas is Archaic Latin, generally used in the period before 75 B.C., but we find it sometimes in supernatural related writings too). It was a little difficult to interpret because the author combined words from each language, creating new words...and some of these combined words don't make sense, but analyzing the combinations, I was able to extract what I assume they mean. I believe it's some sort of prophecy, it says, 'A cambion shall be born on all souls day. He will be a child of great power, born to the risen dead. The dead will die once again and haunt the earth, when the child becomes aware, the dead shall seek it and guide it until the anniversary of the child's 18th year. On the day His faithful honor their beloved dead, the cambion shall merge forever with his father and become one, upon which my ever faithful servant shall be alive once again and with his new power, he shall release the imprisoned souls and give them new life, a life which they will dedicate to my faithful servant who serves me directly.*'"

Eric and Carol simultaneously asked, "What's a cambion?"

Phil smiled. "I had to look that one up too. A cambion is the offspring of a demon and a human."

"If this Aaron person really did converge with Gilles, and he's Calvin's father, that fits...," Eric said offhandedly.

"Well, there's more. I only sent random pages to Boyd, but he said the tail end of one page had symbols on it, and the beginnings of a prayer or incantation. He said other parts were written in Archaic Latin, which he didn't have any trouble with. He said they were like diary entries. The guy who wrote them talked about fleeing to a place where he thought he'd be safe, but the demon showed up again and he isn't strong enough anymore, that the devil's influence was breaking him down. That particular journal wasn't very thick and I'd already digitized the pages because I knew I was going to need help interpreting them, so I emailed the whole thing to Boyd early this morning, and hopefully he can get back to me soon with the translations."

Eric asked, "So you think Vokkel came across this prophecy thing and decided that Calvin was part of it. How did he know Gilles was part of it?"

Phil's head bobbed up and down. "I do, here's why. Remember last night, I initially asked you guys to search Vokkel's papers for references to Drew, then I asked you to stop?"

They all nodded and Eric said, "Yeah, you asked us to start looking for 'A' instead."

"Right, and you found quite a few references, and I took a look at it before I went to bed. The Switzerland notes list an 'A15.' That's a high-level ghost killer and a lower-level longaevus combo, according to Vokkel's coding system. Vokkel says the patient was sent to him because he'd been found wandering around London and was thought to be insane...the ghost-talk insane. Vokkel notes the guy was pretty quiet and reserved most of the time, but had said that he was fleeing a demon created by Satan. Vokkel writes that eventually a demon does show up, and he says...." Phil ruffled through some of his papers. "'*A15 is quite insane. It is unfortunate, as I am told he has a demon by his side at all times now. It would be advantageous if I could communicate with this demon. I would like to know more, and have instructed the nurse to administer a sedative so that I may read his diary, which he keeps close to his person at all times.*'

"So Vokkel gets his hands on this guy's diary and notes some stuff. He says, '*I have read parts of his diary. He writes in a dead language, which I can interpret, but some passages are a language I do not know. A15 states that he performed his duties in San Francisco under God's orders from 1850 until 1910, when he was forced to flee because he was being pursued by Satan's own. Is this the demon that shadows him now?*'

"Vokkel writes more later on about this guy. He says he believes this is the priest in a legend he heard long ago, and now believes it might be true based on the diary writings. He noted that A15 had become very fond of the opiates they'd been giving him, and Vokkel believed he had become an addict. He also said that some of the other GKs thought the demon was haunting, and maybe even possessing A15 on occasion. You guys also tagged the 'A' reference in a couple of Vokkel's journals. One note says that A15 escaped the school and Vokkel was actively looking for him. Then he says that A15 had been found in New York and he believed he'd been converged with his demon. Of course, Vokkel didn't date the journals, but it's too coincidental not to assume he's talking about Aaron and Gilles. Another entry says that A15 had been located again under another name and was fulfilling the prophecy."

Phil paused to drink his coffee. "All right, now there's this story I heard years ago, more like folklore actually, and all of this reminds me of that." He looked around the room and I nodded.

"Okay, by the time the gold rush was in full swing, the city was an intolerable den of iniquity." He winked. "Back in those days, San Francisco was known as the most wicked town in the United States. Anyway, there was a priest who had come to the city to minister to the growing population, but he was distraught by what he saw, because he knew the source. The city was overrun by ghosts and demons. Some haunted people and killed them, but the more powerful were possessing people, turning them into murderous monsters. And of course, since the city had a bad reputation, it attracted all kinds of miscreants, but they weren't haunted or possessed, they were just bad dudes doing bad stuff.

"So this priest decided he had to do something. He prayed to God and God responded by telling him to build a chamber with an inner vault. God told him to lure the ghosts and demons to the chamber with promises of the convergence. At the same time he was to lure the worst of the evil criminals with promises of some sort of riches. He'd take them into the vault, perform the convergence, and kill the combined ghost/criminal on the spot, therefore locking up their eternal souls. A two for one you could say. In addition, the vault served as a place where the souls could repent, and if they did so, God promised to one day release them to Purgatory, where God would decide their eternal fate.

"At some point Satan got wind of all of this and decided he didn't want all those deliciously wicked evil souls to repent, he wanted them back in the general population. So he sent his most powerful demon, one that was capable of possessing someone as powerful as the priest, who was obviously a damn powerful ghost killer. So the demon does what he's supposed to do and tries to force the priest to open the chamber, but God had anticipated this, and He'd had the priest carve a combination of symbols into the vault door that could only be opened by using a special key to read the right combination. Then he had the priest hide the key."

"What happened next?" I asked.

"Well, that's where it gets murky. So, God gives the priest some guidelines as to who can open the vault using the key, but God gets busy and isn't paying attention when the priest writes it all down. And apparently Satan *was* paying attention, so he personally possessed the priest and wrote the guidelines himself, therefore insuring that it would be one of his minions that eventually opened the vault."

"What are these guidelines?" Billy asked.

Phil shrugged. "No one knows. The priest went a bit nutty after Satan's little visit and disappeared."

She frowned, and asked, "Where's this chamber?" He shrugged again. "And you think all of this ties together and that's what Calvin, Gilles, and Edgar want, to find this chamber and open it?"

Phil nodded at her. "Well, that story has been around for a long time, and Vokkel lived for this sort of stuff, so I think we can assume he'd probably heard the tale. Then he comes across this priest and reads his diaries and sees the connection."

Billy looked thoughtful. I asked, "What?"

"Well, I think it's safe to say Edgar knew all about this prophecy stuff too, and Vokkel says that Calvin and Gilles are 'to become one,' and according to what your friend translated, so did this journal." She paused. "Is it possible that journal is actually Aaron's and not Vokkel's?"

Phil's face scrunched up a bit. "You know, I guess it could be. The whole thing is written in these foreign languages and the ink varies, so I just assumed it was one of Vokkel's, but now that I think about it, the journal isn't quite the same as the other ones Vokkel used."

"Okay, well let's assume it's Aaron's and it has the combination to the vault in it. That's what Gilles and Edgar really want...they want that combination so they can open the vault and release the demon souls." She looked around. "That would be Edgar's ultimate revenge, to unleash a whole bunch of angry demons on us." Billy had a sour look on her face, then she snapped her fingers. "The text message on Calvin's phone...the one that said 'they're here.' I bet Calvin was letting Edgar know we had the journals."

I frowned, "How would he know? I thought he just got a quick glance at the library room."

She was shaking her head. "It was quick, but he still walked into the room and had a minute to look around. Some of the journals were stacked on Phil's table. If Vokkel had any of them with him when he was visiting Calvin, maybe he recognized them."

"But you just said Aaron's journal was different." I looked at Phil.

Phil nodded. "It's a little different...the cover was probably a medium grey at one time, but it's darkened from age and handling. It's also just a bit smaller. But if Calvin only got a quick glance at a stack that looked familiar, he might not have noticed."

Billy said, "He sent that text after he grilled Jonas. Maybe he decided Jonas's denial really meant the opposite."

I was shaking my head. We were stepping into a realm of supernatural myths of God-versus-Satan-meets-reality sort of stuff, and I was having difficulty getting my head around it.

Phil said, "What?"

I shook myself and said, "You said it earlier, that story is more like folklore. This is supernatural God versus Satan stuff, and I'm just having trouble buying it. Besides, if Gilles really did converge with Aaron, why wouldn't he already know what's in the journal and therefore know the combination?"

Billy grinned and said, "Really, George? You're okay with ghosts and demons and people that live a long time, and people like us that kill ghosts and demons, or can turn them back into human form, but you're having trouble with other supernatural possibilities?"

Of course she was right... why couldn't it all be true? A blush rose up my cheeks and I shot a contemptuous glare her way.

Phil said, "If Aaron was this priest-ghost killer-longaevus, he was pretty damn strong overall. Maybe Gilles just couldn't penetrate his thoughts. Maybe, drug induced or not, Aaron was able to resist. And Vokkel said he ran away, obviously leaving his journal behind. We know when a demon is converged, the host mind and soul basically dies, so once Gilles got into Aaron for good, he lost all of Aaron's memories. He'd need the journal."

Eric said, "I'm still confused. How did Gilles find the kid in the first place?"

"I think it's the same way GG found me. She was my mother's ghost friend, so maybe it's a familial connection? And Gilles is connected to Calvin through his father... hell, in a way, he sort of is his father." I snapped my fingers. "The kid said as much on his walk with you." I looked at Billy and she nodded. "So, I think we should assume he knows exactly what Gilles was in his last life."

Billy looked downright glum. "And if he does, and he's this powerful, that's going to make him all the more dangerous and determined to get Gilles converged." She was looking at me. "Do you think he can do the convergence now? I mean, he failed the first time."

I thought about my conversations with Calvin. He'd asked, or maybe implied, more than once that he wanted one of us to do it. I shook my head. "No, I don't think so."

Phil looked between Billy and me. "Well, I wouldn't worry about it. I mean, he's seen what you two can do, and he knows the last thing you would do would be to converge that bastard back to human form, so he's screwed on that one!"

Carol's phone dinged and she looked down at it and said, "We need to table this for now. Calvin just opened his door, and might be coming down."

I stood up and Phil said, "Where are you headed?"

"I'm going to see Julie Vokkel," I answered casually.

Billy's head snapped around so fast I thought she might have given herself whiplash. "Why?" she demanded.

"Because I think she knows something about all of this. Like we said earlier, she wouldn't want those journals for herself, so what if it was Edgar that told her to find them? She might know where he is," I replied in the same casual tone, which was clearly ticking her off. I had a second motive for seeing Julie, but I kept that to myself.

"She's not going to tell you anything; she probably won't even let you in," Billy hissed. So much for her new, *pleasant* attitude.

"Maybe not, but I'm still going over there." This time I was firm. I could see an argument brewing in her eyes and I wasn't in the mood, even though I'd more or less provoked it. I decided to escape while I could, and put my cup in the sink and headed up for a shower.

Chapter 28

When I came back from the bathroom, Phil was in our room gathering his own toiletries and fresh clothes so he could hit the shower next.

He whistled when I entered and said, "Man, you really pissed her off."

"I know." I sat on my bed. "What are you up to today?"

"Well, I need to talk to Aris. I got to thinking, if Edgar's plan of revenge includes releasing a bunch of horrible demons, wouldn't it make sense that this chamber/vault place is nearby? Especially if he plans on using these newly released demons to kill you and Billy. He'd want them to be *near* you and Billy, right?"

"I suppose that's plausible...ah hell," I sighed, "anything is plausible at this point."

"So, I'm hoping he might have some ideas on where it might be located." He smiled weakly. "One other thing, which I didn't focus on earlier. It was part of Boyd's translation...it said, '*He shall release the imprisoned souls and give them new life.*'"

I wasn't sure where he was headed and looked at him expectantly.

"They'd need people to converge these newly freed demons into." His eyebrows rose. "What are we missing right now?"

"Holy shit!" I whispered. "You think Edgar has our missing ghost killers?" The thought was unfathomable. Edgar was strong, but as a rule, we were stronger, and I couldn't see how he could be going around capturing our people. I was shaking my head furiously. "No way, Phil; he couldn't overtake our guys like that. Besides, a convergence needs to happen with a weak-minded person, someone who can't mentally fight back. All our missing guys aren't like that. And besides they're all mid-level, they'd be able to resist."

"Yeah, well, Vokkel's notes said that Aaron had become a drug addict...opiates, right? And Gilles managed to converge with Aaron, who was a powerful ghost killer and a longaevus, and I think he was able to do that because of Aaron's diminished condition due to years of drug addiction. What if that's how Edgar is capturing our guys and holding them, by drugging them?"

I rubbed my temples. This conversation was causing *me* to want an opiate or two. "So you think it's possible that Edgar is going around drugging GKs, kidnapping them, and holding them hostage for the awakening of his demon army? Wouldn't that contradict his plans to use the demons to kill us? I mean, they'd want to be converged right away, they wouldn't be in the mood to go around haunting and possessing after being locked up for more than a hundred years."

Phil held his hands out in surrender. "Hey, man, maybe he plans on having them converged after they kill you guys. Or maybe he's gonna do it right away and send the demon/human's after you. Hell," he said in exasperation, "I don't know, it's just a theory. Aris is always saying there's no such thing as coincidence, so..."

He was right. It really couldn't be a coincidence that our guys were suddenly off the radar at the same time Edgar was trying to fulfill some crazy prophecy and exact his revenge.

"Why didn't you mention this earlier?" I asked.

"Honestly, because I knew I'd get the exact same reaction from them as you just gave me." He arched an eyebrow.

"Right, sorry. I think you need to tell Aris and Pete at the very least."

He agreed with me and said, "But there is a silver lining." He waggled his eyebrows. "You guys don't think Calvin is strong enough to perform the convergence, right?" I nodded. "So Edgar is missing a very integral piece of his plan, and I don't think he knows it." Phil smiled. "So regardless, we've got that much in our favor."

It would have been nice if he was right.

Chapter 29

Vokkel's house is in Pacific Heights, not far from my apartment. It's an impressive and rather stunning Second Empire Victorian, with a slate mansard roof, double door entrance, and central tower that rises above the main structure. The rich Charleston Green paint (so dark it was almost black) compliments the rich greens of the ivy-covered brick wall enclosure. I had only been inside once, and I was there against my will, more or less. It was in my early days as a ghost killer and I'd just learned about Vokkel. Stupidity and curiosity spurred me to stake out his house, and I was caught red-handed by Edgar. He used his unusual ability to "persuade" people, and without really knowing what was happening, I found myself inside the house. I'd managed to regain my senses and get the hell out of there before anything bad happened, but it still scared me.

As I approached the gate, a man wearing a crisp black suit, matching tie, and stark white shirt stepped forward. His broad, muscular physique strained against the fabric. We were the same height, and I caught my reflection in his mirrored sunglasses.

I smiled and he brusquely asked, "Can I help you?"

"I'm here to see Julie Vokkel."

"Is Ms. Vokkel expecting you?"

"No, tell her it's George Sinclair. I'm a friend of her daughter's."

He stepped away from the gate and spoke into his cuff. That's when I noticed the earpiece with the curly cord running into his collar, and the shoulder holster and gun under his jacket. Julie's security was very Hollywoodesque, and I smiled at the absurdity of it. When he returned, he scowled at me, but he also unlocked the gate and waved me toward the front door.

At the door I was greeted by another guard wearing the same ensemble, sans the mirrored glasses. I was yet again waved forward. The entry hall hadn't changed since my last visit; same dark wall color, dark wood trim, polished marble floors, and disturbing painting by Wilhelmina Wilkinson hanging in the stairwell. I stared at it—I couldn't seem to stop myself, it was mesmerizing to a certain, creepy, extent. The painting was six feet by four feet, its largesse making it all the more imposing. The edges were dark and faded inward to lighter shades of blues, like a twilight sky. In the center was a grey mist, a ghostlike form that had just received its death stab from the yellowish, more human shape standing off to its side.

The guard, who had been watching me from a few feet away, cleared his throat, startling me out of my reverie. Julie stood in the doorway of one of the rooms that flanked the main hall, her expression of amusement aimed at me. Mockingly, she said, "I'm thinking of giving it to Aunt Justine. I noticed she has the companion piece in her living room." Justine's piece was a fifth of the size and housed in an alcove off her living room. I'd never really understood why she kept it there. It was equally disturbing. Perhaps she needed to be reminded of what we were and the dangers we faced.

I turned to her and curtly said, "We need to talk."

Her eyebrows arched curiously. "Tsk-tsk," she wagged an index finger at me. "Such bad manners. Did you pick those up from my daughter?"

I didn't respond. Instead we stared at each other, uncomfortably, until she finally conceded and directed me into the room behind her. It was a large study with floor-to-ceiling bookcases on one end, a desk off to one side, and two leather wing-back chairs by the window. She waved me towards one of the chairs, and sat in the other.

"I see you've come empty-handed. I've held off on contacting the police as I said I would, but I'm growing quite impatient."

"We already told you that we don't have his stuff," I said, rather obnoxiously. "Why do you want it anyway? What's in these papers that's so important?" I didn't know if she had any idea what her father's papers contained, but it certainly wasn't out of the realm of possibility that she was in on this mess with Edgar.

I did know one thing though…Julie Vokkel considered herself an elite socialite, and based on what I knew of that persona, she was probably accustomed to being spoken to with the sort of reverence many wealthy people expected. Apparently my insubordinate attitude wasn't quite cutting it and she stiffened, her pretty face contorting into something like a sneer.

"That is none of your concern. What should concern you is the police arriving at your home with a search warrant and tearing it apart. Furthermore, I'll ensure they do the same to Aunt Justine's house." It was a silly threat. I had no doubt she'd *try* and sic the cops on me, but I didn't think she'd do that to Justine. Besides all of that, she had no evidence.

I waved my hand in dismissal. "Julie, you've got no proof we took them, so don't try and threaten me with that sort of crap. Back to my original question…why do you want his papers?" She didn't answer, so I waved my hand again and continued. "Well whatever, I'm not here about a bunch of stupid papers anyway, I'm here about Edgar. He's trying to kill us and he's involved in the deaths of at least two other people. Not to mention, he's suspected of kidnapping several people." I still wasn't sure about Phil's theory on the kidnappings, but she didn't know that. "He's very dangerous. In fact, I'm pretty sure he's the reason you've got armed guards here, because you're scared of him."

Her eyes narrowed, disdain and condescension tainting her response. "The guards are here because someone broke into this house once before, and who's to say they won't do it again?" She didn't deny knowing where Edgar was.

"Bullshit," I said vehemently, but quietly. I didn't want the guard rushing in at the sound of raised voices.

She angled her head, her tone a bit odd. "Why would Edgar want to kill either of you?"

"You know why."

She wagged her finger again. "No, George, I don't know why."

She was playing with me, perhaps to see if I'd admit to helping kill Vokkel. She was also ticking me off quite a bit. But there was something else there, and I no longer thought she was working with Edgar. But I did think she'd been in contact with him.

"Here's what I think, Julie. He thinks we killed his mentor, and he wants revenge. He plans on doing that by releasing a torrent of really bad demons and having them kill us." My jaw tightened. "But he can't do it on his own...he needs something in your father's papers. That's why you're looking for them, isn't it?" She looked at me blandly, which only fueled my anger. "I'm pretty sure you don't give a flying f—" I stopped myself before that particularly vulgar word escaped my lips. Taking a breath, I continued. "Look, I doubt you care about Vokkel's papers, so there's no reason, other than Edgar, that you came looking for them. But you need to understand something...Edgar doesn't just want to unleash these demons, he wants to turn them back into humans, to converge them with living, breathing, innocent people. Do you know what happens to the person that receives the demon's mind and soul? *Their* mind and soul dies, meaning they essentially die."

I adjusted my tone to something gentler. "I saw the way you looked at Justine." I was grasping at straws now...they'd been estranged for years, but I'd sensed some affection toward Justine the other night, and she'd asked Justine about Billy's wellbeing. "You still care about her, and I think you even care about Billy a little, at least enough to not want to see her tortured and killed by Edgar. He's hell bent on revenge and he's crazy. He'll do anything to get what he wants, and he wants Billy and me dead. And I wouldn't put it past him to kill Justine just for fun."

Her expression began to change and her hand slowly rose to her throat, as if to hold back a rising sob. I tried to wait her out, but when I couldn't take the silence any longer, I leaned forward and gently asked, "What is it?"

There was fear in her eyes when she said, "A few weeks ago Edgar contacted me. He said he wanted Father's research papers, and more specifically his journals. You are correct...." She shrugged lightly. "I don't care about Father's work, so I agreed to give them to him.

"I told him I'd instruct the attorneys to package them up and send them on. However, when they arrived here, the safe was empty, and they were adamant I come to San Francisco and verify that nothing else was missing from the house. After I arrived and confirmed they were gone, I contacted Edgar." She looked down at her hands, then up at me. "He became very upset. He said you, Billy, and the Watchers had stolen them, and if I didn't locate the papers and get them to him, he'd kill Aunt Justine, Billy, and anyone else I cared about. He knew who my friends and lovers were, and as you said, he is quite insane. I believed him. He said I had forty-eight hours to get the papers back and if I didn't, he'd begin to kill my family and friends one at a time, then he'd come for me. Again, I believed him."

"What day was that?"

"The morning after I arrived, the twenty-eighth."

That would mean the forty-eight hour clock had expired two days ago. I wondered why he hadn't acted. Suddenly it occurred to me... Calvin had come to us three nights ago, and we believed he was there to find the journals, and now, I thought, it was probably Edgar that sent him.

"Do you know where Edgar is now?" She shook her head. "How does he contact you?"

"He called my cell phone." I assumed Edgar probably called from the same number Calvin was texting, but I'd get to that in a minute.

"Julie, did your father ever talk to you about his work?"

"Occasionally. I didn't visit that often, once or twice a year and for short periods of time. But he spoke with Edgar about it frequently."

"So Edgar knows what's in the journals?"

"Yes and no. Father never let anyone see those, so whatever Edgar knows, he was told, but he would never have read them."

"Your father didn't trust him?"

"Oh, he did, to an extent, but Father liked to have secrets as well. The journals contained those secrets."

That was interesting, but I let it go. "Did he ever mention a chamber filled with demons, or a young boy? Well, he's a teenager now."

She shook her head. "He never mentioned a boy or a teenager, but the chamber of demons part is familiar." She paused to concentrate, then snapped her fingers. "He told me this story once, about a priest or something who'd created this chamber." She frowned. "I'm sorry, that was a long time ago. I can't remember how it went...and to be honest, I didn't pay that much attention."

I smiled. "That's okay. Do you recall if he ever said where this chamber is?"

"No, but I seem to remember the story had to do with this city, so I assumed it was here somewhere."

I nodded, and decided to move on to motive number two. "Julie, a few weeks ago," I hesitated, "you were in Paris, with a man. Was he Billy's father?" She stared at me in surprise and I smiled again. "You're very popular on the European paparazzi circuit. They snapped a picture of the two of you meeting in Paris. Billy has enough of his physical traits… it wasn't hard to figure out who he was."

A small amount of embarrassment crept up her cheeks, then she nodded.

"Does he know about Billy?"

She nodded again. Her face paled and she looked like she was going to cry.

I said, "Tell me."

She took a deep breath. "I knew what and who Andrew was and why Father wanted us together… it was a business arrangement." She smiled demurely. "But I never expected to fall in love with him."

The idea that Julie was capable of being in love almost shocked me, but she'd softened up in the last few minutes, so I decided to give her the benefit of the doubt.

"Father and Andrew crossed paths during Father's years at the school in Switzerland. Andrew is not only a ghost killer but a longaevus, and he wasn't averse to doing work for either side, as long as it wasn't too ugly and the price was right. When Father wanted to test his hypothesis regarding the creation of the ultimate ghost killer, he called Andrew and paid the two of us to be together. Unexpectedly, we fell in love, and since we both knew what Father wanted with our child, we hid from him.

"Andrew and I stayed together until Billy was two, then one day he disappeared. I couldn't believe he'd leave us willingly and assumed that Father had caught up with him and probably killed him. I was broke and alone and needed help, but I knew what Father wanted and I knew that Andrew didn't want our child anywhere near him. That's the reason I came back to Aunt

Justine. I couldn't turn Billy over to my father…at least not in the beginning." She batted her eyelashes quickly in an attempt to stave off the tears that were forming.

"I tried to be a mother to Billy, but…," she paused, "I wasn't cut out for it and had begun to spend more and more time with my friends… drinking, drugs, the whole privileged world of the twenty-something rich girl." Her face was a jumble of embarrassment and shame. "I more or less left Billy to Aunt Justine. She and I had begun to fight constantly, and it was easier to be away than it was to be home. When Billy began to show signs of her abilities, Edgar came to me. He said that Andrew was not dead, that he left because Father paid him a great deal of money to disappear. He said that I had two choices…turn the child over willingly and Father would pay handsomely for her, or Father would simply take her and I'd never see her or his money again. I was devastated at the news of Andrew's betrayal, and shortly after Edgar's proclamation, Aunt Justine and I had a horrible, vicious argument, which spurred me to act irrationally, vengefully. I went to my father and turned Billy over to him." She looked up at me. Her shame had turned to anguish and tears were streaming down her face.

"Um, I don't mean to be…." I wasn't sure how to ask the next question. "Have you two been in contact for a while?"

She smiled again. "No, we haven't. That was the first time I've seen him since we parted thirty some-odd years ago."

"Why now? I mean, did he look you up, or the other way around?"

"He found me. He'd heard of Father's death and decided it was safe to make contact. It turns out that he left us because Father had found us and threatened to kill Billy and me if he didn't leave us." She angled her head and smiled. "There's no need to beat around the bush, George…I can see it in your eyes. You want to know if he wants to see his daughter, and you want to know if that's a good idea..." Another slight smile. "Letting Billy know about him. Am I correct?"

I nodded.

"I told him what I knew of her, but it was unnecessary. He's been keeping tabs on her. He's so proud of who she's become. However, he also knows what we did—more specifically, what I did—to her, and he's afraid to come forward...that she'll reject him." She leaned toward me a bit. "What do you think he should do?"

"Well, I think first we need to deal with Edgar, then I think you should tell Billy everything you just told me and let her decide if she wants to see him."

A look of fear crossed her face quickly, then she relaxed a little and said, "She hates me, justifiably. I don't think it would be a good idea for me to be the one to tell her."

"Julie, you obviously want to...." I actually wasn't sure what she wanted, so I guessed. "Make amends, right?" She nodded. "Well, there's a much better chance of that if *you* tell her everything."

She nodded again and relaxed into her chair thoughtfully. That was a good start, and I made a mental promise to bring all this up with Billy when I had time. I switched gears. "When was the last time you talked to Edgar?"

"It was the evening I went to Justine's. I believe he's watching my movements...he called the minute I left, when I was in the car."

"And you told him we denied any involvement in the disappearance of the papers?" She nodded. "What did he say to that?"

"He said you were lying and he'd give me a little more time to convince you. I expect to hear from him today."

"How did he sound?" I was hoping she knew him well enough to gauge his mental state at this point. His initial plan to get the documents and kill or kidnap one of us had failed. Now we had the kid—who was his weapon du jour—and the papers, and he had nothing. I was concerned that any rational thinking he might have had was out the window, and the threat level, at least from Edgar directly, had probably reached DEFCON2 and was accelerating.

She angled her head, thinking back to their last conversation, I assumed. "He sounded angry, a bit anxious, and perhaps a little frustrated. It was…," she hesitated, "very unlike him. As unstable as he is, he's always shown remarkable emotional control."

"Could I have the number he's using?"

She nodded and left to retrieve her phone.

While I waited for Julie to return I took a walk around the room, stopping at the bookshelves. They were loaded with volumes of books ranging from classic literature to modern-day science tomes, and just about everything in between. Sporadically placed, almost like bookends, were various pieces of sculpture in a variety of mediums. A tall metallic object caught my eye—silver, I thought. It resembled a column with an identical pedestal and capital. The shaft was etched, but the silver was badly tarnished and difficult to interpret. I was about to reach for it when Julie came back.

"Interesting, isn't it?"

"What is it?" I asked.

"I'm not sure, some sort of late 19th century artifact, I believe. I think Father said it's used to read magic spells or something like that." She shrugged. "He had a propensity for collecting odd things that pertained to the supernatural world. That box up there," she pointed to a top shelf where an ornately carved wooden box sat, "supposedly it's full of human bone fragments that are used to ward off evil spirits or some nonsense of that sort." She had an amused look on her face and I couldn't tell if she was serious.

Grimacing, I said, "That's just gross."

She walked over to the wingback chairs and sat. When I joined her she handed me her phone; the screen reflected a recent incoming number. I called Carol and briefly explained the situation. She told me to hold on. I listened to muffled voices, probably Pete and Billy, and when she came back on the line she recited a series of instructions and hung up.

"We think Edgar is probably starting to lose it, which makes him all the more dangerous. I'd love to tell you to get out of town and lay low, but we need you here." She nodded lightly. "How many security men do you have on the premises?" She held up two fingers.

"If it's all right with you, we're going to send over some more people. They'll be armed, and they'll be instructed to shoot Edgar on sight, and they'll be ghost killers. We need you to stay locked up in this house until further notice... it's the only way we can protect you." She nodded again.

As I got up to leave, she said, "George." I turned to her. "Thank you for not...," she paused and smiled, "openly passing judgment on me. I know that I've been a horrible mother *and* niece." This time she laughed. "A horrible person all around. I can't make up for what I've done, but I hope what I've told you helps. Please keep them safe."

I nodded and left.

Chapter 30

Since I was so close to home I decided to stop at my building to check on Justine and Margie. When I came through the garage entrance that led to the lobby, I was intercepted by Kevin Riley, our building maintenance man and self-appointed building manager.

"Hey, George, I'm glad I caught you. I was just going to call you."

"You were? Is everything all right?"

"Oh sure, but remember that guy from a few months back—bald black guy, kind of mean looking?"

Doing my best to keep my voice steady, I said, "I do. Was he here?"

"Yeah, about ten minutes ago. I was checking my mail and saw him outside. He was just standing in the courtyard, like he was waiting for someone. Anyway, I poked my head out and asked what he wanted. He said to give you this." Kevin handed over a slip of paper. He had a perplexed look on his face. "What's it mean?"

It was a receipt from a grocery and liquor market. Under the address it said, Corner of 42nd Avenue and Irving Street. It was only a block and a half away from the Lincoln Way house. There were two items on it, a bottle of water and a bag of chips. I flipped it over to find a crude drawing that I didn't recognize at first.

Kevin said, "It kind of looks like a top hat."

The top hat was Phil's signature look when he did his ghost tours, and Edgar was well aware of that. Swallowing down the rising panic in my chest, I pulled my phone from my pocket and dialed Phil. It rang several times before going to voicemail.

My voice trembled slightly when I spoke. "Kevin, take this number down." I recited Aris's cell number and name and he put it in his phone. "If that guy shows up again, call him. He's a detective…he'll know what to do. If you can't get him, just call 911."

Not wanting to wait for our old and painfully slow elevator, I started to sprint up the stairs when Kevin called after me. "Is everything okay?"

I yelled over my shoulder. "I think so. Just keep an eye out for him." I was hitting the second flight when Kevin yelled something else that I didn't catch.

Six flights of stairs later, I was out of breath and panting heavily when I pounded on Justine's door. Margie answered quickly, a look of annoyance on her face. "George!" She paused, taking in my panicked look. "What's wrong?"

"Is Justine here?" I asked, pushing past her toward the living room. Justine was sitting on the couch and looked up at me, her expression turning to immediate concern.

I held my hand up. "Hold on, I'll explain in a minute." I dialed Billy's cell phone. She picked up on the second ring.

"Billy, where's Phil?" I was still out of breath and it came out like a wheeze.

"He should be back any minute. He went to his house to grab some things. What's wrong?"

"Shit," I hissed. "How long has he been gone?"

"He left about an hour ago…George, what's wrong?!" she asked, this time with more vigor.

"I think Edgar has him." I explained the visit and the receipt, and she echoed my previous expletive. I asked "Where's Calvin?"

"He's upstairs."

"Who else is there with you?" I asked.

"Eric, Carol, Pete, and Pete's men."

"Okay, I'm on my way. Do not let Calvin out of your sight...I mean literally out of your sight. I'll call Aris." I didn't wait for her reply, just hung up.

I turned to Justine and Margie, both of whom looked horrified. I quickly briefed them and asked, "Aris said he'd get some extra security for you. Did he get in touch?"

Margie's eyebrows rose and she arched her head toward the reading alcove that held Grandma Billy's painting and a large collection of books. The man standing in the entrance towered over my six foot frame by at least another four inches. His shoulders and chest were so broad he appeared to fill the ten by ten space. He had an open book dangling from one hand, and his other was hovering near his holstered gun.

He started to smile, seemed to realize the magnitude of the situation, and turned serious. "Hey, George, what can I do to help?" I knew him. His name was John Kempt, not just a mid-level ghost killer, but a semi-retired WWF wrestler. I didn't care how strong Edgar was, John could *and* definitely would crack his head wide open.

Margie was suddenly at my side, her hand on my shoulder. "George, sit for a minute, you're going to hyperventilate." I didn't realize how heavily I was still breathing. She was right and I sat down, put my head in my hands, and worked on controlling my breathing. There was a tray on the coffee table with a water pitcher and accompanying glassware. She poured me a glass and said, "Drink, slowly."

After a few moments, I dialed Aris, explained the situation, and told him I'd be heading back to the house in a few minutes.

I also confirmed he had extra security on my dad too. We knew Edgar was in California, but who knew what contacts he still had. I wouldn't put it past him if he'd sent someone up to Idaho to kill my dad just out of spite.

I asked Justine and Margie to come with me—I'd feel better if they were with us at the house where we could keep an eye on them. They declined. I would be glad about that later. After assurances from Margie and John that they'd be safe, I left for Lincoln Way.

I took the stairs again, slower this time, and when I arrived in the lobby, Kevin was waiting for me. I apologized to him. "I'm sorry for running out on you like that. I just needed to make some calls."

"Sure, no problem... do I need to be worried about anything?" He took his responsibilities seriously, and the safety of the residents was high priority in his book.

"I don't think so. I doubt he'll be back, but better safe than sorry." I remembered that he'd shouted something earlier and I asked, "You said something before, but I didn't hear it. Did it have to do with that guy?"

Kevin frowned, then brightened. "Oh yeah, this probably isn't anything, but since you've already had one suspicious visitor today, I thought I'd mention it. The security cameras record 24/7 as you know. I check them frequently throughout the day to see if anyone is lingering around the building entrances." He liked to remind us as often as possible that he was doing his job above and beyond the call of duty. "You know, in case they're checking the place out to rob it or something." He smiled proudly. "A few days ago, a teenage kid pulled up on a motorcycle and parked in front of the building. He lingered there for a while, then got off the bike and walked around the corner and checked out the garage entrance.

"That night I was walking back from the market and the same kid was sitting on the bike at the corner. He kept looking from the front of the building to the garages, like he was waiting for someone. Before I could approach him, you pulled out of the garage and drove down the street; the kid waited a second and followed in the same direction."

I asked for a description of the kid, but it wasn't really necessary. However, it did explain how Calvin found us, and I assumed it was Edgar that gave him our address. But none of that really mattered now. Phil was what mattered now.

I was getting anxious to get back to Lincoln Way. I thanked Kevin and started toward the garage. Kevin grabbed my arm lightly and asked, "George, do we have a security problem? I mean...," he stuttered, "I haven't seen the kid since, so I didn't think it was a concern."

"Uh, no." I had to think quickly...he wasn't stupid, and now I thought he was worried. "The kid won't be back, but the other guy might. Just call that detective or 911 if he does show up. If you don't run into him, but you catch him on your security cameras, call me right away."

"Okay, but what's the story here?" he asked suspiciously.

"The bald guy was an acquaintance of mine...we had a fight. He's holding a grudge...I guess." I thought it was a believable lie. Kevin didn't look all that convinced.

"So that note has something to do with your fight?" He looked confused, which was understandable.

I smiled. "Yeah, listen, I really need to go. Just keep your eyes open." Thanking him again, I turned and left before he could say another word.

Chapter 31

I broke just about every traffic law getting over to the house on Lincoln Way, making it there in record time, only to be thwarted by a full driveway and no nearby street parking. I circled around the block, finally finding a spot someone had vacated seconds before. I was feeling frantic by the time I bounded up the front steps. The door opened before I reached it and Dave waved me through.

"Thanks, Dave. Where is every—?" He pointed down the hall to the kitchen. I entered the room and focused on Pete and Aris. "Did someone go to his house?"

Pete replied, "I just came from there. His car is parked out front and the front door had been busted open. There are signs of a struggle in the house, his cell phone was crushed to bits and left on the floor, but otherwise the place was empty."

"Did you see any…," I hesitated, "signs that he was hurt?" Pete shook his head.

I fell into the nearest chair, which happened to be next to Billy. She grabbed my hand and squeezed it. The next thing I knew a glass of whiskey was placed in front of me. Eric said, "Drink that. I can see your veins pulsing in your neck and forehead…you need to calm down." I swallowed it in one gulp and almost threw it back up just as quickly, but a minute later the calming effect of the Bushmills was working.

I pulled out the receipt, handed it to Aris, and said, "The timestamp is from this morning. I don't think the items he purchased mean anything, it's the fact that he was just down the street and the sketch on the back." Aris turned it over, briefly examined the crude top hat drawing, and handed it to Pete, who did the same and passed it around.

"Why Phil?" I asked no one in particular.

Pete said, "Julie told you that Edgar was agitated. I'm guessing he's growing pretty impatient too. He was most likely watching the house and saw Phil leave. He knows Phil isn't a ghost killer, meaning he isn't trained or strong like we are, and he was all by himself." Pete shrugged. "I think he just wanted to get things moving and he saw an opportunity, so he took it."

Carol said, "I think it's more than that." She looked around the room. "That stuff Phil told us about this morning, one of the things he said sort of stuck with me, but I guess I was too tired earlier to realize why it was bothering me. Anyway, it hit me a little while ago…that prophecy thing he read us, it said something about the cambion being born on all souls day and something about its eighteenth anniversary." A touch of panic lit her eyes. "I checked Calvin's license…he was born on November 2nd, 1997. He'll be eighteen tomorrow, or if you follow the prophecy, at midnight tonight…."

Billy let out a hissing sigh. "Edgar doesn't think Calvin can get the journal. He kidnapped Phil because he's running out of time and he needs leverage."

I ran my hands down my face and groaned. It also probably meant that Edgar was even more volatile than we thought, because now he was up against an impending deadline and he didn't have Calvin or the journal. I asked, "What was Phil going home for, anyway?"

Eric answered, "He was hunkered down in the library after you left. When I went in to check my email, he was excited…mumbling something about it being a map. Then he jumped up and said he had to go get some papers he left at his house."

I turned to Pete. "Did you see any papers at his house?"

Pete frowned. "Yeah. Like I said, it looked like there was a struggle of some sort. There were papers and books scattered all over the floor near the desk."

I stood up and paced. I was too keyed-up, whiskey or not, to sit down. Something got him excited, something that made him rush home to find something else. I walked out of the room and headed to the library. I heard chairs scraping as the others got up to follow me.

The library table that Phil used as a desk was strewn with papers and journals. His laptop sat off to the side, a cartoon ghost lazily drifting across the screen every few seconds. I tapped the keyboard and the screensaver ghost was replaced with an open email. It was from his friend Boyd, the subject line said, "RE: writings", it was dated this morning.

It read: *P, thanks for the new scans, that's a pretty interesting theory you have. Since you said this was important and you were in a hurry, I got right on it, but you owe me big time! Anyway, based on what your email said, I outlined the stuff that directly pertains. I'll send you a word for word translation later.*

Since "RE:" was in the subject line, I assumed Boyd just replied to Phil's email and I scrolled to the bottom so I could figure out what Boyd meant by "interesting theory". Phil's email to Boyd regaled him with the folklore tale he'd told us that morning. Phil went on to say that he'd been given the strange writings by a police friend who knew about Phil's interest in the supernatural, they had belonged to a man that was suspected of kidnapping people for some sort of Satanic ritual, and that the prophecy Boyd had already deciphered indicated something was to happen on November second (Phil had obviously reached the same conclusion as Carol). I scrolled back to the beginning and started to read.

The stuff in Archaic Latin appears to be diary entries of some sort. This guy was a priest and he was sent to San Francisco during the gold rush. Most of his entries are more like complaints about the people here, how bad they were, etc. He does mention ghosts and demons too. Then the entries more or less follow that story you mentioned (although there are some minor differences). Anyway, he got a call from God, built a chamber with an inner vault, and apparently lured demons and bad men to their deaths, and entrapped their eternal, and evil, souls (he did note that he was saving their souls if they took the time to repent while they were imprisoned...).

He says that God had him carve symbols into the door of the vault, but that only some of them actually open the vault door. Then "by God's hand" he created two drawings of the strangest and most undecipherable nature, which God stated were the map to the chamber and the combination to the vault door, and he carved a special key that would interpret both (he notes that he has no memory of doing this, but knows it was God who guided his hand). But in order to use the key, a special prayer had to be recited, and it could only be recited by an emissary sent by God. He then hides the key in a sacred and holy place.

The next entry states that Satan had come to him in the night and overtaken him, and used his knowledge of the chamber and the vault to rewrite God's instructions on opening the vault. He said that Satan had used the priest's own "unwilling hand" to write out a prophecy, which depicted his (as in Satan's) emissary (instead of God's) would rise one day and open the vault.

There's one last entry that might have to do with this... it's sort of manic though. "I cannot resist Satan's servant. He enters my mind often—he claws at my thoughts and memories—he has glimpsed the reflective eye. Oh I pray She can protect it.... Son, Observe the Time and Fly from Evil!"

The rest of the entries don't seem to pertain to the story, but like I said, I'll send over the complete translation later.

On to the Enochian/prisca Latinitas entries. Aside from the prophecy part that I already sent over, there was another paragraph that discusses how this will all go down. It says, "My faithful servant shall guide them to the key, and with the reflective eye they shall see all. Upon the stroke of midnight of the eighteenth anniversary of the cambion's birth, he shall sacrifice himself to his father and become my most powerful servant, at which time the combination shall be read by my own prayer and the vault shall be opened." (There's no mention of this prayer though.)

There is one last part. If you sent the pages in order, I assume this is towards the back of the journal. It's also written in Latin, but I don't think the priest wrote it. The writing looks different and it's more like a notation. It said, "Old St. Mary's?"

That got me thinking…the priest said he hid the key in a holy place, and since he lived in the city, I looked up Old St. Mary's. It's the oldest church in town, and the Bible verse, "Son, Observe the Time and Fly from Evil" is quoted under the clock face on the tower of the church, so that fits into what I translated.

I did a quick little search on the church just for fun. The interior wall of the tower is exposed brick, and several random bricks were imprinted with a variety of religious symbols. In the 1990s the church was broken into and vandalized. The vandals had chiseled out several of these imprinted bricks, all of which had small cavities behind them. The church said nothing was stolen, but the rumor mill thought perhaps something had been hidden in those cavities and that's what the thieves were after. Maybe that's where your priest hid his key thing?

I reread it out loud and turned to Aris. "Did Phil call you this morning?" He nodded. "Did he tell you about this folktale and his other theory?" Aris nodded solemnly.

Billy said, "What other theory?"

"Phil thought if this chamber was real, it would be nearby because Edgar would want to release the demons, and they'd need to be close to us so they could help him with his revenge plan. The prophecy said the imprisoned souls would be given new life." I looked around. "So maybe Edgar was kidnapping our GKs—"

Billy interrupted me before I could finish. "Uh-uh. I don't care how strong he is. Even if he managed to capture one of us, even our lowest level guy is too strong, mentally, to allow a demon in—"

It was my turn to interrupt. "I know, but here's the thing... the stuff you guys found last night talked about Aaron's drug addiction. Phil was pretty sure Aaron's diminished capacity from his drug use was how Gilles was able to converge with him. Phil thinks maybe Edgar is using drugs on our guys. That's how he's going to make them pliable, able to be converged."

Eric said, "But I thought we decided Calvin wasn't capable of doing the convergence yet?"

Carol said, "Damn, why didn't we catch this before?" She looked around. "The prophecy said that the cambion shall merge forever with his father and become one, and as one they'd be powerful enough to open the vault and converge the imprisoncd demons."

Pete said, "Okay, I'll buy that becoming one with Gilles, etc. would increase Calvin's power to that level, but who's going to converge *them*?"

"There was nothing in those writings about that, so I'm guessing Edgar is going to need one of you to do it," Carol said as she looked from Billy to me.

Eric sighed. "No wonder Edgar's so desperate...he's up against the clock, and he's missing," he started ticking off his fingers, "the journal with the combination, Calvin and Gilles, and one of you two."

Pete cleared his throat and said, "All right, we've established that Edgar probably has our guys, and we know he has Phil, but where is he? Where are they?"

Billy said, "Vokkel mentioned that they found the chamber, so I'm going to assume that's where Edgar's hiding out."

I looked at the papers strewn all over the center of the table. A yellow pad was on top of the mess, and Phil had scribbled a few things on it. A couple of words stuck out… *reflective eye=anamorphic drawing? Maps? Edge of cemetery—it means something!!!!*

The journals were stacked on one end and I started flipping through them, but none of them contained strange words or drawings. "I think he went home for the other journal, the one that has all the drawings in it. It's not here."

Carol was standing near me and read the words on the yellow pad. "Anamorphic…." She slapped her head lightly. "Of course! They're mirror anamorphic drawings. I knew they looked familiar."

Eric frowned. "What are you talking about?"

She pointed at the yellow pad. "He wrote 'anamorphic'… it's a form of art. The artist creates a deformed image on a plane surface surrounding a cylindrical mirror. The drawing can only be viewed clearly through the mirror though, so when you remove it, all you have is a distorted image that doesn't resemble anything. But replace the cylinder and a three-dimensional picture that can be viewed from various angles comes to life." She looked down at me, a slight smile on her face. "The translation Boyd sent said that God had him create drawings of the strangest and most undecipherable nature. He also said something about the reflective eye, which could mean the cylinder or whatever you need to interpret the drawings. I'm guessing Phil thinks the drawings in the journal are the maps and the combination."

Eric said, "I think we need someone to go back over to Phil's house to see what they can find. Hopefully, Edgar didn't see the journal and take it with him."

"I'll go," Carol said matter-of-factly.

Aris looked concerned. "Perhaps you should take someone with you, one of Pete's men."

Carol smiled and said, "Don't worry. One of Pete's guys is stationed at Phil's until further notice. And if anyone wanted to follow me when I leave here," she winked, "they'd have to catch me first." She was right…her driving skills consisted of speed and rapid lane changes. There was no way a car could follow her, and even an experienced motorcycle driver would have a hard time keeping up with her and her Ducati.

Carol didn't wait for more argument; she left the room, and within a minute, we heard the front door open and close, and soon after the roar of her motorcycle as she took off for Phil's.

I leaned back in the chair and ran my hands down my face. "What now?"

Aris said, "I believe it is time to speak with Calvin."

Pete growled, "I'll get him," as he left the room.

I looked at Billy. She was staring at the papers on Phil's table, her brow wrinkled, and I asked, "What?"

She pointed to the notepad. "Edge of the cemetery." Her brow wrinkled. "Something Calvin said the day we walked through the park. He asked where the cemetery was. I told him there wasn't one, that there weren't any cemeteries anywhere in the city except the Presidio and Mission Dolores. He started to argue, then he just dropped it."

Pete popped his head into the room. "The kid's waiting in the den. I think he knows something's up."

Aris nodded and turned to the rest of us. "I'd like both of you to join me, as well as Pete. Eric, I'd like you, Jonas, and Dave to stay in the hallway, but be on guard…this boy is quite unpredictable."

Chapter 32

When we entered the den Calvin was standing next to Pete. He didn't look nervous or worried...he actually looked quite relaxed. It's always nice when your psychopathic houseguest feels comfortable.

"Please have a seat, Mr. Brelong," Aris said as he walked over to one of the sofas and sat. Calvin did as he was told while looking around the room. Billy had moved toward the corner, her arms firmly crossed under her breasts, her expression hard, almost callous. I walked over and sat near Aris. Pete stood behind Calvin's sofa, his pose similar to Billy's.

"I must admit, Mr. Brelong, your ability to portray yourself as a feeble-minded boy, lost in a world he does not understand, is quite impressive. However, it is no longer necessary. What is necessary is the location of Edgar and Mr. James."

The green flash came, but so did a slight twinge of surprise. He asked, "What makes you think I know where either of them are?"

Aris angled his head and said, "Ah, you weren't aware of his plans to kidnap Mr. James, were you?" Calvin's eyes narrowed slightly and Aris continued. "I think I understand. Edgar is concerned, much like Vokkel had been, that you hadn't reached the proper maturity level to fulfill your destiny. You've been unable to accomplish your mission here, is that not correct?"

Calvin's eyes became slits, giving them a reptilian appearance. Aris kept going. "We are aware that you came to us with the intention of obtaining a particular journal that was in the possession of Mr. Vokkel. In addition, we are aware of the contents of said journal. It appears however, that you are not fully aware," he gave Calvin a condescending smile, "of its contents."

"Oh, I know exactly what's in it," Calvin sneered.

"Ah," Aris said disbelievingly. He arched an eyebrow lightly. "Based on the information we have gathered about you, I would not have thought such a selfishly impetuous young man as yourself would be willing to give up his life so easily."

"What are you talking about?" Calvin's voice had a touch of concern to it.

"Your mother told us you were smart and manipulative. That indicates that you are also, most likely, quite selfish. I believe you went to Sam to confront him, and when he told you he would be turning you in to us, you killed him. But it was done without forethought, thus your attempt to have it appear as an accident."

"Sam was a traitor, and an asshole. He was gonna ruin it all," Calvin spat out.

"Yes, of course, he was going to do the right thing…I suppose that would appear traitorous to someone such as yourself. But let us get to the point of the matter. The true prophecy states 'that the cambion,' which is you…," he pointed to Calvin, "'shall merge forever with his father and become one, upon which my ever faithful servant'—that is Gilles, by the way—'shall live once again.' There is only one way to interpret this part of the prophecy…Gilles will converge with your body and discard your mind and soul for the devil to deal with at his leisure. In essence, you shall die."

He was baiting Calvin and I was enjoying every minute of it. Aris kept going. "You have been betrayed, by Mr. Vokkel, by Edgar, and most importantly, by Gilles. However, you are here, with us, and we have no intention of allowing this prophecy to come to fruition."

"You're lying," he hissed.

Aris stood, smoothed his pant legs, and said, "No, Mr. Brelong, I am not." He turned to Pete and said, "I am sure the others have a few questions. When they are finished, please escort him to his room and post guards inside and out." He turned and left the room.

I leaned forward. "So, he's right, I would like to clear some stuff up. Why'd you kill Leo? I mean, if you knew the part in the prophecy about when and where, you knew you couldn't converge Gilles yet."

Calvin had regained his composure and said, "Leo could see the ghosts, he was just too stupid to know what to do about it. But he wasn't so stupid that he didn't realize Gilles was doing something to him, and he said he was going to tell my mom. She would've freaked out, and that was the last thing I needed." He shrugged. "So we took care of him." He grinned wickedly. I really hated this kid.

"Well, that clears that up. But I'm confused about these other attacks. What was the point?"

Another wicked grin. "In the beginning I was just having fun." He winked. "I mean, Vokkel and Edgar kept me on a pretty tight leash, and I needed to see what I could do." He laughed. "Edgar didn't even know Gilles and I were out playing; he was too busy hiding out and planning."

"All right, so what changed? Why'd you try and kidnap Billy in Marin?"

He pointed. "Now that *was* mostly Edgar, although the killing part was all me." The green flash intensified, sparked maliciously, and this time it didn't leave. "See, Edgar said we were going to need someone to perform the convergence for Gilles...I didn't lie about that part. So the plan was to attract your attention and take one of you, and like I said before, then the other would do what we wanted. But you guys were much stronger than I anticipated, and then Edgar found out you'd stolen the journals, so we came up with a new plan." He smiled. "And you bought it, until now."

Billy moved forward and placed her hands on the back of the couch, leaning a little closer in as she did so. "Calvin, I'm confused; who did you think we'd be converging Gilles into?"

Then it hit me, and I said, "You didn't know, but you thought it had to be Edgar. Oh hell, maybe Gilles told you it *would* be Edgar so you'd keep playing along, but you also realized that you couldn't do the convergence." And with that I realized something else, something that terrified me. I took a breath and said, "I'm beginning to think you didn't know shit about this prophecy, so let me tell you exactly what it's about. The actual prophecy, the one you know nothing of, clearly states that the cambion shall sacrifice himself to his father, meaning you give *your* body to Gilles, and you just," I threw my hands up, "poof, you go away. You told us that Edgar and Gilles have been chatting without you, so they probably hatched a plan to keep you in check, let you believe that Edgar would be Gilles's new body. And I'm thinking that you've been allowing Gilles into your head for so long, and with each visit, he's secretly breaking down any resistance, so when the time comes, he's going to get in your head one last time and kick you to the curb and take up full-time residency. He doesn't need us...only Edgar needs us for his revenge plan. But Gilles, he only needs you!"

Gilles was the ultimate demon. Everything about him screamed intense power, and that kind of power would surely be able to take over a kid like Calvin, especially a kid that the ultimate demon created just for this purpose.

My phone chirped with a text message, and a second later I heard two other alerts coming from Billy and Pete's phones. Calvin was staring off into space...I thought he was thinking through what I'd said. I pulled my phone out just as Pete and Billy did the same and checked the text; it was from Carol.

It's not here. I think Edgar must have found it, but I found something else, and if I'm right, he won't be able to read it. On my way back now.

Billy mumbled "shit" and I looked back at her, then over to Pete. He angled his head toward the door and said, "Go, I'll stay with him." We both left the room and moved down the hallway, out of earshot from Calvin.

I said, "If Edgar has that journal, he only needs Calvin now."

Billy nodded. "Yeah, I think we should talk to Aris and Pete about making a trade," she said in a defeated tone.

"Billy, didn't you hear what I just said? Gilles doesn't need us to converge with Calvin, he's so damn strong he can do it himself!"

"You can't be sure of that."

I grabbed her by the shoulders. I could tell by the look on her face that she knew I was right. "Aris said a demon that converged with one of us would have exponential power. Gilles converged with a man of God, who was a longaevus and a ghost killer. It's like a trifecta! He can do it on his own!"

She slumped. "What now?"

"Let's get this kid locked up and we'll go from there." We walked back into the living room. Calvin was picking his nails and looked up as we entered.

"Bad news?" He had an unbearable smirk on his face and I wanted to rip him limb from limb. He moved to the edge of the couch, as if to stand, and said, "So this has all been fun, but it's time for me to go." He rubbed his hands together. "Here's the plan... one of you will come with me and bring the journal, we'll go find Edgar, and once you've done what you're supposed to do, I'll let you and Phil go on your merry way." He winked. I couldn't believe this kid; had he not heard a word we'd said?

I shook my head. "You're an idiot." Turning to Pete, I said, "Lock him up."

"With pleasure." He grabbed Calvin under the arm and dragged him from the room. Billy and I went to the kitchen, where I assumed Aris was.

Chapter 33

Aris was sitting at the table, drinking coffee, and looked up when we entered the room. I poured a cup for myself and Billy and joined them at the table. A minute later Pete came into the room.

I asked, "Is he secure...I mean, with just three people watching him?"

Pete nodded. "For now, but I think we should either move him or call in more reinforcements." Aris agreed with a nod.

Suddenly the house shook as several loud crashing noises from above rattled the walls, followed by a tortured masculine scream and what sounded like someone being thrown down the stairs. Pete turned and ran to the front of the house, with the rest of us in his wake.

When we reached the staircase, a body was heaped face down on the landing. Only he wasn't really face down...his neck had been twisted so viciously that the head was now backwards, staring at us with dead eyes. It was Jonas.

I looked up. Calvin stood on the stairs between the first landing and the second floor. His green eyes had darkened...the color reminded me of Vokkel's house, that Charleston green, so dark it was almost black. The irises were expanding into the white, and then that was all, this dark malicious green. He looked haunted, and then I saw it...not an aura so much as a silhouette surrounding him; another form, that of Gilles, the alive and the dead, now enmeshed together. Was this what it looked like when a ghost killer was possessed by a demon? It wasn't like this with normal people…the demons stood in their wake, but with Calvin, with Gilles, they'd almost become one.

Calvin and Gilles grinned together and raised their hands, summoning. The air shimmered, hummed, and sizzled, and I knew what was happening…it had happened before, when Vokkel summoned his surge of demons to kill Billy and me in the garage on Bush Street.

Behind Calvin, heaped on the upper landing, Eric groaned…at least he was alive. Dave stumbled into view at the top of the stairs. A large gash ran across his forehead, and his face was covered in blood. He grabbed the banister to steady himself, then, realizing what was happening, launched himself at Calvin. But Calvin wasn't a gangly teenage boy anymore; he was the possessed and invincible monster Aris had warned us about. Without looking, Calvin simply swatted Dave away and leapt down the stairs, over the railing, and into the library.

The hallway was now filled with demons. I could barely see through them…they grabbed at us, trying to zap us with their electroplasmic juice, and for a fleeting moment I thought maybe they were drawing on Gilles's strength; they were that powerful. I stabbed without thinking, taking a jolt each time, but somehow managing to push through to the library.

When I entered the room, Calvin was pulling the journals off the desk, one by one, flipping through them quickly and tossing them aside viciously. He turned abruptly, the most evil, ghoulish scowl on his lips, and screamed in a voice that wasn't all his, "WHERE ARE THEY?!"

I stopped. The jolts of demon juice I'd received had jarred me, my breath was ragged, and blood pounded in my ears, but I could still hear the sound of furniture breaking and pain-filled screaming from the hallway. I hesitated, not sure what to do...fight Calvin or help save my friends? He made the decision for both of us...he lunged. He was incredibly fast, and his formerly adolescent-strength hands were around my neck and squeezing like a vice before I could react. I kneed him in the balls. Demon or not, it hurt him and he went down, letting go of my throat. Unfortunately, he also recovered quickly, jumped up, and ran back into the hallway and out the front door. I did my best to follow, but he was so incredibly fast and I was having trouble breathing, not just from the demons' jolts, but from Calvin's assault on my trachea. Before I made it to the curb, he'd crossed the street and was entering the park at the intersection of Lincoln Way and 41st Avenue, headed towards Martin Luther King Jr. Drive and a very thick mini-forest within the park. If he got to those trees I'd probably lose him. Mustering up everything I had, I ran. It felt like I was breaking the speed barrier, but he was still faster, and by the time I got to the trees, he was gone.

I searched for ten minutes, but I knew it was useless. I headed back to the house, hoping that the others had managed to tackle the demon storm I'd left behind.

Chapter 34

The front hall was torn apart; the artwork hung askew, a small table was reduced to kindling, and the runner was bunched up at the end of the hall leading to the kitchen. There was a head-sized hole in the plaster at the top of the stairs where I'd last seen Eric. Aris was on his phone; his suit jacket was gone and his crisp white shirt was torn and scorched in places. Pete was helping Eric down the stairs, plaster dust covering his head and shirt. Dave was sitting on the step, holding his hand to his head, blood oozing between his fingers. There was no sign of Billy and I started to panic; then she came through the kitchen door holding a first aid kit and a blanket. I sighed in relief. She handed me the blanket and pointed to Jonas's mangled body. I could feel tears of frustration, anger, and sadness building, and I didn't think I'd be able to stop them—Jonas was dead, the kid got away, Edgar had the journal, and we had no idea where he was holding Phil. I realized we'd probably never see him alive again. I covered Jonas up and walked back into the library and tried to compose myself.

A few minutes later I heard the roar of Carol's bike and walked back out to the hallway. Eric was holding an icepack to his head, but he looked otherwise unharmed. Billy had bandaged Dave's wound and was helping him clean the blood off his face. Pete was at the front door, talking to his men that had been on guard on the street. I hadn't seen them when I went out or came in, but I assumed they must have seen us run into the park. Pete and Carol came into the house and after he explained what had happened, she exhaled an expletive in response.

Pete looked down the hall to Aris. "They saw which way he went, but I called them back. I'm not risking any more lives." Aris nodded.

Carol looked around and settled on Eric and Dave. They were sitting side by side on the step. "You two okay?" They nodded. Liars…none of us were okay.

Aris headed to the kitchen and we all followed, taking seats at the table. Billy went to the fridge and pulled out several beers, handing them to each of us. Now really wasn't the time to imbibe, but they'd help slow down the raging adrenaline.

Carol said, "Okay, listen." She pulled two rolled-up pieces of paper from her jacket and spread them open. They were about eleven by sixteen inches each and crumpled, as if they'd been balled up. "Phil must have copied and enlarged the drawings in the journal. I found these on the floor next to his trashcan. I'm thinking Edgar starts to bust the door down and Phil realizes what's happening and balls them up and tosses them, in the hopes that whoever is coming in won't notice them." Everyone appeared to agree with that theory, and leaned in to take a closer look. I had no idea what I was seeing though. They resembled nothing as far as I could tell. The images were a half circular pattern that took up most of the page, with the exception of the upper center portion, which was blank.

Carol pulled a shiny stainless steel cup from her pocket. "This was on the floor too, and I think he was trying to use it to read the drawings." She looked up. "The reflective eye." She placed it on the clear semi-circular section at the top of one of the papers and motioned us to gather around her. "Look at the cup straight on." This required us to hunch down to counter level, and we each did it in turn. The image developed into something, but it still wasn't quite clear.

"I know, it's not right. But I remembered something else Boyd had translated. Aaron wrote that God had him create the two drawings, but he also had him carve a special key. So I think somewhere out there is a reflective cylinder with etchings on it, and when you pair it with these, it reveals the location of the chamber and the order of the combination."

Eric dejectedly said, "I'm guessing Boyd was right and that's what was chiseled out of the walls of St. Mary's tower, and since Vokkel wrote that he'd found the chamber," he pointed at the drawings, "he must have had that cylinder and now I guess Edgar has it. Which means, if Calvin catches up with him, he's got everything he needs."

Considering I was still riding an emotional roller coaster and not thinking anywhere near straight, I was surprised at how bright and furious the light bulb moment was that suddenly hit me. I smiled and said, "He doesn't have it!" Pulling my phone out, I dialed Julie Vokkel. She answered on the second ring and I put her on speaker.

"Hi Julie, it's George. I've got you on speaker...is that okay?"

"I suppose." She sounded hesitant.

"Sorry, I just don't want to repeat myself after we hang up. Is everything okay? Has Edgar contacted you?"

"Not yet. You don't sound well...is everything all right?"

"No, Edgar kidnapped our friend and we've had...some trouble on top of that."

There was panic in her tone when she asked, "Billy and Justine?"

I looked over at Billy; she looked utterly confused at the concern in her mother's voice. "They're fine. Listen, Edgar is about to realize, if he hasn't already, that there's something in the house he desperately needs. Remember that silver thing I was looking at this morning?"

"Yes."

"Well, I need that, but so does he, and he might be watching the house at this point, so I need a distraction so we can extract it."

"Hmm," she paused a moment. "I have an idea. Who do you want me to give it to?"

I looked at Pete and he mouthed the name Morris. "Not sure if introductions were made, but one of the guys we sent over is named Morris."

"Oh yes, actually he's standing right here. He hasn't left my side since he arrived."

"Great. Can you give it to him and tell him Pete will be calling?" As if on cue, I heard a phone ring in the background and looked at Pete, who was, not coincidentally, on his phone.

"What's your idea?"

"Father has an elaborate alarm system for both police and fire. I'm going to trigger the fire alarm. This is Pacific Heights… the response will be immediate, and there will be swarms and swarms of responders. The confusion will be enormous, and Morris can make his escape then." I could hear the amusement in her voice.

"That's actually a great idea, but I need you to remain safe, protected from Edgar if he's in the vicinity."

"Don't worry. I'll be sure my guards and your guards keep me surrounded until the mayhem dies down and we can lock ourselves back in the house."

"Thanks, Julie. We'll be in touch later… keep your phone with you and stay safe." I hung up.

Billy had folded her arms across her chest and was eyeing me suspiciously. I knew what she wanted to know, but now wasn't the time. Instead, I said, "Julie told me that Vokkel never let anyone see the journals, including Edgar, but she was sure he discussed them with Edgar, and if they found the chamber, I'm guessing he would have sent Edgar to check it out, so he would have told him where it was. But if he never saw the journals, or the drawings, he wouldn't know you need something special to read them. But he's not stupid, so I think we should assume he's going to figure it out quickly. I saw this etched, but badly tarnished, silver cylinder on Vokkel's bookcase this morning, and asked Julie about it. She said Vokkel told her it was some artifact that was used to read magic spells. And I'm guessing Edgar will come to, or already has come to, the same conclusion I just did."

Chapter 35

As we waited for Morris to arrive, we did our best to straighten up the mess left by Calvin and Gilles. A van arrived and was ushered into the garage. Two stoic men came up the back stairs and gently removed Jonas from the landing. They left as quickly and quietly as they'd come.

In all the excitement, no one had bothered to check Calvin's room, so Carol took on the task and returned with the cell phone he'd been using to contact Edgar. "He got a text from Edgar about thirty minutes after I left for Phil's house. It said, '*leave now.*'"

I looked at Dave and Eric. I didn't want to appear accusatory, but they were supposed to be in the room with Calvin, so how was he able to check the phone? Eric must have sensed the question. He said, "It beeped, like a reminder that there was a text. I started towards the sound...I knew it was under the mattress. He was sitting on the bed and casually pulled it out and looked at it, and then he smiled all crazy like. He tossed the phone on the bed and just went nuts. He threw me out the door. I hit my head, blacked out for a minute...."

Dave picked up the rest. "I tried to stop him, but he grabbed me too, like I was nothing." He shook his head. "I outweigh that little shit by a hundred and twenty pounds...I'm not sure what happened next." He hung his head in unjustified shame. Carol placed her hand on his arm reassuringly.

Forty-five minutes later, Morris arrived with the column. Billy volunteered to polish it, and a half-hour later, she had it down to a mirror finish. She brought it over to the counter and placed it, like Carol had done with the cup, in the upper portion of one of the papers. We all hovered around, and lowered ourselves so we were looking at it straight on. It was a map.

I'd spent most of my adult life in the commercial real estate field and was adept at reading old parcel maps. This resembled that. There were faint grid lines, what appeared to be individual parcels marked out, and a bolder outline with the word "cemetery" in the center. Inside that outline were several intertwining double lines that resembled pathways or small roadways. Between those were numbers, ranging from one to thirteen…I assumed they designated the cemetery sections. The lower left of the cemetery outline had a shaded section carved out, with a U and S in it, but nothing else. The upper half of the map had a wavy bold line running across it, with a shaded area above the line.

However, aside from that, there were no street names, and no other identifying markings. I looked closer; there was something else, and I said, "Eric, do you have a magnifying glass?" He nodded and left the room, returning a minute later.

I held the lens over the area I thought I'd seen something in, and it came to life nicely. It was very light but it resembled an arch of some sort, and was located to the northwest of the area with the U and the S.

I stood up and said, "Nothing here tells us where it is…there's no street names, nothing. But this," I pointed to the letters, "U and S, could be for the United States, and the Presidio was a military base and has one of the oldest and still remaining cemeteries in the city. I think we should start there." Billy had swapped out the map for the other drawing and was studying it closely. "Well?" I asked.

She said, "They look like symbols…not sure of what, but they're clear enough. They're in a particular order, so I'm guessing it's the combination." She stood up and stretched her back.

My phone rang…it was Julie. I put her on speaker.

"Hi Julie, everything all right?"

"No." Her voice hitched. "He called. I…he sounded angry. He rattled me a bit and I think I answered wrong…."

"Okay, slow down. Tell me what he said."

"He said, 'There was something else with the journals, I need it now.' I wasn't thinking and I replied that I didn't have it. He knew right away that I knew what he was talking about." I heard a slight sob. "He actually hissed at me and said, 'You traitorous bitch, you gave it to them!' Then he said, 'They die, then you die,' and he hung up."

"It's all right, he's not coming after you anytime soon. We'll get you out of there, where he can't find you—"

She cut me off. "George, I heard someone scream in the background. They were trying to say something, but they were stopped. It sounded like flesh hitting flesh, then there was a whimper."

I looked around the room. "Stay put, Julie. He's got other things to worry about at the moment. He doesn't have time right now to come after you. It's going to be okay," I lied.

"What about Aunt Justine?"

I looked at Billy, who was frowning. I could tell Julie's new "concerned and cooperative mother" persona was confusing the hell out of her. I smiled lightly at her reaction and turned back to the phone. "We'll take care of her too. I need to go, please don't worry." I hung up.

I sighed heavily; we needed a plan, it was already past 4 p.m., and we had less than eight hours to find the chamber and save Phil, and hopefully kill Edgar. I turned to Aris and Pete, who were standing next to each other, and said, "I think we should use Calvin's phone to send Edgar a text, let him know we're willing to negotiate."

Billy said, "Are you crazy?!"

"What the hell else are we going to do? We don't know where he is, he's got Phil, and he's going to kill him. And I'm guessing he's got Calvin by now, too!"

Aris held his hand up. "Please, calm down. I agree that we should text him, start a dialogue with him. Perhaps he'll inadvertently say something that will help us find him."

Carol had been furiously tapping at her tablet. She stopped and sullenly said, "It's not the Presidio…Phil's copy doesn't resemble any maps, old or new, of that area."

Billy's phone rang. She looked down at the caller ID and said, "It's Justine." She hit the ignore button and turned to Aris. "If we're going to do this, then let's do it!"

Calvin's phone was sitting on the table. I pulled it forward and said, "What do we say?"

Aris was thoughtful, finally saying, "Identify yourself and ask him what he wants."

I tapped in the text and held the phone while I waited for Edgar to respond. Seconds stretched into minutes, and when the phone did beep with an incoming message, I jumped.

I want the key and boy.

Pete said, "He doesn't have Calvin?"

Billy tilted her head. "I don't think Calvin knows where Edgar is." She snorted. "I guess Edgar didn't trust him enough to tell him where the chamber was."

"That is unfortunate. If the boy is lost somewhere in the city, it will infuriate Edgar even more, because it is an additional piece that he needs and does not have." Aris turned to me and said, "Respond to him—tell him we will negotiate the boy and the key for Phil's safety."

"What about our other guys?" Pete asked.

"It is unlikely he will agree to that. He must have bodies for the demons to converge with." Pete started to argue, but Aris held his hand up. "We will not abandon them." Turning back to me, he said, "Tell him you want proof of life…video, not a picture."

I did as I was told and again we waited. Ten minutes later another text arrived, containing only the video we'd requested. Phil was bound to a chair of some kind, his hat was gone, and his hair was matted and tangled. Both eyes were badly swollen and bruised, as were his lips. Blood trickled down the left side of his chin. Edgar growled in the background and told Phil to speak. He looked at the camera and slurred, "Ges me ousta here, there are rodens esvrywhere." Then he attempted a wink.

"Is he trying to tell us something?" Eric asked.

"Mr. James is quite clever, and I am sure that is exactly what he was trying to do. Carol, can you analyze the background and other sounds? Perhaps they will tell us something of where he's being held." I handed her the phone.

"Should we respond first?" Billy asked.

"Yes, tell him we will be in touch within the hour." Carol texted the message and left the room with the phone, I assumed to go to her bank of computers in the library.

I started pacing around the room, pulling my hands through my hair in frustration. There's a certain amount of inner strength that comes with knowing you can save a life, or just make one better; there's even more strength in actually doing it. For the last several months I'd had a sense of empowerment and confidence in what I was doing. But now I felt useless and out of control. I was terrified of what Edgar was going to do, not just to Phil but to the other ghost killers. I couldn't see how we could fight something as powerful as Gilles and Calvin, because no matter how strong we were, he was stronger…and he was evil on top of all that.

Billy said, "You okay?"

I looked up and realized everyone was staring at me. I said, "I need some air," and left the room, headed for the front door.

Chapter 36

I wasn't sure how long I'd been sitting on the front stoop—feeling sorry for myself and desperately trying to hold back tears of frustration, which was only causing more frustration since I was too damn old to be crying in the first place—when the door opened and closed behind me.

Billy sat down next to me, so close I could feel her body heat and smell her shampoo. She put her head on my shoulder and gently said, "We're going to save them."

I laughed; the sound was wild, bordering on insane. "That isn't going to be easy...we have no idea where to look."

"Actually, we do. I just talked to Aunt Justine. If you recall, we filled her in the other day on what we'd learned so far, including Vokkel's mention of the 'edge of the cemetery.' She'd heard that before, but couldn't remember where until just a little while ago."

I turned to face her. "And?"

"Back when my grandmother was in her late teens and still living in the city, Justine took her to an event at the Legion of Honor. Grandma Billy was in one of her ranting moods that night, and kept going on about how close the horrible demons were, trapped right there at the edge of the cemetery." I looked at her now, eyebrows raised. She smiled and said, "Carol did some checking. The Legion of Honor and Lincoln Park Golf Course were built on the site of a former cemetery. It was condemned in the early 1900s, the bodies supposedly relocated to Colma. But when they renovated the museum in the 1990s, they found a bunch of corpses, and it's rumored there are still quite a few buried on the grounds."

The Legion of Honor was one of the city's most renowned museums. It also held a large collection of sculpture. I laughed again... still wild, but the touch of insanity was gone. "I thought he was trying to say rodents, he was really saying Rodin. The museum is loaded with his sculptures... there's even a few galleries named after him."

She elbowed me lightly in the ribs and said, "Yep. Now come on, we've got some guys to rescue, and if I have my way," her green eyes sparkled viciously, "a man that needs to be put out of our misery."

When we entered the kitchen, Carol was hovered over the map copy again. She had printed out two other maps as well. One was similar to our anamorphic map copy as seen in the silver column, but with more detail and all the appropriate street names and markers in place. The other was more recent and showed the museum and the surrounding areas, which included Lincoln Park Golf Course to the east and the Veterans Administration Medical Center to the west. Billy stared at it for a long moment, then started laughing. It was a dark and bitter sound.

Carol said, "You want to share with the class?"

Billy pointed at the recent map, specifically the area to southeast of the museum where Lincoln Park Golf Course was, then she pointed at the old map Carol had printed out, which not only showed the cemetery, but its name, Golden Gate Cemetery.

I definitely needed to get a grip... it took me entirely too long to grasp what had amused her, but when I did, I laughed too. "He had bits and pieces of the chamber location; 'park,' 'Lincoln,' 'Golden Gate.' He asked Billy where the cemetery was when they walked in the park. He doesn't know the city and he put it all together wrong. I think he assumed that Golden Gate meant the park, and this house is on Lincoln Way, so he assumed the 'edge of the cemetery' and therefore the chamber, were in Golden Gate Park."

Pete moved forward, looked at the maps, and said, "You think he's wandering around the park, trying to find it?"

A phoned beeped somewhere and Carol turned around, looking at a phone on the table… Calvin's. Aris picked it up, read the text, and said, "No, he is no longer searching for the chamber, and I believe we need to act quickly."

"What did he say?" I asked.

Aris read the message. "'*Bring the key, 11:40pm, eagles point, or he dies.*' I believe Calvin has found him."

I frowned. "Why so late? I thought this had to go down by midnight?"

Pete said, "Edgar probably thinks we don't know where the chamber is, but he's also cautious, so in the unlikely event we do know, he doesn't want to risk us getting to them before midnight, when Calvin needs to read the combination. Eagles Point is just down the road from the museum. Edgar's fast like us; he could get back to the chamber in ten minutes or so. I'm guessing he doesn't want to be too far away from Calvin. He's got at least seven men in that chamber with him. Our systems have a way of fighting things off, healing quickly. If Phil was right and Edgar drugged our guys, there's a chance the stronger of them could fight off the effects of the drugs. I don't think Edgar wants to leave them alone for too long."

Aris agreed with Pete and turned to Carol. "What have you found?"

Carol said, "Right. So the video of Phil shows rough stone walls in the background. They looked damp and slimy, and when I amplified the background noise I heard moaning, probably from our kidnapped GKs, and what I thought was trickling water. So I'm assuming this chamber is underground; in fact, it has to be."

She laid the most recent map on the table and ran her finger around the area where the golf course was. "I tapped into the city's website and pulled the utility plans for the golf course. There are no large underground areas...it's all pretty solid ground with the exception of some utility piping, so that's a no go. However, I also pulled the plans for the museum. This area...." She ran her finger between the back side of the museum and the VA campus. There was a strip of land running between the two. I knew from our frequent visits to the VA that the piece of land she was referring to was at the bottom of a small hill, and the museum was perched on top of the hill. "The location of the cemetery was here. This area in between would have been reserved by the government back then, so the cemetery wouldn't have extended into that. Thus, the edge of the cemetery." She looked up, a broad smile across her lips.

"All right, there's a large interior loading and storage bay under the museum here, and some old storm water tunnels here, here, and here." She jabbed the map at intervals. "They're no longer in use, but according to this map, there are access points here and here." She pointed to a spot inside the loading bay, and another on the strip of land at the base of the hill. "I think we can access them from inside the storage area under the museum. And this...," she pointed at a little mark, "is an exterior auxiliary access tunnel that would have been accessible from this back side, by the VA. I did a Google Earth search; there's something there that looks like a concrete arch with a large steel door. I think there's probably an entrance somewhere inside these tunnels that wasn't obvious to anyone, and it will lead to the chamber."

Pete blew out a breath. "All right, what's your idea on getting in?"

"Well, if we assume Edgar is holding everyone in the chamber, I'm guessing he's been coming and going here." She pointed to the part between the museum and the VA. It was the general area where I'd seen the arch from the anamorphic map. "It's pretty wooded and secluded. He wouldn't want to access the tunnels through the museum, it's too public. But I think we should use that one, because I'm betting he has this entrance guarded."

It never occurred to me that Edgar would call in reinforcements. Carol continued. "The museum closed," she glanced at the clock on the wall, "twenty minutes ago, but there's probably still a few employees running around. And of course there's going to be security guards to deal with."

Pete said, "We need to do some recon…this is too vague!"

"What do you propose?" Aris asked.

"After Calvin attacked I called in two more guys, which makes six total. As soon as Carol identified the chamber location, I sent two over to check things out. I'm going to have them get into those tunnels through the loading bay entrance and scout around inside." He pulled his phone out and started texting.

"How are they going to do that without getting caught by the museum security or attracting Edgar's attention?" Billy asked.

Pete smiled at her and said, "Darlin', two things to ease your mind. The guys I've got assigned to this house were all military, with *very* special skills." He winked. "Second, getting in and out of dangerous places unseen was my specialty back in the day." Regardless of how concerned Pete was, he was in his element now and that made me feel a little better. I'd heard a story or two about his Special Forces days, and I believed every one of them.

Turning to Carol, he said, "Can I borrow those maps for a bit?" She nodded and he gathered them up and left the room. A few minutes later I heard Dave greeting people at the door. The voices faded quickly and I assumed Pete had them in the library, where tactical instructions were being doled out.

Any confidence I had gained by learning the location of the chamber seemed to suddenly fade away, and exhaustion and doubt seeped in. Anxiety and fear were hitting me in waves, especially when I thought about the enormous strength that the combined Gilles and Calvin had displayed earlier.

Eric said, "What's wrong? You went all pale."

"Gilles and Calvin together are monstrously strong, and that demon storm they called in, they were drawing off their strength. Calvin damn near killed me, and he did it with ease. Even with Pete's little band of ghost killing soldiers, I just can't see how we can win against them."

Billy said, "Well, I say we start with the obvious; we shoot Calvin and Edgar the minute we lay eyes on them."

"Yeah, that's good for them, but Gilles can't be shot."

"There is another way," Aris said. His eyes moved to something behind me and I turned around to find GG standing in the corner of the room. She smiled at me, then looked up to Aris and nodded.

"As you know, Gilles was, in a way, possessing Calvin, amplifying the boy's ghost killing strength, which I believe is a great deal more advanced than we all initially thought. I believe he is very close to your and Billy's level. However, in their case, it isn't so much a possession as it is a shared consciousness. They are both present and in control, together." He looked at Carol painfully. I had no idea why, but her sad smile said it was something important, and she nodded at him.

"This must happen willingly...both the ghost—or in Calvin's case, the demon—and the ghost killer must accept each other. Once that is complete, your combined power is amplified beyond anything you shall ever experience." He glanced at GG again. "I believe GG is willing to do this with you, and together you will defeat Gilles and Calvin."

I couldn't believe what he was proposing, and I stuttered. "Uh...are you saying you want GG to possess me? What about what's happening with Calvin? I mean, he doesn't seem that in control when Gilles gets in him." I knew it was different with them, but still....

Billy said, "George, you said it yourself... Gilles has been stepping into Calvin's head for so long that he can't resist him anymore. This isn't going to be like that... this is a one-time thing, and GG isn't some son-of-Satan demon like Gilles."

I turned to her. "So you think I should do it?"

"I will if you won't," she replied quietly.

I turned to Aris. "How does it work?"

"GG will show you. I believe you should initiate it now. It can take some adjustment."

I had no idea what to expect with all of this, and I was scared, damn scared. Billy could tell too, and she said, "You want me to be there, you know, for moral support or whatever?" I nodded and headed to the den.

* * *

GG was waiting for us, hovering anxiously near the far wall. I said, "I have no idea how to do this." She smiled and came towards me.

I closed my eyes, and within seconds I felt something odd. An overwhelming sense of intrusion, of not being alone, overcame me, like a shadow was living in the corner of my mind. Then a sudden flood of images and information rushed me; laughter, tears, joy, and days flying by, my vision taking a higher stance with each image, as if I was growing. It was someone's life and I was reliving it. Then I felt excruciating pain and I knew I was dying, and then nothing... blackness.

The darkness started to fade as fast it came, and images and emotions once again took shape; sadness and loneliness, a feeling of being lost. Then I saw a little girl, smiling, but I could sense the unhappiness in her. I knew her, but as an adult... it was my mother. When GG's entire living and dead existence had run its course there was yet another sensation. An incredible surge of strength—her strength—coursed through me. It was the most exhilarating thing I'd ever felt. I opened my eyes... Billy stood to the side, staring, a combination of horror and awe lighting her face.

"I'm okay." I smiled. "We're okay. Can you see her, like with Gilles and Calvin?" I couldn't recall if she'd seen what I had when they attacked. She must have though; she nodded her head ever so slowly.

"Does it hurt?" she almost whispered.

GG and I smiled together, then she stepped away and I felt this strange loss. But she wasn't completely gone... there was a hint of her still left in my consciousness. She was now standing near Billy, smiling her own sweet smile.

I asked, "Have you ever done that before?" GG shook her head. "That was... I don't know, weird, kind of intoxicating. I could feel the power and strength, like I... we could take out an army single handed." GG was nodding and smiling, then she did something very un-GG like... she held up both hands and gave me an enthusiastic double thumbs-up.

Chapter 37

Billy and I went back to the kitchen. I grabbed another beer, not because I was thirsty, but because I was shaking slightly from having a ghost in my machine...I needed it to steady myself.

Pete was back as well, and Billy asked, "So what's the plan? Did Aris tell you about our new secret weapon?"

Pete nodded and turned to me with a serious and concerned expression. I put him at ease. "Don't worry, this is a one-off—well, two-off if you count our little introductory crash course a few minutes ago—but after we take care of this business, I'm done. It's...too weird, and honestly, I think it would be like taking a really good hallucinogenic drug. The sensation could be very addicting." He nodded, but I didn't think he was convinced about the safety of it all.

"All right, my guys just reported in," Pete said. I looked at the clock on the wall and was shocked to see how fast the time had gone by. It was now almost 10 p.m.

"We've got a problem," Pete continued glumly. "Like Carol suspected, Edgar didn't come alone. Men were posted in the little park area outside of the VA access point and in the area where the museum access point is located. My guys got into the storage bay without being seen, but once they got inside the tunnels, there wasn't much cover, so they couldn't get far. About twenty feet into the tunnels, it becomes a dead zone as far as cell and radio are concerned, so Edgar won't be able to communicate with the men inside; that's an advantage once we take them out. But we're going in blind. We have no idea where to go once we get into the tunnels."

The connection GG and I had shared earlier was still lingering, like a tenuous length of spider silk; delicate, yet strong. I concentrated on that. I wanted her back in the room…I had an idea. When she appeared, I motioned her over.

"GG, when you helped us with Vokkel, you were traveling between the ballpark and our location, remember?" She nodded. "I need you to do that again, but I need you to go to Edgar and the chamber. We need to know exactly where it is."

Fear filled her eyes and I remembered our conversation the other day about Gilles…she was terrified of him. I frowned. "Can Gilles sense you?" She nodded. "Can he hurt you?" If he could, I didn't see how our earlier plan to fight as one would work. She shrugged, which didn't tell me much of anything. I said, "GG, we need the element of surprise. If we can't get to the chamber undetected, I don't think we can win, or save Phil and the others."

She sighed sadly, a forlorn look on her face. Finally she nodded and disappeared.

Aris said, "George, I think we should ask her if she can bring reinforcements again. Perhaps creating our own chaos upon entering the chamber would work to our advantage."

I thought about it for a moment, and something came to me, another moment of great sadness. This time the image was the garage on Bush Street where we had fought Vokkel and his surge of demons. I sighed. "I don't think she'll be able to do that again. I have this…impression, from her…her memories. I think we inadvertently vanquished many of the good ghosts she brought. I don't think she can get them to come this time, especially because of Gilles and whatever is in that vault."

GG rematerialized and looked around. Settling on the maps that Pete had returned to the counter, she pointed to them. I went over and touched each one until she nodded; it was the map that reflected the unused storm water tunnels. She put her ghostly finger on the area where the museum entrance was, then ran it along the tunnel outlines. She kept going, even after the outlines stopped, and I said, "Hold on...are there tunnels beyond these, that aren't on here?" She nodded. "Okay, wait a second." Turning to Eric, I asked, "Got a pencil?" He arched his head with a look that said, "Seriously, you're asking me for a pencil?" I smiled and pulled out a stash of trusty number twos from my back pocket. I'd loaded up on them after Calvin and Gilles pulled their stunt earlier...I didn't want any more electroplasmic shocks today. Holding them up, I said, "Unsharpened." He rolled his eyes and walked over to a drawer, pulled out a mechanical pencil, and tossed it to me.

Turning back to GG and the map, I asked, "Can you trace that again and I'll follow along and mark it out?" She nodded, and when we were done, a whole new network of tunnels appeared on the map. "You're amazing," I said affectionately. "So where's the chamber door?" She pointed to a spot and I put an "x" on it.

Dave came into the room smiling. "It's done." He held up a silver column, similar, but not exact, to the key from Vokkel's house.

"Where did that come from?" I asked.

"I got a jeweler buddy over in West Portal. Pete had me call in a favor, and I had him create this. It isn't exact—we didn't have time for that—but it should fool Edgar for a little while."

I started shaking my head furiously. "No, no way...that key sat on Vokkel's bookshelf for God knows how many years. Edgar might not have known what it was for, but he definitely knows what it looks like." Pete started to say something and I interrupted. "If he realizes it's fake, he'll kill Phil on the spot!"

"Calm down," Pete said firmly. "The hand off is being made in a dark place. Even if he shines a light on it, he won't be able to see that much, but it's close enough to fool him in the short run. While the hand off is happening we'll be infiltrating the tunnels, and before Edgar even gets back to them, we should have the situation in the chamber controlled."

I wanted to protest, but he was right and we were running out of time. He spent twenty minutes going over everything. It felt rushed and inadequate.

Since we now knew Edgar had help, we assumed he was watching the house too. Eric was to do the hand off, so he was the only one going out the front door. The rest of us were to leave by the back, going over the fence, through the neighbor's yard, and into waiting cars one block over on Irving Street. Pete gave us five minutes to change into dark clothing, after which we reassembled in the kitchen for final instructions. Aris was the last to return, and I did a double-take when he walked in. I'd never seen him in anything other than his tailored suits and crisp white shirts. Now he wore black fatigues, a black sweater, and a holster, complete with a gun and extra clips.

Pete's final instructions consisted of handing out weapons to those of us that didn't already have one. Each one was equipped with a silencer. He explained that we'd most likely have to shoot our way in, and we needed to do it quietly. I knew Billy was familiar with firearms, and based on Carol and Eric's reactions, they were too. Phil, who had a small collection of guns, had insisted a few months back that I join him at the shooting range just in case I ever needed to use one. I still didn't feel all that comfortable with them, but I wasn't going to turn it down tonight.

Chapter 38

There were two black SUVs waiting for us on Irving Street. I felt like I was entering some strange covert ops movie. To think I'd mentally made fun of Julie's Hollywood style security just that morning, and here I was going full Hollywood to infiltrate a secret supernatural chamber next to a condemned cemetery—which was rumored to still be full of bodies—and defeat a demon and his newly risen army. And let's not forget we had every intention of killing the psychopathic villains of this little skit from hell, Edgar and Calvin. The whole situation dripped with irony, and I gulped hard to choke down the hysterical laughter I could feel building.

The quickest way to get to the museum would have been to go through Golden Gate Park, but Pete wanted to avoid driving by the front of the house, so he headed west to the Great Highway and turned north until he reached Geary Boulevard, from which point he cut over on 44th Avenue and into the VA Medical Center. I thought that was risky. It was a government facility and I was sure they had security. He killed the lights and drove to the northern most parking lot. When we got out of the car and started toward a path he indicated, I glanced back. The SUV had government plates on it, thus his lack of concern... it would look like it belonged. Pete's bag of tricks seemed bottomless.

The moon was full, but there were scattered clouds, causing our only source of light to blink in and out, making the trek down the dark, steep path a little treacherous. The path opened up to another parking lot, which was at the end of El Camino Del Mar and a short walk from the loading bay of the museum. Pete held his fist up, silently commanding us to stop. He checked his watch; the dial glowed an eerie green. It was twenty-five minutes to midnight.

He was wearing a wireless earpiece and microphone, and spoke softly, "status." He listened for a moment, huddled us together, and whispered, "Edgar's walking toward Eagles Point now. My men already took out his guards watching the loading bay. Let's move, quick and silent."

We hugged the hillside and walk-ran until we reached the loading bay. The large roll-up door was closed, but the man-sized steel door was slightly ajar. Pete whispered something into his headset and a man appeared and waved us through, then led the way to another door on the far side of the cavernous bay. Through that we found ourselves in one of the tunnels Carol had shown us. I was surprised to see it was lit, although the fixtures were ancient and very few had working bulbs in place. Pete stopped again…he was listening, and hissed "damn-it." I tapped him on the shoulder and mouthed "what?" Pulling us back toward the door to the bay, he said, "Edgar's on the way back."

"And Phil?" I asked. Pete shook his head. "Is he dead?!"

Pete scowled. "Keep your voice down. I don't know, but don't shoot until you're sure who you're shooting at."

Billy whispered, "Is Eric okay?"

"I don't know that either…my guy had to keep his distance. He heard a scream, then saw Edgar sprinting back this way. Look, we need to move. Eagle's Point is on this side of the museum, so there's a good chance Edgar would come in this way too, and it's getting close to midnight…we need to move fast. I don't want him catching up until we've secured the chamber.

He's already going to be suspicious when he notices his guards are gone."

Pete started moving again. It was damp and smelly in the tunnel, and the dim industrial lights running down the center of the ceiling did little to dispel the creepy feeling I was getting. It felt like we walked for a long time. The tunnels were a labyrinth, and I was pretty much lost at that point. The man who'd been leading us stopped abruptly and opened another door. It was steel like the first one, but this one was rusty and pitted...I was surprised it had managed to stay intact. An equally rusty padlock lay to the side. This new tunnel was much older than the ones we'd just come from. Instead of semi-smooth concrete walls, these were some kind of stacked stone, slimy with moisture and a dark, foul smelling moss. Based on how old the walls looked, I assumed we'd now entered the tunnels GG had pointed out. There were no lights here, and Pete and his man pulled out pen lights and continued on until we reached yet another door. When I started to go through, I realized the door itself was made of the same stacked stone, and I guessed that when it was closed, you probably wouldn't know it was a door at all, just part of the wall. A man was lying just inside the door and Billy pointed down at him. Pete mouthed, "Edgar's guard." I couldn't tell if he was dead or just unconscious, and decided it didn't really matter.

The new tunnel was considerably narrower, the air thick and almost electrified, and I knew we were closing in on Gilles and he was amping up. I tapped Pete's shoulder. He turned, his pen light shining just past me so he wouldn't blind me. I mouthed, "GG." He nodded and stepped back, waving for the others to move back too.

I concentrated on that silky thin connection, and although there was barely any light in the tunnel, I could see GG materialize before me. She came to me—into me—and I felt that surge of power again. The flashes of her previous existence came again too, but the feeling wasn't nearly as jarring as it had been before. I heard a voice, sweet and shy, but the message and images it portrayed were horrifying and I could feel my eyes widen.

Pete mouthed, "What?" I waved them all back to the stacked stone door of the chamber tunnel, and whispered, "GG, she spoke to me. She said...," I hesitated, "if they try and open the vault with the wrong combination, she said it would be like an explosion. The vision she sent me was like a mushroom cloud...it would destroy everything for a mile in either direction." The city wasn't that big—seven by seven miles—and it was densely populated. If GG was right and they tried to open the chamber using the fake key, it would kill thousands and thousands of people, including us.

I grabbed Pete's arm and looked at his watch; it was nine minutes to midnight. If the offshoot tunnels bypassed the ones we had used, it was possible Edgar had gotten ahead of us. He'd had time to explore all the routes, and he'd be very motivated to move fast if he realized his guards were gone.

Pete motioned for us to move and we traversed the last tunnel quickly, coming upon an arch with a solid wooden door, light seeping from underneath it. The air was now so charged with the electrical energy of demons I could feel GG shudder inside me. She was afraid, but it seemed to strengthen her too. Pete didn't hesitate...he pulled the door open and burst through with the rest of us right behind him.

The chamber was so full of demons that I could barely see. I immediately grabbed a pencil from my pocket and started stabbing, moving fast and efficiently, but with every demon I killed, it seemed like three more appeared. Demons weren't the only things moving in the chamber, and the punch to the kidneys that I received was unexpected, but not debilitating. I turned quickly, bashing the large man in the face, feeling his nose shatter. He staggered back and I turned to the next guy, doing about the same damage. I couldn't say how many or how long this went on...it seemed like forever, but could only have been a few minutes. The surge of power I was getting from GG was incredible and very useful. The electrical sizzle was dying down, and now I saw our men, bound and gagged on the floor by the far wall. I also saw Pete's man, the one who'd led us in, lying in a pile on the floor near the door.

Someone screamed, "STOP!" and I turned to find Edgar with his muscular arm around Phil's neck, holding him like a shield. In his free hand he held a gun pointed at Phil's temple. He waved the gun toward the chamber door and said, "Back over there, NOW!"

Billy and I were standing on the far side of the chamber. I looked over and saw Calvin and Gilles; they weren't together yet, but were standing very close to each other. Calvin held the fake key and the journal. He was reading the second drawing, the one with the combination, and glancing at a door nearest him...it was the vault door. I had expected it to be larger. It was made of a smooth white stone, free from the moisture and residue that had caked all the other surfaces in the tunnels. The door was so clean and bright that it appeared to glow. A square sat in the upper center, and inside that were sixteen smaller squares with intricate carvings in each of them. Calvin moved to the door and rubbed his hand over the carvings. Then he turned to Gilles, who immediately began to merge with him.

Calvin's eyes started to turn that dark green again, the irises expanding. Suddenly his eyes themselves bulged and his expression changed to horror, and it occurred to me that it had to be seconds from midnight. Now, suddenly, he realized we were right...Gilles was taking him over and casting him out.

I heard a sharp poof sound and turned to see Edgar—a dark hole in the center of his forehead—begin to fall. He still held Phil by the neck, but his arm started to loosen and Phil pulled away. Aris was at the chamber entrance, his arm, silenced gun in hand, still extended.

I turned back to Calvin. Gilles's silhouette was now shrinking as he converged with Calvin. If he completed the process and we killed Calvin, there was a chance that someday Gilles could rise again as a demon, and I wanted him gone for good. I knew what had to be done, and although I'd only shot a gun a few times and this was close range and it was unlikely I'd miss, still I hesitated. Calvin/Gilles registered my hesitation. They began to lunge, and suddenly Calvin's eyes widened, his mouth forming an O. Billy was right beside me. I could smell the gunpowder from her weapon, and now I saw the hole in Calvin's chest, the blood spreading in a wide circle around the impact wound. Gilles and Calvin began to shake and shudder. I could actually feel the power and anger emanating from them, and then Gilles began to separate from Calvin, whose body was beginning to slump to the floor.

This time there was no hesitation...Billy and I lunged. The moment we made contact with his spectral form several things happened simultaneously; my pencil and her chopstick disintegrated, Gilles swirled away into a grey mist, and a massive jolt of his electroplasmic juice shot through us. It was so powerful that we both flew back, hitting the farthest wall hard.

Stunned, but not unconscious, I looked around. The vibration that had begun with Calvin's death was now amplifying and had moved into the ground and walls of the chamber. Mortar dust started to rain all around us, and a faint foul odor began to permeate the room. Someone—Pete, I think—screamed, "Grab a man and get out NOW!"

We ran, each of us dragging a semi-conscious ghost killer with us. Even Phil, who'd been beaten rather badly by Edgar, managed to muster enough strength to help. We hit the museum storage bay just as the chamber and vault exploded, causing the ground to shake and ripple.

I had no idea where the museum security guards were, but I was sure they'd be showing up any second. The explosion had triggered an alarm and it was blaring loudly. We exited through the steel outer door. The two SUVs were waiting, and we piled in and drove down El Camino Del Mar and disappeared into Sea Cliff, where we made our way back to Lincoln Way.

Phil was seated next to me in the back, and I said, "Are you okay?"

He smiled and said, "No, but I will be." Then he leaned his head back and sighed painfully.

Chapter 39

When we arrived at Lincoln Way there was no sign of Eric, and I turned to Aris for an answer. He said, "Edgar broke Eric's arm; he's being treated now."

"Why did the chamber explode? Calvin never got a chance to read the combination."

Pete answered, "When the outer chamber started to vibrate violently, I caught a whiff of rotten eggs...hydrogen sulfide, probably. Brief exposure to the smallest amounts can kill you, and it's explosive when it reaches somewhere around 4,500 parts per million. I think as the walls started to disintegrate, it began to seep in more rapidly, reaching the explosive level. There was still an electrical charge down there from Gilles, and it would have ignited the gas."

Carol's forehead creased. "I still don't understand why it didn't kill us."

"We got out fast, within seconds of smelling it. When we reached the newer tunnels, I closed the chamber tunnel entrance, which probably contained the blast to some extent. Not only that, but we didn't hear the explosion until we were at the museum entrance, so we also had several hundred yards of concrete tunnels between us and the blast." Pete shrugged his shoulders. "Basically, we got damn lucky."

"What about the vault itself? Assuming it was destroyed in the explosion, wouldn't the demons have been released anyway?" I asked.

No one seemed to have an answer to that question. Finally Aris said, "I asked two of Pete's men to remain in the area. So far they have not seen any additional ghosts or demons. We can only hope the vault itself remained intact and is buried forever in the rubble."

Billy turned to Pete. "The man that led us into the tunnels, he was killed?" Pete nodded solemnly. "Did we lose anyone else?" she asked. He shook his head.

"What about Edgar's men?" I asked.

Aris replied, "The authorities will naturally investigate. They will most likely discover a museum guard was bribed to allow access to the tunnels. If any of Edgar's men were in the tunnels at the time of the explosion and died because of it, it will most certainly be assumed they were the perpetrators. However, I will monitor the situation closely and if needed, instigate any necessary damage control."

I had no idea how he'd manage any sort of damage control and I didn't actually care. I was exhausted and just wanted sleep. Our drugged ghost killers had been brought to the house and were currently being given medical attention. It would have been better if we could have taken them to a hospital, but that would have spurred questions that we couldn't answer. One of Pete's men had medical training and took everyone's vitals, declaring they'd be all right in a day or so.

Phil gave us a brief rundown on what had transpired at his house. As we already knew, he'd gone home for Aaron's journal and the enlarged drawings. He'd finally figured out what they were and was using the silver cup to interpret them when Edgar and one of his minions broke in. Phil didn't have time to access his small arsenal, but did have the presence of mind to crumple the drawings and toss them aside in the hopes that we'd discover them.

Lincoln Way, a house that had been occupied by a party of one a short week ago, was now filled to the gills, and I saw no point in staying there for the night. Besides, I wanted my own bed. I headed upstairs for our bags and brought them down. Turning to Phil, I said, "Why don't you stay with me tonight? Your place is kind of a mess right now." He smiled and thanked me.

On the drive home, Billy asked, "What happened to GG?"

The electroplasmic jolt I'd received from Gilles was incredible, stronger than anything I'd felt before, and I assumed its strength had also jolted GG right out of me, because she wasn't there when I fully regained my senses. However, I was hopeful I'd see her in the next day or so.

* * *

The following morning I was awoken by the heavenly smell of frying bacon and brewing coffee. I found Phil in the kitchen happily humming while cracking eggs into a bowl; the man was nothing if not resilient. Billy was there too, and said, "'Bout time you got up." I looked at the clock...it was almost 11 a.m.

I frowned, not at her snide remark—that was expected—but at the fact that she was up too...yesterday had been long and exhausting. "Why are you up so early? I thought you'd sleep until dinner time."

"I would have, but Kevin showed up about an hour ago with this." She tapped an envelope that was lying on the table. I picked it up...it was addressed to Billy, the handwriting was elegant, and I knew right away that it was from Julie. I looked at Billy. She didn't seem upset, and I wondered what Julie had written. I'd texted Julie when we arrived at Lincoln Way in the wee hours of the morning, letting her know that Edgar was gone and everyone was safe, but Billy and I hadn't had the time or inclination to go into my conversation with Julie from the day before.

"What's it say?"

Billy's eyes darkened slightly. "Well, you probably already know most it." There was a slight twinge of anger in her voice, but it wasn't murderous, which was always a good thing. "In a nut shell, she told me she was sorry for everything, and that she always loved me. She said Andrew had been in touch with her and wanted to speak to me...she gave me his contact details. She asked if we could get together in a few weeks, when she comes back to town to finalize Vokkel's estate."

The raw emotion that I expected wasn't there. Instead, there was almost an air of acceptance about her, like she was pleased...or at the very least, considering Julie's offer.

I asked, "What are you going to do?"

She shrugged. "Don't know. I need to think about it."

My cell phone, which was plugged in and charging on the counter, rang...it was Aris. I put him on speaker.

Greetings and queries about our various conditions were exchanged, then he said, "Phil, I have arranged for the repair of your front door...it is now secure again. Perhaps it would be best if you all take the next several days off. We can gather at the end of the week at Lincoln Way to discuss any loose ends."

Epilogue

A few days after our foray into the tunnels, we met at Lincoln Way again. Billy and I came bearing gifts for the man of the house. We'd taken a little trip to the SPCA and picked out two kittens, both males...one orange and white, one black and white. They'd been given names, but we assumed Eric would change those to something more to his liking. We were right...he named the black one Jonas and the orange one Winston, after the other man we lost that night. You can't show up to a cat-less house without supplies, so we purchased all the feline necessities. Unfortunately, Billy had gone a bit overboard on our shopping trip, and while she carried the box containing the two lightweight mewling furballs, I was laden down with bags of food, toys, bowls, cat litter, and a large litter box. I could barely make it through the front door. Eric's arm was still in a cast and sling, and by the time we left the house, both kittens had crawled up into the sling and were snuggled up cozily, right along with Eric's plastered arm.

Although the city was far from completing their investigation into the explosion, Aris had been able to obtain a few details. Edgar had broken into the tunnels via the access point between the VA and the museum. The authorities, having found evidence of this, assumed that an unknown person entered there and had somehow caused the explosion. No bodies had been found so far, and the older tunnels were reduced to rubble and inaccessible. There was no mention of the vault. GG had told me the chamber would explode if the combination was read incorrectly, but since the combination was never actually read, we could only hope the vault was buried forever.

Curiosity was killing me, and I asked Pete how he had managed to bypass the guards at the museum. It turned out to be quite simple; since we only wanted into the loading area, the guard on duty didn't see a problem with allowing it, as long as he was handsomely paid, which he was. Apparently Carol had hacked into the security cameras and altered the recording so that our entrance and exit didn't appear. The guard was questioned, but there was no evidence to indicate anyone had penetrated the tunnels through the loading bay, so that line of inquiry was quickly dropped.

A few hours after Calvin's escape, a woman jogger reported being accosted by a teenager who stole her phone. The phone was found, via its "find my phone" app, a short time later. One call had been placed to a prepaid cell number before the phone was ditched in the bushes near the northwest part of the park. The number was Edgar's.

Before leaving Lincoln Way, I asked Aris about the merger with GG and the reaction he and Carol had. Although it had been his idea, they were both clearly uncomfortable about it, and I needed to know why.

Carol's mother had been Aris's sister. She was ten years younger than he, and when he left for college, she hadn't begun to show any ghost killing abilities. His parents were not ghost killers, but had come from a long line of them and knew all about it. When his sister began to see the ghosts, she kept it to herself, because she not only saw them, but she had befriended one.

Unbeknownst to Aris, this ghost was a demon and it was slowly infiltrating her consciousness. By the time he realized what was happening, she was a young wife and mother and almost completely under the control of her demon. When Aris tried to intervene, she went on a rampage, killing her husband and almost killing her daughter. Aris became Carol's guardian and swore to protect and guide ghost killers from that day forward.

Two days after our last meeting at Lincoln Way, GG returned. She looked horrible, and it alarmed me. I was still feeling that tenuous thread, but it had been getting weaker and weaker with every passing day.

"Are you okay?" I asked. She shook her head and pointed at me, then at herself, intertwining her fingers. "You want to merge?" I didn't want to do it...twice was enough, and as I said, it was an addicting sensation. She sensed it and nodded sadly, but her eyes were pleading, and I felt like there was something important she needed to say. The joining only lasted a few seconds, but it was long enough. She extracted herself and stood staring, waiting for my reply.

She'd been dead for some time...since 1924 to be exact. She had no idea why she'd never moved on, but she was thankful when my mother came along...at least she had a friend. After our first merger, she was immediately terrified at how wonderful it felt to be human again, even if she was sharing her consciousness with someone else. But the second time she wasn't sure she could leave; the desire was too strong. Gilles's juice was the catalyst that sent her packing from my body and mind, and she'd been wandering aimlessly since then, trying to decide what to do.

She only had one solution, and it was her salvation. She wanted—no, *needed*—me to vanquish her. I'd felt her anguish the moment before, but I'd also felt her weakness, and I knew she was right. If I didn't kill her, she might not be able to resist the pull, and that could lead her down the path of possession. As I reached for my pencil, I smiled sadly and allowed the tears to flow.

* * *

It had been a several days since my last moments with GG, and I hadn't been in the mood to do anything but mope around my apartment. Billy and Phil knew what happened, but had been kind enough to leave me be while I mourned. After the fourth day, Phil decided enough was enough and rang my cell phone five or six times in a row. I finally picked up.

"Dude, what's up?" His exuberant tone was more than just cheerfulness…he had something exciting to tell me.

"Sorry, didn't hear the phone ringing," I lied. "What's up with you? You sound a little keyed up."

"Oh man, I found something in one of the boxes from the attic…you gotta see this! Meet me at Seymour's in an hour."

As I was leaving my apartment, Justine's front door opened and Billy stepped out. She was wearing a pencil skirt with a front slit, a pair of high-heeled calf-length boots, and a rather fitted sweater. I said hello, then realized she was also wearing a touch of makeup—lipstick—and her hair, which was normally mostly straight, was lightly curled. She looked incredible and completely un-Billy like. I eyed her suspiciously, arching an eyebrow questionably.

She sighed. Clearly she had hoped to make her escape from the building unseen. "I'm meeting Mike for dinner," she said nonchalantly.

I felt my eyes widen, and much to my surprise *and* embarrassment, I also felt a twinge of jealousy. I shook myself and said, "Ah, that's great."

"Yeah, whatever," she said, and took the stairs, obviously so she could avoid talking about her pending date. I just smiled and took the elevator.

When I arrived at Seymour's, Phil was already at our regular booth and I waved, stopping at the bar to get a beer and say hi to Ed. When I sat down, I handed a flash drive to Phil.

He said, "What's this?"

When GG was in my head, her entire life and death was shared with me. She was gone now, and although I wasn't a diarist like most ghost killers, I decided in honor of everything she had done for us, the least I could do was write down everything I knew about her. I'd spent the previous twelve hours typing furiously on my laptop. The information flowed flawlessly, as if GG was guiding my fingers as I typed.

"It's the entire life and death of Amelia Santorino... you knew her as GG."

Phil's eyes bulged dangerously, "Dude...." He shook his head. "Right, she shared everything with you." He glanced at the flash drive, then smiled up at me brightly and said, "This might be the most important diary the sanctum has ever received."

We sipped our beers in silence for a few minutes, then turned to the box on the table.

Phil was right; what he'd found was incredible. The cardboard box was old and crumbly. Inside was a diary and a large collection of letters, still in their original envelopes, all postmarked in 1915. There were also several sepia-toned photographs.

The inside cover of the diary had the name George Sinclair written in neat print. The photographs were the most telling though; the man in each of them was probably in his late teens or early twenties, and much to my surprise, my father bore a very strong resemblance to this man.

Phil said, "Flip to the back of the diary and read it."

The men that hunt us will eventually succeed in capturing us. Mary and I cannot keep our son, it is too dangerous. My cousin Charles will take him. He will say that he adopted the boy from an orphanage. No one will ever know, including the boy, who his real parents were. It must be this way... the evil men and their demons will not give up; they want our power. Charles is not like us... he can raise the boy in a safe and ordinary home.

The entry was dated in mid-1920. I looked up at Phil. "You think this is a relative of mine?"

Phil splayed his hands out. "Dude, no such thing as a coincidence. I mean, the guy's name was George Sinclair, for God's sake. And come on, you can't tell me you don't see the resemblance to your dad in those photos. This dude was probably your great-grandfather!"

* * *

The Legion of Honor was indeed built on the remains of many of San Francisco's dead, and that cemetery was called Golden Gate Cemetery (aka City Cemetery). It is also true that during the museum renovation in 1993, many of those dead were uncovered. I think it would be safe to assume, if there are ghosts in our fair city, they probably wander the links of Lincoln Park Golf Course and the great halls and galleries of the Legion of Honor. Is there a chamber full of evil souls buried at the edge of Golden Gate Cemetery? Let's hope we never find out....

If you're (morbidly) curious, see below:

- http://www.nps.gov/goga/learn/historyculture/upload/Property_Golden_Gate_Cemetery_sr_2014_v2.pdf
- http://www.sfgenealogy.com/sf/history/hcmcit.htm
- http://richmondsfblog.com/2013/10/29/halloween-special-what-or-whom-lies-beneath-the-legion-of-honor/

Lightning Source UK Ltd.
Milton Keynes UK
UKHW020633161120
373485UK00010B/257

9 781715 783051